EQUINOX

A Lake Prophet Mystery

The Lake Prophet Mysteries
Book 2

ELI EASTON

RJ SCOTT

Love Lane Books

Copyright

Equinox - A Lake Prophet Mystery

The Lake Prophet Mysteries, 2

Copyright ©2023 Eli Easton, Copyright ©2023 RJ Scott

Cover design by Anna Tif Sikorska

Edited by Sue Laybourn

Equinox

The tranquility of Prophet is shattered when a local trail rider is killed and whispers of wolf packs and murder spread like wildfire.

Three months after the murder of Mike Bressett, the sleepy town of Prophet faces another tragedy—the death of Billy Odette, a well-liked Makah man who ran trail rides for the tourists. When Billy is discovered to have been the victim of a vicious animal attack, dragged right off a popular trail, angry locals are quick to blame a wolf pack that's recently moved into the area. But Sheriff Gabriel Thompson learns that the death isn't as simple as it seems when decades-long animosities and secrets come to light.

A figure from Tiber Russo's past cast a shadow over his blossoming friendship with Gabriel and dashed any hope for a meaningful relationship. However, as Tiber confronts the demon on his doorstep he turns to Gabriel for help, and all the reasons he has to stay apart become nothing at all.

While Tiber and a local wildlife painter fight to protect the wolves, Gabriel has to unravel a tangled web of deception, betrayal, and long-held grudges and as the mystery unfolds, he discovers Billy's death is part of a larger plot that threatens his town and beyond, and when Tiber's life is threatened, will Gabriel lose everything?

To Lola. who taught me how to talk to animals
~Eli Easton

Always for my family
~RJ Scott

Equinox

Chapter One

Tiber

DUKE WAS a streak of lightning as he ran down the rocky shore of Lake Prophet after the ball. It'd been three months since the murder of the Labrador retriever's owner, Mike Bressett, and since Duke and I had helped the sheriff find his killer. Duke was part of my pack now. And on most days, he was a happy dog. But there were times when he would retreat into a ball of yellow-furred sadness, and I could tell he was thinking about Mike.

That was not today. He sent pebbles flying as he skidded to a stop near the ball, snatched it up in his mouth, and raced back towards me, eyes alight.

Gracie, a wolfhound, loped the last few strides with Duke. As inseparable as they were, Duke's energy was too much for her and for Leo, a fifteen-pound mutt who dug around the rocky shore hoping for crumbs left by picnickers, and for Ferdinand, a chunky basset hound who lay on his back, sunbathing, and sometimes even for me. I threw the ball again.

Leo barked.

I glanced over at him. "What did you find? Salami?"

He barked again.

"Well, there probably isn't anymore, Leo. Someone must have dropped it."

His yip went higher.

"Yes, they have it at the market. Maybe we'll get some as a special treat. But processed meats are super bad for your health, you know."

Leo expressed his opinion with a growl and went back to sniffing around.

It was one of those perfect afternoons you never wanted to end. It was October, and we were having a late summer in this normally wet and overcast part of Washington state. Lake Prophet shimmered blue-green in the golden sunlight, the evergreens and oaks and birch crowding the lakeshore were like a painter's palette daubed with green and orange and yellow. Fluffy white clouds floated like ice cubes in a deep blue sky. Heaven.

Something caught my peripheral vision, and I turned my head to see a crow land on a larger rock on the shore. Another joined it, and a third. All three stared at me.

I eyed them warily. "I hope you're here for the fish."

One of them cawed in response.

My cell phone rang. I took it out of my pocket and glanced at it, not intending to answer. But it was a 360 area code—someone local. I accepted the call. "Hello?"

"Hey, is this Tiber?"

"Yes." I didn't recognize the man's voice. For a

second, my brain hiccupped, and I thought it was my ex, Jeff. A chill of dread passed over me. *Please God, no.*

"It's Sam, over at the riding stables."

"Oh. Hey! Sam." My relief was immediate but short-lived. It wasn't Jeff, because I wasn't asleep, and this wasn't a nightmare. But why would Sam be calling me?

When I'd first moved to Prophet, I'd opened a customer account at the local trail rides stables up at the Thompson Cabins and I'd gone out a dozen times. It had been a big ticket item on the 'pro' list when I'd contemplated moving to Prophet, honestly. I'd gotten into horses on the rez in Arizona when I'd stayed with my Navajo grandma during the summers. It was one of the best things to do there, and popular with natives and tourists alike. The red rock landscape had that Old Western movie vibe and that was compounded on horseback. But since I'd taken in Duke, I hadn't had the extra time or energy to go riding.

As for Sam, who owned the Thompson Cabins and the adjacent stables, I didn't know him well. but I knew he was Gabriel's brother. Gabriel—the hot sheriff of Prophet. The hot, *gay* sheriff, and a man I'd put firmly in the friend zone. The thought something had happened to him made my blood run cold. "Is Gabriel okay?"

"What? Oh. Yeah, Gabriel's fine as far as I know. He's over in Seattle for some law enforcement training today. I'm really sorry to bother you." Sam sounded upset. "I just didn't know who else to call who's a strong rider. And Gabriel thinks the world of you."

I looked across at the three crows. Two had jumped off

the rock and were now pecking at the ground but one was still eyeing me. *Thanks for the heads up.*

"Sure. What do you need?"

"It's Billy." I heard Sam take a shaky breath. "He took River out this morning about eight a.m., and he hasn't come back yet."

I checked my watch. It was almost four. "That's not good."

"No. I'm getting really worried. I thought I'd better do something about it before it gets dark. It'd be good to have someone along, just in case. And with Gabriel away and the fact that Deputy Devin doesn't ride, I didn't know who else to ask. But if you're busy, I totally—"

"No problem. I'll be there as soon as I can."

Sam gave me directions to the trailhead where he wanted to search. I gathered the troops and headed back up the game trail through the woods to my house. The dogs seemed to sense my mood had shifted, and that we were in a hurry. They came along quietly and without their usual reluctance to leave the lake.

I had time enough to worry as we hiked home. Billy Odette was the trail master for the Thompson stables. He was a Makah man in his forties—wiry, strong, and an excellent horseman. He'd grown up in nearby Neah Bay and knew the area well. There was no way he'd be out this long—for the horse's sake, if not for his own.

I couldn't help but flash back to the murder we'd had in Prophet just three months ago. Prophet, to all appearances, was a sleepy little town. It was historically an artist's community. We were separated from the busy towns and cities around Puget Sound—including Seattle—

by the Olympic Mountains, one of the densest, wildest, and wettest mountain ranges in the United States. On this side of them, in the open land between the mountains and the western seaboard, the population was sparse. As my mom put it, I'd moved to the ass-end of nowhere.

You'd think that would make Prophet a safe place to live. But lately, I'd begun to see the dark side of that isolation. People moved here who didn't want to be found —me included. Maybe some of those people weren't running from an abusive ex, or even themselves, but from the law. It drew people hoping to hide their sins in the deep, shadowed forests of the Olympics.

People who came here to escape the rules were especially angry when the local law tried to enforce them. As Mike Bressett had learned.

I prayed nothing like that had happened to Billy Odette.

WHEN I PULLED in at the Clear Creek Falls trailhead, Sam was waiting with his pickup, a horse trailer, and two horses already out of the trailer and ready to ride. Another older red pickup with a small horse trailer was also parked there —probably Billy's. The sight of it struck a note of fear in my soul. It seemed abandoned, bereft.

"Hey, Tiber," Sam said as I got out of the car. "Thanks for coming."

"Sure."

"This is Conway and Biscuit," Sam introduced me to a chestnut gelding and yellow mare. "Biscuit can be a bit headstrong, but I thought you could handle her. She's fast."

"No problem."

I understood why he'd brought her. The horses you could take out on trail rides were rescues—older and slow. And that was fine with me normally. But today we had a purpose.

I took Biscuit's reins and Sam mounted Conway. I could tell he was in a hurry by the tension in his voice and around his eyes, but I took a moment to feed Biscuit a bit of apple I'd brought with me, stroke her jaw then met and held her gaze. "We're going to search for Billy and River. It's important that we find them. I know you can help."

Sam no doubt thought I was as weird as rumor would have it, talking to animals. But he didn't say anything as I gave Biscuit a final scratch. She wouldn't understand my words, but she might pick up a sense that this was more than a routine outing, and that would be helpful.

I hopped up into the saddle. "Did Billy tell you where he was going? There're several trail branches up there."

Sam shook his head. "He just said he was gonna check out some trails near Clear Creek Falls. He thought it might be a good addition to our roster. I figured we could ride up to the falls and then check out the side trails if we have time." He checked his watch. "We've got almost two hours before sunset."

"Let's go."

It was a steady mile-and-a-half climb to the falls, and Sam led the way. We went as fast as safety allowed, which was pretty fast, maybe five or six miles per hour. I'd hiked this trail a few times, so I was familiar with it. But I'd never done it in the fall. The air was already crisp with the promise of a cold night, and the woods were dotted with color. We came across a section of yellow birch that had littered the trail with golden coins. Biscuit seemed to be delighted, her step growing livelier when she saw the leaves ahead, and then slowing as we moved through them. She danced sideways, as if she wanted to run, but I sat deeper in my saddle and relaxed my legs, stroking her neck to calm her, and we went on.

I kept an eye out for any signs of disturbance on the trail but didn't see anything amiss. We came upon fresh horse droppings and paused. I hopped down to examine them. They weren't baked dry, but neither were they still warm.

"Might be from this morning," I said. "I haven't seen a lot of horses on this trail."

Sam nodded. "Billy came this way then."

We went on.

We passed several trail junctions. There were two main loops you could make that included this trail—one went up on a ridgeline and another to a small mountain lake. But we ignored the offshoots and continued on up to the falls.

We reached the bridge. It stood over a deep ravine where Clear Creek ran cold and bitter over the long drop of Clear Creek Falls. It sounded like a locomotive passing below. The horses were breathing hard from the climb when we dismounted. Sam tied his horse to a nearby tree, so I did the same. We headed over to the bridge to look around.

The bridge was a worry in and of itself. But seeing at it with fresh eyes, I knew they couldn't have gone over the side. It had a wooden guardrail as high as my chest, and it showed no damage. Besides, an experienced horseman like

Billy would have walked his horse across, taking care she didn't get startled. There were no droppings on the bridge, either, but that didn't mean anything.

Back where the horses were tethered, Sam put his hands on his hips, his expression frustrated. "Crap. I knew it was unlikely to be this easy, but I'd hoped…"

"Yeah." I pushed my long hair back. "He likely did come this way. Maybe he was doing a loop." I pointed across the bridge. "There's a trail junction about a mile over that way. It takes you down to a lake and then you can—"

Biscuit's high whinny got my attention. She was dancing on the tether, anxious. She sensed something, but she didn't strike me as fearful, more anticipatory. I watched her closely.

"What is it?" Sam asked.

I held up a hand to quiet him.

Biscuit tossed her head, straining towards the north where the trail reentered the woods, heading up to a ridgeline. She whinnied again and I heard it echoed, faintly.

I walked as silently as I could to where the trail disappeared into the trees and looked down the path. I couldn't see her, but I knew she was there.

I clicked my tongue. "River. C'mere, girl. Come, River. It's okay." I dug out another slice of apple and offered it on my palm. It wasn't a very impressive offering, and if River was hurt, she couldn't come, or wouldn't. But I waited and listened.

Sam came up behind me, but he didn't speak.

After several long minutes, a horse appeared a ways

down the trail. She trotted closer but stopped a good fifty feet away. She was a black mare, saddled, her reins hanging. Foam flecked her mouth. Her eyes were wide with fear as she considered us. Then she turned and bolted away again.

"Shit," Sam breathed in my ear, and there was a hiccup in the word.

Yeah. Not good.

"Where's Billy?" he asked, but it was rhetorical.

"Wait here." I snuck forward.

It took a while to get River to let me close—time, soft words, the slice of apple, and radiating what I hoped was calm and reassurance—but I finally got hold of her reins. With more soothing words, and strokes of her lathered neck, I managed to lead her down the trail toward the bridge. I didn't attempt to ride her. She was too distraught.

When River saw Biscuit and Conway, she pulled the reins from my hands, frantic to reach them. I let her go, knowing she'd stick by her friends. They greeted each other with head bobs and neck nibbles. River gave them a few fearful-sounding whinnies, maybe telling them in horse language what had happened to her. But Sam and I were none the wiser.

"Where is he, Tiber?" Sam asked. "Could he have had a heart attack? Or fell and was injured? We have to find him."

"We do."

It was then I saw the blood. With River's black coat, it hadn't been immediately apparent. I moved closer, Sam following me.

On River's right flank was a large patch of reddish

wetness. I traced my fingers through it and held them up to
the fading light. Blood.

"Oh my God," Sam said. "Is it hers? Or—"

"Take her reins."

He held her steady while I checked her flanks and her
underbelly. "It's not hers," I decided, heart sinking.

"Crap. What happened to him, Tiber?" Sam's voice
shook and his eyes were damp. I felt his pain in my heart.

"I don't know," I said. "But I think we'd better call
Gabriel."

Chapter Two

Gabriel

Seattle sucked.

It was different, but not necessarily in a bad way after all the tall glass and steel hotel where I stayed offered excellent coffee, a definite plus. The city had a vibe nothing at all like LA, so it wasn't as if I was getting flashbacks of the heat and dirt and pain I'd run from. The other law enforcement officers at this professional development day were friendly enough, so that wasn't the issue either.

But there was one thing, and one thing only—Seattle wasn't Prophet.

There was no Tiber in Seattle.

The moment I'd crossed county boundaries away from the forest and lake, I wanted to turn back, and it hadn't boded well for me attending an event designed to hone my skills and bolster my network of contacts. Attendance would mean talking to people, and I didn't want to do that.

Particularly at the less than gentle introduction to the other delegates at the meet and greet last night, which had been nothing but a cacophony of people talking over each other just to be heard. I'd lasted ten minutes in that busy space, then taken my plate of nibbles through the nearest door and ending up by accident (of course) back at my room.

I'd eaten my shrimp in peace, and not one useful professional networking relationship had been made. The instinct to seek solitude and fall into a state of avoidance was central to my sessions with my counselor, Cliff. It was self-preservation, and we both knew that until I processed my conflicted feelings about my father, my disconnect from my family, or worse, the city where I'd broken apart, I'd never move forward. I needed to process my past before I could embrace the future.

A future where Tiber Russo was front and center.

The same man who'd shown me what peace could taste like before he placed me in the friend zone in his own act of self-preservation. Turned out we were both scared of everything, me with my nightmares and the horrors I'd seen and dealt out, him with an abusive ex, which meant he couldn't trust easily.

Worst-case scenario we'd never find a middle ground where we could be together, but that didn't stop me craving it.

I wanted to be back home with Tiber, not standing around with other cops bragging about the worst crime scene they'd found, or making connections so they could move up the ranks. I was happy back in Prophet, or at least I was heading along the path to being happy. My brother was kind of talking to me, my job had settled down, and there'd been no more major crime scenes after the case this past summer where a local park ranger had been murdered. No more deaths, and I'd almost fooled myself that I was working my way through my issues.

But I clearly hadn't because I avoided everyone at breakfast by going down way earlier than anyone else, and then same again at the first training session where I sat at the back of the room and left as it ended.

I just wanted silence, and the desperate need to not be here ate at me more than I'd expected it to. What if someone here recognized me? What if there was another cop up here from LA who wanted to talk about things they'd heard? Why was I here?

Because I'm trying to be normal.

Prophet wasn't silent, least of all in the sheriff's office where Hen could talk all day, but the buzz of work and gossip at least made sense to me. I was beginning to relearn the town I'd been born in, understanding the mechanics of it, and slotting myself back in.

All I could think, as I avoided everyone, was that I had a lot to talk to Cliff about in our next session, because maybe I was broken, and I'd go back to Prophet and never leave again.

Maybe Tiber saw this avoidance in me and that was why he'd pushed me away. Perhaps with his instincts and his soul-searching gaze he saw I was damaged goods. I bet when we kissed he could feel the darkness inside me.

Stop spiraling, fuck's sake. Tiber needs space, I need space, it's okay. It's normal and healthy to have space.

At least this was the last session of the day, an interdepartment working group focusing on a case very similar to one I'd cleared three months ago, led by no other than Hudson Reid himself. A law enforcement ranger for the National Park Service, he was the very same ISB agent who'd never quite made it to Prophet to take over the murder investigation of Mike Bressett. He'd emailed me after our single call—a perfunctory congratulations for helping and solving and a summary of the information he required so he could close the file, but we'd never met. I'd sent what he'd wanted, got a thank-you in return, but our murder wasn't quite as big as the right-wing activists' standoff in Idaho he'd been working on, and was filed away as done.

Or done in terms of the crime. Although, I wasn't sure it would ever be forgotten in Prophet, as the town gossip was never-ending.

Still, after all this time and despite my avoidance tactics, it was both good and bad to meet Hudson, ISB agent extraordinaire with perfectly styled blond hair, a body built by a god, and piercing blue eyes that stared right through me. He was the kind of guy I'd have hooked up with—*before*—all flirty and suggestive, temporary, a one-night stand. He was someone I might have had some easy no-strings fun with back before my life had changed.

Before the undercover case broke me and sent me running from LA.

Before Prophet.

Before Tiber.

I wish I was back home. I knew Tiber had called a halt to *us*, but we shared Duke, hiked as a pack—his words not mine—skimmed stones on Lake Prophet, then sat in silence as we watched the storm petrels wheeling in the leaden skies above the verdant rainforest.

Tiber and I had kissed exactly three times since he'd said we shouldn't. The first was after we'd eaten a bucket of popcorn while watching animal documentaries at his home—my favorite place to be. He'd definitely leaned in first and kissed *me* before sitting back, flustered, and fussing around Patch as if the sleeping cat needed the attention. I'd loved the buttery kiss but had to leave soon after because otherwise I would have begged for more. The second had happened when I'd lost my cool as he laughed at something Duke had been doing. I'd wanted to kiss the smile, and lurched clumsily at him, only to mash our lips together in the most unsexy way ever, then step back because he was shocked.

After all, friends don't kiss friends.

Right?

The third, last Sunday, happened outside my house when he came to drop off Duke. The rain was out of a romance novel, or a post-apocalyptic movie, so heavy it drenched us in seconds, but when he smiled his goodbye, his long hair plastered around his face, I'd gripped his yellow slicker, and we'd met in the middle.

A kiss for the ages, soft, then hard, wet from the rain, and so hot.

When we separated Tiber stared at me wide-eyed, touching his lips before he turned and left. I'd wanted to call after him, suggest maybe being friends wasn't enough, and that I'd be good with more kisses. I'd said nothing, watching his tail lights vanishing into the rain, because he'd asked me to back off.

So that was what I'd done. My heart hurt that I could see him and not hold him, but that was something else to unpick in counseling.

"… Sheriff Thompson out of Prophet. Sheriff, do you perhaps have a few words to say on this?"

Fuck. ISB McSexy was talking to me.

"Sorry?" I asked as Hudson smiled in encouragement, and I felt everyone in the room focus on me. I had the semi-hysterical thought that they wondered who I was and what I was doing in the room, given my avoidance tactics so far.

I will not lose my cool. I'm a hardened former cop with years undercover, and I can handle a room full of my equals without going red.

Nope. The pep talk didn't help as Hudson was still giving me the reassuring smile, as if we were connected, and then cleared his throat.

"Small-town policing," he encouraged, which I assume summarized in three words all the bits I'd missed when daydreaming about Tiber. I stopped myself from asking what he wanted to know about small town policing.

"Sure," I threw out, and heard a snigger from behind me.

"Exactly," Hudson said, as if I'd given the right answer, which I probably hadn't but clearly he was a good guy who wouldn't throw me under a bus. Sue me, I was tired, I wanted to be at Tiber's place snuggled on the sofa, a cat on my lap, and a dog under my arm. I'd hug a tortoise if it meant I could sink into the peace I only seemed to find when I was around the cute, frustrating, sexy, kissable Tiber and his pack of animals.

Hudson tapped a pen on the podium and all fifty people in the room turned to look back at him, and *thankfully* away from me. "So that wraps up the questions —how about we call it a day and get out of here early?" His suggestion was met by enthusiasm and the shuffling of chairs on the wooden floor, and I almost made it to the door in among the herd.

Almost got away.

"Gabriel? Sheriff Thompson? Can I have a moment of your time?" Hudson called, and my heart sank. Great. So much for getting on the road ahead of rush hour and making it home in good time. I pasted a smile on my face as the last of the other delegates left and then turned to face him.

"Sorry about before," I apologized, and waved to indicate my daydreaming earlier, but he shrugged.

"It's all good, this is the last session of the day, I'm surprised people are even awake given the drinking last night." He leaned back against a desk filled with flyers, then crossed his arms over his very impressive chest which I could discern through his white shirt. He wasn't wearing a tie, and the top two buttons were undone, showing a hint of chest hair.

Tiber was smooth-skinned.

So smooth. So perfect.

"… although, I didn't see you last night."

Shit he was talking again, and I needed to focus if I was going to get out of here.

"I had a date with a plate of shrimp and reruns of *The Simpsons*," I joked—sort of—and he laughed. It was a very nice laugh, but not the kind that came from the heart along with hugs and grins, not like Tiber's.

Fuck's sake, stop thinking about Tiber.

"Quality programing," Hudson said. "*The Simpsons*, I mean."

"Oh, yeah." And great conversation was had by all. *Not.*

He studied me for a moment, and I met his steady gaze. "I wanted to thank you face-to-face for having our back in the Bressett case."

I stiffened. It hadn't been just *the Bressett case* to me, or to Prophet, it had been personal, it had been too many lies, and an uneasy fear that refused to leave town. Everyone looked at the visiting tourists in camper vans as potential murderers, the gossip still hadn't died down, and with the accused in court in a few weeks, it was a story still on everyone's lips, embellished as it passed from one person to another.

Turned out the word was Tiber and I had fought off actual bad guys—ten of them. Or at least that was how I'd last heard it from a woman when she'd accosted me on the street as she explained she was the second cousin of someone, who knew someone, who'd heard how brave we'd been.

"Sorry, I know it wasn't *just* a case for you," Hudson apologized and threw me a rueful smile. Shit? Had I spoken some of my thoughts out loud? "It's worse when you're personally involved, but I wanted to reassure you that my team and I couldn't have done a better job at tracking down the person responsible. If you ever..." He paused, and glanced at his feet, giving himself time to think. "I read your personnel file."

"My file," I said in a dead tone. Shit. Fuck.

"The parts that weren't redacted at least," he amended, and gave me a moment to hear his words and calm the fuck down. "Look, we always have vacancies with ISB, hardly any benefits, lousy money, but a worthwhile job. Even undercover work if you wanted that."

My chest tightened so much that I couldn't breathe, and I rubbed the place over my heart. "I'm the sheriff for Prophet," I forced out. *I'm not leaving. You can't suggest anything that will make me leave.*

He gave a shrug but carried on. "Your experience with gangs, and trafficking would benefit us enormously, so if it your latest role gets too small for you…" He left the rest hanging; the suggestion Prophet wasn't big enough for me to get job satisfaction was right there in the empty space.

I sought to quiet the demons in my head, then forced a casual indifference and quirked an eyebrow. "If I left my town, who would break up the land disputes between Old Man Frazier and his neighbors?" I was joking, and I hoped he heard more than me choosing to live a quiet life, and all the bits I wasn't saying about how freaking happy I was in Prophet—or at least how happy I would be when I figured out my place in the world. He didn't have to know I was a work in progress. So much of this conversation was unspoken that I was starting to feel like running before I agreed to something I shouldn't.

"Sure, sure," he said, and laughed. "Hey, and no pressure, but shall we get out of here? Find a hot bar and a cold beer?"

Oh, the temptation laid right there in my path. The drink wouldn't just be a drink, not if the way he raked his gaze from my head to my toes and back up again was anything to go by. Yes, he was handsome, impossibly so, but his hair wasn't dark and long, it didn't frame angular features, nor did he have piercing dark eyes, or a smile that spoke to my heart.

Not even the offer of *something* got me going, because he wasn't Tiber.

"No. Thank you, but I have to get back." I was firm, and we shook hands only long enough to extend the courtesy of a goodbye. If he was disappointed he didn't say so, and I was happy to get out of there.

By the time I was back on the ferry, crossing Puget Sound, I was over the event, all my mental notes of things I'd learned tucked away for tomorrow, and with every watery moment that passed the strain of the city slipped away.

I was going home, with touristy Seattle gifts for my niblings, Sarah and Aaron, which would give me the excuse of visiting with my brother, another step in mending a relationship that was still new. At least he let me into his house now, which was one step up from completely ignoring me. Then I planned on heading straight over to Tiber's place with the stuffed state animal —a marmot or so the guy behind the hotel counter said— just to see Duke, of course.

Although if kissing Tiber was on the agenda, I wouldn't say no.

I almost made it home, was a mere thirty minutes away, when a call came through on my cell. Devin had already messaged me seven times in the twenty-four hours I'd been in Seattle, each time with various questions that could have waited if he hadn't been a rookie still. I could have left it, but I had nothing else to do except get mesmerized by windshield wipers flicking away the persistent rain into the darkness swallowing the tree-lined road.

I answered hands free, as I guided my car around the puddle at the turning to Bear Creek campgrounds, and had my smiling, soothing tone all ready to go. If this was another filing question I might just laugh.

"Billy Odette is missing!" Devin exclaimed with all the drama I'd become used to from my rookie. He was a good kid, would make a fine sheriff one day, but he really needed to stow the excitement when a case hit our desks.

"Billy Odette?" I knew him a little, and placed his face, Makah, quiet, worked with my brother Sam up at the Thompson cabins, assisting with trail rides. My first instinct was that there was nothing to worry about because Billy knew the forest and knew horses.

"You need to come back!" Devin added with a hint of panic.

"I'll be with you in thirty—"

"Sam says it's not right, so him and Tiber went out on horseback looking for Billy, and they found his horse. No rider, just the horse, and there's blood."

An icy chill skittered up my spine, but finding a horse, albeit mentioning blood, didn't add up to Billy actually being missing—horses got loose and walked off all the time then cut themselves on branches. Billy was an experienced rider and knew the forest around Prophet like the back of his hand, taking all kinds of folk out on tours.

"Okay—"

Devin talked over me. "Sam said I should call, or Tiber did. They both did. I think—"

"Focus, Devin."

"Okay, sorry." He took a moment. "I'm thinking as soon as you get here, we saddle up and go out as well? Or should I go out on my own now? Like straight away? I could take a flashlight. Should we set up a search party? What do I need to do?" His words tumbled out and I could imagine him up on his toes bouncing with coiled anxiety and probably no small amount of excitement as he offered his plans and asked questions.

"First off, it's a hell no to randomly riding out in the dark, Devin. Okay?"

"But surely—"

"No buts, start from the beginning. Where did Sam and Tiber find the horse?"

By the time Devin spilled everything he knew about the horse, the blood, the missing Billy, it tumbled out in a mess of thoughts that I made him go back over and put in order. I drove past the sign for Prophet, and met Devin outside the office, with no immediate signs of Tiber or Sam, and by the time I got there he'd calmed down and was much more clinical in what he said. In the SUV we headed toward the Thompson cabins which were about a half mile away—about the only thing we could do right now—but met Sam and Tiber, walking down the hill, and so many mixed emotions hit me. I stopped the car and jumped out so fast I almost fell on my face.

"Are you okay?" I blurted to them both.

I wanted to hug Sam and tell him I was here now, and he shouldn't worry, and then as sheriff I wanted to find his friend. Neither of them answered my question; Sam was upset and stressed, Tiber was focused, but frowning.

I wanted to hug my brother.

And I really wanted to kiss that frown from Tiber's face.

"We need to go back out," Sam announced without even a hello. Tiber and I exchanged glances—he knew as well as I did that a search party in the dark was a no go. Particularly when faced with the tangled depth of ancient undergrowth where moonlight was blocked by heavy clouds and the dense canopy of trees.

"First light," I said, and waited for Sam to rail at me.

All he did was close his eyes. "What if that's too late, Gabe?"

I wished I could tell him it wouldn't be. Had to hope that Billy was safe and had found cover from the persistent rain and the tending toward chilly September nights.

Had to hope he was alive.

And would stay that way until morning.

Chapter Three

Tiber

IT WAS a relief to see Gabriel. We needed help—Billy needed help—and there was no one I trusted more.

While Sam got the horses back into the horse trailer, I pulled Gabriel a few feet away in the gravel parking lot so the others couldn't hear.

"Are you okay?" Gabriel asked.

I shook my head impatiently. "Me? Yeah, of course. Listen. I didn't want to scare Sam but... something dragged Billy off his horse. Something terrifying. It attacked them while Billy was in the saddle, and he was pulled off. Then River bolted."

"How do you know that?"

I stared at Gabriel; my lips pressed tight.

"The horse told you," he said. He didn't sound sarcastic or skeptical. His expression was grim.

"I just... got that vibe. Strongly."

In fact, the horse *had* told me. Not in words, of course,

but I'd gotten a flash of her terror, I'd felt the familiar man being dragged off the saddle. It was a horrible feeling.

"Who did it?" Gabriel asked. "Was it a person? An animal? A bear, maybe?"

"I don't know." I hadn't gotten a visual on the attacker. All I could sense was shock and terror and a need to get away.

Gabriel rubbed his chin thoughtfully. I couldn't help noticing his five o'clock shadow. He was a good-looking man, but that stubble tipped him over into territory I didn't need to be thinking about right now. Or ever.

"If he was dragged off his horse," he said, "Could it have been a tree limb or something like that? Something they ran into?"

I shook my head. An experienced horse like River wouldn't lead its rider into a low-hanging branch. Nor would the result have been so terrifying to the horse. "It wasn't a branch."

"Maybe the horse bolted, like from seeing a snake or something else that spooked it? And Billy fell off?"

I shook my head again. That didn't fit the flash I'd gotten. Besides—"Billy wouldn't have bled on the horse if that was the case."

"Good point," Gabriel said. "Well, that narrows down the options. Bear? Mountain lion? What about a coyote?"

"Coyotes wouldn't attack something as large as a man on a horse. Besides, there's plenty of deer and smaller game in these woods." That was true. But then, bears and mountain lions weren't likely to attack a man on horseback either. More likely than a coyote, yes. It wasn't impossible.

What would cause an animal to do that? Rabies,

maybe. Or an animal wounded and unable to hunt their usual prey. I recalled reading about the famous grizzly attacks in Glacier National Park in 1967. One of the bears that had killed a camper had been emaciated and had glass embedded in her gums, probably gotten while foraging in human dumpsters. She'd been in constant pain for months, maybe years, and unable to feed normally. It could be something like that.

But it could also be a man. One thing I knew for certain—humans were, by far, the most dangerous species on the planet.

"It might have been a person."

"Well, that settles it," Gabriel said. "I don't want people blundering around in the dark with something—or someone—that dangerous on the loose. How much blood did you find?"

"Not a lot."

"So, Billy's unlikely to bleed out."

"Not from the wound he got while on the horse. I have no idea what happened to him after he fell off. But, Gabriel, if he wasn't badly hurt, he would have walked back to the trailhead by now. Or found his horse back up in there, the way I did, and ridden out."

"Right." We exchanged a worried glance. I wasn't willing to go to as dark as to assume Billy was dead. But whatever had happened, it wasn't good. It wasn't good at all.

Sam walked up to us. "What's next?"

"I'll organize a search party for first light," Gabriel said. "I'll start making phone calls now."

Sam's eyes grew damp. He looked towards the woods.

"God, I hate to leave him out here. I feel like we're letting him down."

Gabriel put a hand on Sam's shoulder. "Billy's a strong guy. He knows these woods. He'll know how to take shelter. It's not going to help to get more people in trouble blundering around in the dark."

Sam nodded reluctantly "I know. First light."

"I'll be here," I said.

There wasn't a lot more to be done, so I drove home. I fed my animals and got them bedded down for the night. But I couldn't sleep. I lay there, staring at the ceiling, surrounded by snoring animals, and thought about Billy being lost in the woods, in the dark. It was unbearable. I told myself that Gabriel was right—Billy, being local and Makah, and having ridden and hiked all over this area and the Olympic National Park, no doubt had wilderness survival skills. And the temperature tonight was low fifties —not freezing. And it wasn't as if he'd die of dehydration. The trail ran right along a freshwater stream—Clear Creek.

My mind went back to the summers I'd spent in Arizona. My grandmother lived in Window Rock, on the Navajo reservation, not far from Gallup. She wasn't the most popular woman on the rez. She'd married a Mexican man in her youth—my grandpa, Jose. He'd been crazy handsome according to his pictures. He could have been a movie star instead of a rodeo cowboy. But women who married outsiders were regarded with suspicion by other Navajo. It didn't matter that Jose had died in his thirties from a blow he'd sustained bull riding, and that my grandmother had remarried a Navajo man. Her youthful *wildness* would never be forgotten.

I grew up knowing her second husband, Albert Lapahie. I called him my grandfather because Navajo called their elders my grandfather or my grandmother as a sign of respect, whether they were related or not.

Grandfather Albert was a good man, even though he rarely spoke. Every summer, he built a hogan out in the canyons during my visits, and we'd hunt and fish there. He'd taught me basic survival skills. Of course, they were skills for the desert, and I'd moved to one of the wettest spots on the planet. But still. I'd be willing to bet the Makah valued self-sufficiency as much as the Navajo did. Billy could take care of himself.

As long as he wasn't badly hurt. But the ache in my heart said otherwise.

If I slept at all, it was the restless, uneasy sleep of a man who knows a horrible day lies ahead. The next morning, I pulled into the trailhead just as dawn was breaking. There was no horizon here that wasn't blocked by green trees, but a glow of yellow to the east told me the sun had made an appearance. There were half a dozen cars already in the parking lot, and a group of men and women stood around, grave and silent townspeople. I was glad to see them.

Sam had six horses lined up at his horse trailer. When I walked up to him with Duke on leash, he raised an eyebrow at me. "So that's why you wanted it." He handed me a plastic grocery bag. I looked inside. There was a bandana in there. I'd requested something of Billy's in a text I'd fired off to Sam in the middle of the night.

"This is perfect. Thanks."

"You really think your dog can find Billy's scent?" Sam glanced at Duke doubtfully.

Duke wasn't the typical bloodhound you'd see in the movies. But I knew for a fact he had an excellent nose. "It's worth a try."

"Okay. You going on foot, then?"

"That'd be best. Unless you really need me to lead a group on horseback. But then I wouldn't be able to take Duke."

"No, we've got this. Mark Grable is a good rider, so he can help out. Take the dog. I hope you find him."

Gabriel pulled into the parking lot carrying his deputy, Devin, and three other men in his official SUV. He organized teams. There'd be a group on horseback—led by Sam and Mark. And a group on foot—led by Gabriel and Devin. At each trail junction, the teams would split, but we were never to get below two on a team. His manner was firm and efficient, and it was impressive to see him at work. But I was anxious to get moving and so was Duke.

Devin handed out maps, radios, and whistles. The group on horseback started out first.

Gabriel came over to talk to me while we gave them a head start. Duke went into spasms of joy seeing him, and Gabriel gave him some pets and a treat. He always seemed to have them in his pockets—just like me.

"You brought Duke," Gabriel said, straightening up from greeting the dog. "Think he can track Billy?"

I showed him the baggie Sam had given me. "I have his bandana. Dogs are supposed to be able to detect a person's scent up to a half mile away, so maybe if we get close enough. But Duke's not trained for this."

"It worked with Mike," Gabriel pointed out, and I remembered the day Duke had shown us the location where Mike Bressett had died.

The parallels to today made me feel sick. I took a deep breath to quell it.

"True," I said. "But Mike was Duke's owner. I guess we'll see if he'll track a stranger's scent."

Gabriel put a hand on my shoulder and rubbed a thumb there. "Stick with me. Okay?"

I nodded and looked away. After a sleepless night, my emotions were too close to the surface. Including those for Sheriff Gabriel Thompson.

We started out. Everyone was quiet, staring into the trees intently. But I knew we wouldn't find Billy this close to the trailhead, and I was impatient to move faster. When we reached the first trail junction, we split, Devin taking a group to the left while Gabriel, me, and Duke, and three other men went on towards Clear Creek Falls.

I let Duke sniff the bandana a few times. He continued to want to go straight ahead, but I wasn't sure if he was following Billy's scent or if he was scenting the horses. There wasn't much I could do but wait and see where he led us.

It was full daylight by the time we reached the falls. There were fresh droppings in the clearing—Sam or Mark's search group on horseback had been here. But there was no one there now.

We stopped for a water break, and I told Gabriel about where I'd found River on the trail. He nodded and walked out onto the bridge, turning to study our side of the falls from the bridge's expanse. His gaze dropped to the stream below.

I knew what he was thinking—could Billy have fallen over the edge? But that wasn't what I'd gotten from River.

Still. Gabriel stood at the railing and scanned the bank. Duke strained on his leash for the trail straight ahead. He wanted to keep going.

Gabriel walked back; expression thoughtful. "Okay. You guys cross the bridge and go that way. Tiber and I will continue on."

"Sure thing," said a tall man in his fifties wearing a red flannel shirt. I didn't know his name. A second man nodded.

But a big, burly guy with white hair, a young face, and uncanny blue eyes took a step toward Gabriel. "I wanna continue on with you two, Sheriff."

I could tell Gabriel wanted to protest. But there were two of the other guys, and two of us. So, the white-haired guy could go with either team of two. "Okay, Dell. You come with us then."

I gave Duke another sniff of the contents of the baggie, and he led the way.

We'd gone uphill on the trail for maybe ten minutes. I knew we were close to a right-hand turn onto a ridgeline trail. But before we got there, Duke reversed course, turning abruptly on the leash, and heading back down the trail, pulling hard.

Gabriel and I exchanged a quizzical glance, but I went along with Duke. He stopped near a rock at the side of the trail and sniffed the ground in big, greedy huffs and snorts. Gabriel squatted to get a closer look, motioning me to get

Duke back, which I did. And yeah, there was something there.

"Is that a footprint?" I asked.

Gabriel nodded. "Looks like a boot." He took out his camera and took some photos.

Dell scoffed. "It's a hiking trail, Sheriff. There're gonna be prints all over the place. Hell, some of these trails are like Grand Central Station these days."

I was starting to dislike Dell. He struck me as a blowhard. More than that, his tone felt off. I stared at him, but he just rolled his eyes and crossed his arms. I decided he was one of those men who had to be the know-it-all in any situation. As if he was an expert on missing persons investigations.

Gabriel ignored him, taking his time photographing the prints and checking the pictures on the phone's viewscreen. When he stood and nodded to me, I gave Duke some slack on the leash and he headed into the woods, bounding over the underbrush. I followed, barely having time to choose my footfalls as Duke's pace grew more frantic.

"Hope that dog knows what he's doin'," I heard Dell mutter from behind me.

I kept going. I prayed Duke hadn't scented a rabbit or deer or otherwise gotten distracted.

There might or might not have been blood, or broken twigs or other sign of something coming this way. The morning light was dim under the cover of the dense, green trees, and I didn't have time to do anything but hang on.

And then Duke stopped. He sniffed around a fallen, rotting log, in deep huffs.

That was when I saw a bit of red shirt on the other side.

"Gabriel," I said in a warning voice. I held Duke back as he tried to climb over the log. If Billy was there, I didn't want Duke getting any closer.

Gabriel went around us and over the log, taking careful steps, and studied whatever was there. I saw his face drain of color. He moved closer and dropped to his knees, reached out. My head swam. I didn't want to see it. Or begin to think about what had happened.

It was Billy—Gabriel's face told me. But why was Billy *here*?

Dell had no such compunctions. He put a hand on the log and swung his bulk over with a grunt.

I heard Gabriel on the radio. "Search teams, this is Sheriff Thompson. We've located Billy. I repeat, we've located Billy. Devin, you there? Over."

"Here, Sheriff. Oh, um, over."

"Devin, call for an ambulance. Over and out."

"Is he hurt? Where is he? Where are you?" Sam's voice.

I swallowed down my empathy and horror as best I could. I had to be stronger than this. Gabriel shouldn't have to deal with it alone.

His gaze was on me as he held the radio at his lips. I knew he was conflicted about what to say to Sam. What to say to anyone who could hear his radio signal. He spoke. "We're off-trail, Sam, maybe ten minutes up from the Falls. I'll send Tiber back to the trail to meet you. Everyone else, thank you for your help. You can go on home."

He lowered the radio, expression defeated. This wasn't the way this search was supposed to end.

"Wolves," said Dell, his lip curling with disgust. He was staring at whatever lay on the other side of the log. He raised a white finger and pointed at what I presumed was the body. "Goddamn wolves did that."

Gabriel and I exchanged a confused look.

Wolves?

It hadn't occurred to me. I wasn't used to thinking about wolves. But now that Dell had said it, I remembered hearing something about a small wolf pack moving into the Olympic National Park. Hell, I'd admired a painting in the window of the gallery on Main Street—a white wolf standing proudly on a rock in a glowing green landscape. It had been done by Libby Smith, our famous local wildlife painter. I knew gray wolves had been reintroduced to Yellowstone National Park and parts of Idaho in 1995, and their offspring had spread, worked their way west. This was about as far west as it was possible to go.

But even if there was a small pack in the Olympic mountains, why would they come this close to Prophet? They'd avoid people.

"I doubt it was a wolf," I said.

"Well, sure it was!" Dell insisted. He waved a hand at the log. "Throat's all ripped out. That's what they do. Come look at 'im! It sure as shit was a wolf."

"You don't have to," Gabriel said. He glared at Dell. "We won't know what did this until we get a full autopsy."

Dell huffed. "Well, I can tell you right now. You don't have to pay me, neither."

I didn't want to see it. But Dell was pissing me off.

And I thought, too, of that painting on Main Street. Unease sent cold prickles along the back of my neck.

I tied Duke to a nearby tree. He'd had enough trauma with Mike's death; I didn't want him to see the body. Then I climbed over the log a few feet down.

"You don't need to look," Gabriel repeated, but I ignored him and walked to where he stood. I glanced at the body.

Billy was on his side. He wore jeans, boots, and a red canvas shirt under a puffy blue vest. One arm was outstretched as if he'd been reaching for something—or fighting something off. His face was turned so I could only see half of it. One dark eye was open. His skin was pale and waxy. He didn't look real.

At one of his calves, the jeans were ripped and bloody. *That's the bite that dragged him off his horse.* But it hadn't killed him. He had more bites on his arms.

His throat had been torn out.

There was no sign that whatever killed him had made a meal of him. It had been a vicious attack, but not by an animal intent on feeding.

I swallowed hard and met Gabriel's eyes. I wanted to fall against him, hold him. But neither of us moved to touch. Not with Dell there.

"It does look like an animal attack. Huh?" Gabriel murmured.

I nodded.

"I'd better radio it in to Fish and Wildlife. They'll have a procedure, probably send someone out."

I nodded again, not trusting my voice.

I heard crunching twigs and turned to see Dell scramble over the log. He started back towards the trail.

"It *was* a wolf!" Dell called out, sounding pleased with himself, as if he were informing the rest of the group.

And I knew, right then, this was going to end badly.

Chapter Four

Gabriel

As soon as we got back to the cabins Sam pulled me to one side—shaky but determined. "Gabe, can we talk?"

"Sure?" Was it wrong to think that maybe I'd fucked up again somehow with my brother? He gestured for me to follow him toward the trees behind the house, where we couldn't be heard. I registered Tiber's frown, but it was Sam I focused on.

"It's about Billy." Sam remained as pale as he'd been after finding out Billy was dead, and now he seemed uncertain. Worried.

"What's wrong?"

Sam lowered his voice. "Something's not right." I waited for more. "One day he tells me he'd been recommended to check out this new trail, and the first time he rides here, this happens."

I wasn't sure I saw the connection between a trail recommendation and being attacked by a wild animal. But it was my job to gather information and besides—this was my little brother. I'd spent a long time just getting him to talk to me again. I was damn well gonna listen.

"Who recommended the trail to Billy?" I asked.

Sam shook his head. "He never said. But it seems like a heck of a coincidence to me. And it's not just that." Sam carded a hand through his hair and gripped it. "He'd been on edge for a few months, now, started wearing this pouch around his neck. Said it was 'protection.' When I casually asked from what, he didn't answer, and I didn't push, because why would I? Only, once, when we were out riding, he got really nervous and clutched the pouch, looking around and muttering in Makah. I don't know. Maybe all of this means nothing, but I think he had troubles." Sam dropped his hands to his sides, and then locked his gaze to mine. "Maybe his fear and the pouch and him getting attacked was related to his time in prison."

This was news to me. "Billy did time?"

Sam nodded. "Did a stretch for marijuana possession, way back. He'd lost everything, including his wife, and turned up here looking for work. He was good with horses, sincere, friendly, and we all know that marijuana was a bum charge, so I wanted to give him a second chance, you know?"

My head spun—Sam had let a convicted felon near his family? What the hell—

"You're doing that thing," Sam said, and poked me in the chest, which served to get my flare of shock under control.

"What thing?"

"The thing where you silently judge me for my choices."

"You hired an ex-con," I summarized, and yes I sounded judgey and I winced. In a perfect world, those who'd done their time, paid for their crimes, been rehabilitated, should be given a second chance. But I'd seen the imperfect, and what if Billy was like one of the cons back in LA who were in and out of prison as if the place had a revolving door? *Stop it. Stop treating Sam as if he isn't a grown man with a family who's run this place on his own since I left town.* I remembered him as my kid brother, but he was an adult now, and I had to trust he knew what he was doing.

Sam sighed and his eyes shone with grief. "He was a good man, Gabe. Loved the kids in small doses, I'll miss the ornery bastard."

"I'm sorry for your loss," I repeated again. I knew my brother's heart was big given he was slowly forgiving *me* for fucking up, and that it must be hurting.

"Just, please, find out what really happened, okay? The fact that Billy had a record doesn't mean he's not worthy of due care and investigation."

Hurt flooded me at the veiled implication. "That's not how I work."

Sam gripped my arm. "I'm not talking about you. I trust *you*, but this town… it gets something in its head and then everything goes to shit. I've seen the way people treated Billy." He stopped and tightened his hold for a brief moment. "Work for him, yeah? Do it for Billy. And do it for me."

I nodded, and patted his hand, a connection I'd missed so much. Sam was trusting me, and it was everything.

Of course, I'd run Billy through the database, and of course I'd follow up any leads from the coroner and from his background, even if this did look like a wild animal attack.

But it wasn't for Sam I was focused that way.

It was the poor soul who had lost their life near my town.

"THE TOXICOLOGY REPORT WAS CLEAN," Amelia started.

I nodded. We'd headed to her office in Port Angeles first thing Monday morning, hoping that after two days of fruitless searching for anything to support a crime, a face-to-face meeting would give us more information on whether this was a criminal act or an accident.

"Completely clean?" It wasn't that I doubted the coroner, after all I'd never caught Billy with a beer let alone drugs or worse, but I just needed to make sure.

"Yes. There were defensive wounds on both hands—Mr. Odette wasn't going down without a fight. The wound on his leg isn't deep enough to puncture an artery, teeth marks have punctured the skin through the denim, and we've taken a cast of the area and extensive scans. At this point he was still alive as the damage caused was superficial compared to what happened next."

"He didn't bleed out from that wound?" I'd held onto the hope that somehow Billy's death had been quick, and he wouldn't have known what was happening to him.

"No. There is extensive bruising on the same side of his body as the leg wound, consistent with him being dragged from the horse and falling from that height. I can hypothesize with a fair degree of certainty that the killing wound was the one around the neck." She pointed at Billy's head; his face covered with a cloth. "Drag marks appear on his back where his shirt rode up, the carotid artery was torn cleanly, his windpipe and carotid arteries severed, with major blood loss, and marks on his C5 and C6 vertebrae are suggestive of damage caused by biting. It was definitely an animal attack, but I can't positively ID the species from the visual assessment."

"Are there tests you can—"

"Yes. I've sent in tissue samples from the wounds for DNA testing—the results should show not only Billy's DNA but the DNA from the saliva of the attacker. I found two hairs on the body that I sent along with the tissue samples. And I've also submitted samples for a rabies test. Those results will take a good week to come in, though. Longer if the lab is busy."

"Are you sure there were no signs that a human was involved?"

She shot me a glance of frustration. "Not that the body showed. Why do you ask?"

I thought about Sam's suspicions. "Just dotting all the Is. But… could it have been something like a wolf?"

She raised an eyebrow at me. "You *know* I can't give you a definitive answer until results are back, Sheriff. Meanwhile, I suggest you contact Fish and Wildlife. The WDFW should be involved if it's a wild animal attack." She huffed at a stray red hair escaping from the bun where she'd removed her cap and waited for me to ask some more inane questions. I stayed quiet because Devin was standing next to me, and I didn't want him to see me eviscerated by our feisty coroner.

"Already did. They're sending someone. You mentioned finding hairs on the body. Animal hair?"

"Two hairs, about one point five centimeters long and gray. But I understand from the work up that Mr. Odette spent a lot of time around animals, so at this point we can't suggest it's fur from whatever killed him. Although I have ruled out one suggestion."

Hope flared. "And that is?"

"Bigfoot." Amelia leveled a look at me after indirectly referencing the park ranger case where bigfoot had been a momentary suspect—not by me, but by bigfoot hunters everywhere. "Anyway, what I have so far is in the file that I'm emailing you, and for what it's worth to his family, whatever did this didn't play with the victim, in fact the bite on his neck caused catastrophic blood loss and would have killed him instantly. He wouldn't have suffered for long."

Next to me Devin moaned and held his stomach, and the last thing I needed was for my rookie to lose his lunch on the pristine tiles. The first time I'd seen a dead body—a jumper from the roof of a glass and steel office block—I'd managed to hold my stomach for as long as it took to get around the corner and to the nearest open drain. He'd seen Mike's body, but Billy's had been torn apart, which was a new one for Devin, whereas Mike Bressett's corpse had been icy cold and bloodless, and the *X* carved into his chest had been done post-mortem.

"Is there any sign that whatever killed him ate any part of him?"

Devin gagged and excused himself, and both myself and Amelia sent a fond look after the kid.

"Took me three autopsies before I could keep my food where it belonged," Amelia murmured.

"Yeah," I agreed.

"And no, to your question, There's not enough of him missing to suggest his attacker made a meal of what they cut out. Whatever did this was all about killing, it wasn't food."

Now I felt sick. When I played with Duke—when I loved on Duke, and we roughhoused, or indeed when I saw any of Tiber's little family—I never imagined any of them tearing a throat out. In a quiet LA suburb, when I'd been training, and before the undercover fallout, I'd seen what a trio of Chihuahuas had done to their owner's arm when she died and hadn't been found for five days, where nature overcame nurture. Dogs were creatures who operated on instinct, and hunger was a compulsion—even humans grew desperate when hungry.

But what would cause any sort of animal to drag a man from a horse, tear his throat out, and then not eat at least some of the remains? It certainly crossed the starvation imperative off my very short list of reasons why an animal attacked a human. Was it just for sport? Was it a game to whatever animal had done this? Had Billy crossed into a parcel of land that was something's territory?

Head full of unanswered questions I found Devin leaning on the wall outside the bathroom, pale and dabbing a tissue at his bloodless lips.

"Sorry," he mumbled.

"It's all good," I reassured him and patted his shoulder. "We all have that one time." Or two, or three, or ten.

"So it gets better?" he asked, with a note of desperation. "Because that wasn't my finest hour."

"Sure, it gets better," I hedged.

"Does Amelia think it was a wolf?" he asked.

"She doesn't know yet."

"Dell Prosser is convinced it's a wolf, he's riling up people in town," Devin said, and I shot him a glance. I knew Dell was convinced that a wolf pack had done this to Billy, but there was no evidence to back this up. "Hen said he's going to talk at the town meeting later."

I massaged the bridge of my nose. "For real?"

"Yep."

"Great." A town meeting stirring up yet more anger and worry that hadn't begun to die down from Mike Bressett's murder. Just what we needed. "Guess I know where I'll be tonight then."

"What if it is wolves and it's a pack and they come into town?"

I knew he was playing devil's advocate, but he had to realize that wouldn't occur.

Would it?

"Not gonna happen, Tiber said wolves normally avoid people, they wouldn't stroll into town."

"Hmmm." Devin didn't sound convinced.

By the time we hit the parking lot, he'd inhaled lungs full of fresh air and had color back in his cheeks, but the clouds were gathering, a storm threatened over Port Angeles, and there was no time to be standing outside waiting for a cloudburst. We hurried into the SUV, closing the doors as the rain began, and then sat for a while as I skimmed the report on my phone. I don't know what I was searching for—maybe a clue Amelia had neglected to hand to us, maybe some trace DNA that could solve the whole thing.

But I found nothing apart from a clinical report about the remains and it was one more horror I'd never forget.

WE HEADED BACK TO PROPHET, both silent, the sound of the local radio station ebbing and flowing where there was reception. Neither of us reached to fix white noise when it happened—happy to process thoughts on our own.

When we were five minutes from town I sensed Devin had something to say, and I braced myself for the worst. Death was hard on every cop, hell, every first responder, and the poor kid had gone through a trial by fire in what was supposed to be the sleepy Olympic Peninsula.

"We'll find what did this," he murmured.

"We will."

The rain had eased when I parked the car, and we split in different directions, me heading up to the cabins, Devin into the office. I could have taken the SUV, but I had my slicker, and I needed the air as much as Devin had, also I needed the time to school my thoughts and not imagine poor Billy on the table, because I was going up to see Sam, and the last thing I needed was to carry those images with me. We may be struggling to get back to being brothers, but Sam knew me, and would read my expression, then losing Billy would hurt all over again. I wish I had something to tell him, but it had been two days since we'd found the body, and we had no hint of why he'd been pulled from the horse, no firm leads on his killer other than the coroner not being able to ID the species, and I knew Sam was as exasperated as me.

Somehow it didn't surprise me to see Tiber at the stables behind the cabins, and to say I'd been hoping to see him as well was an understatement. Dressed in his usual jeans and yellow coat, he'd tied his long hair back and I'd never seen anything more beautiful since... well, since the last time I'd seen him. My heart swelled a little, despite the fact we were *just friends*, because I was a patient man, and I hoped that one day he'd want to kiss me again and this time not to back off. He gave me a small wave as I passed where he was working with River. I'd seen his empathy with dogs, cats, rabbits, and tortoises. Hell, he probably even had it with Sid the spider who, thankfully, I'd yet to meet. I'd just never extended his intuition and love for animals to horses, although with River staring at the ground, it didn't seem like Tiber was winning today.

I waved back at him and threw him what I hoped was a smile of reassurance and not one that showed me wanting to go over and kiss him senseless.

"Any news?" Sam called from the far stable.

I pulled my attention away from the man I was falling for, and to the brother I needed to mend bridges with. I didn't want to destroy Sam's hope, but what could I say? It wasn't as if the coroner had anything to add that would make sense of what happened to Billy.

"Nothing concrete," I summarized, and his shoulders fell. "We need to get back up there in the morning with a biologist from Fish and Wildlife and I'm hoping she'll know more."

"So Dell is shouting off about wolves. Is he right?"

I shook my head. "I don't know. For the moment everything points to a wild animal attack, and unless I camp out up there and wait for something to stroll on by, I'm at a loss."

"Shit. I really thought…" Sam stopped and scrubbed at his face, smudges of exhaustion under his eyes. I knew he'd relied on Billy for the stable help, plus he was having to deal with the cabins, and we were at peak leaf-peeping season so I guessed all cabins would be full. "… never mind. Thank you for coming up and letting me know."

"Sam, I'm going to continue to look into it. If there's anything to find, I'll find it."

"Thanks," Sam sighed.

Conversation over, he went inside the stable and I followed him, which got me a weary smile.

"So Tiber's up here then?"

"Yeah, working with River, on and off, when he can. Poor horse is really traumatized by what happened. I never realized Tiber was a freaking horse whisperer, but he has this connection which is kind of intense," Sam said as we headed straight over to a small table in the tack room. It held the coffee machine I recalled from years ago that sat next to a see-through box holding three chipped mugs and my other brother's travel mug—leave it up to Ezra to be all efficient with a lid and everything.

Mine was the mug at the back, and it probably hadn't moved since I'd left town. I felt a twinge of something at seeing the mug next to mine—a bright neon-green Greatest

Dad mug. Dad had been gone a few years now, yet Sam had kept the mug out here?

Well, he kept mine as well. What do I expect?

"Tiber's good with all animals," I said, and could hear the pride in my tone.

Sam shot me a sharp look but focused on picking up my mug. He peered inside and gasped theatrically, then shook his head as he tipped out the remains of a big-ass spider.

Fuck. My. Life.

I will *never* use that mug again.

Catching my grimace he raised an eyebrow—he'd never understood my hatred of all things arachnid— then pulled out Ezra's travel mug instead. He sluiced out the inside with hot water before handing me coffee and he did all of that in silence.

"How are you doing?" he asked me, when I took my first sip of the dark, grainy brew.

I recalled being out here with Dad and my brothers as a kid, feeling so grown up when I was the first of us to get to taste coffee. I'd been eleven, Sam nine, Ezra still a baby, and Dad had told me it would put hairs on my chest, which for every pre-pubescent boy was a dream. Of course, his casual referencing of what happened as boys became men soon stopped when I'd told him I was gay. Then he'd called me unnatural, and wrong, and called on God to show me the error of my ways. *Stop thinking about the past, because sure as shit I'll spiral.*

"Shouldn't I be asking you that question?" I hedged because I didn't want to talk about me.

"Me?" he asked, surprised.

"You lost a friend, and you're picking up the slack and—"

"Don't change the subject," Sam said, and I clammed up. "When you told me... implied stuff about LA... you said you were seeing someone, and you... " He dipped his head, about as happy to be talking emotions as I was. "I just wanted to check that you were okay."

Something passed between us then, a thread of connection I thought I might have lost all together. I could lie and say I was all fixed, but I still didn't sleep, and I had a head full of flashbacks and regret.

"I'm getting there." *Change the subject.* "Can I ask you something?" I didn't want to start a fight, and my relationship with Sam was still in its infancy, but I needed to get something out of my head.

"Sure, can't promise I'll answer." He half smiled—he was teasing me. I loved that glimpse of us as we used to be.

"What does Ezra think... I mean... where..." Jesus, why did my question come out in a tumble of nonsense.

"Ezra was only ten when you left, he just remembers you as the big brother who never came home." That was sharp and it dug into my heart. For a moment all the stupid decisions I had made were front and center, and the regrets chased right after them.

"He's happy at NYU. We don't see him much because he's interning at a law office there, pays his own way, got a full ride because he clearly got all of the Thompson brains."

I was so proud of Ezra, the first in our family to go to

college, making something of himself. "But you talk to him, yeah? He's not on his own."

Sam's expression turned flinty. "We're close—he's never *alone*."

I deserved that. "Does he... do you ever talk about me."

Sam sighed. "What do you want me to say? That we sit around chatting about our awesome big brother and how much we miss him?"

Jeez, I deserved that too. What was I doing to myself?

"I'm sorry Sam, I'm so damn sorry."

"Look, he says he's coming back for Thanksgiving, has this thing in Seattle, maybe he'll talk to you then. Emphasis on the *maybe*, because let's face it, I've not been kind to you in your absence."

Sam—"

"You left us to deal with Dad at his worst, and we were on our own." Sam rubbed a hand on his chest, and I didn't have to look hard to see the tension in him. "I can't say sorry for how I felt at the time, but I regret how I felt because it was just a waste of everything."

"I don't expect you to apologize, I was the one who left."

"But I will explain to Ezra that you're making a difference here, that you're trying, and that you're hurting. What he does with that, I don't know."

"Thank you, Sam."

"Don't thank me yet."

"Can I help... here I mean. I'm all yours for the rest of the day, nothing I can do until the morning when someone from Fish and Wildlife is supposed to show up, so can I help here?"

His eyes widened, and he sipped at his coffee to give himself time to process.

"You're gonna shovel shit in that?" Sam gestured at my uniform.

"You have some old clothes hanging about?"

He headed into the small office that had once been Dad's but now sat empty, came back, and tossed me a bag with some joggers and a long-sleeved shirt. I recognized them as mine from way back but they'd both been freshly laundered.

"Thought you'd make it up here one day," Sam explained.

"But not enough to wash the spider from my mug?"

Sam snorted a laugh. "Be thankful I didn't leave it in your coffee."

"Asshole."

"Back at ya."

Buoyed by that glimpse of normal we had going on between us and feeling as though I'd ripped the bandage off the Ezra thing, I shook out the clothes, waiting to see if anything crawled out from them. Then I changed, the pants a little tighter now I was much older, but the shirt hung loose on me. I didn't recall losing muscle mass, but I didn't eat as well as I should unless it was Tiber dishing up the food. So yeah, maybe I was getting skinny?

"Hey, Sarah and Aaron want you to come over for their birthday, for lunch, you, and Tiber. You up for it?"

"Of course, yes, I'd love to. October sixth, right? Friday. What time?"

He arched an eyebrow that I'd recalled the date, but the date I'd become an uncle wasn't one I was going to forget in a hurry. I hadn't been here for them, but I'd gotten a message through control when my job was done in LA, and the date would never leave me.

"Lunch?" he asked. "I dunno, twelve or so?"

"I'll ask Tiber. I can't wait."

Sam wondered off and left me mucking out stables, and I stopped to talk to each of the horses, spending most of the time chatting away to Sam's horse Conway who nudged my arm as I worked and made me smile. I took a few moments to rub his nose and buried my face in his mane.

"There's something so uncomplicated about horses," Tiber said from behind me, and it didn't startle me, almost as if I knew he'd be checking up on me, or maybe I sensed he was there. "They never lose their wild spirit, no matter how domesticated they've become. They aren't easily won over, but when one gifts you their trust it's magical."

He smiled at me, scratching Conway's nose and laughing as Conway hunted out treats.

His uncomplicated, real joy at petting a horse, was everything.

It alleviated my worries about not knowing what had happened to Billy, it made sense of why I was standing here, and I couldn't help myself. I cradled his face and kissed him. This time when we separated he didn't step away, nor did he go wide-eyed and surprised.

But he *did* change the subject.

"I'm thinking we turn out Conway with River into the

back pasture tomorrow—he'll be a steady calming influence."

I blinked at the redirect, and wished we were kissing again. He patted my arm and wandered back out, and it was only then I noticed that Fluffy the barn cat was at his heels. Seemed that even Fluffy was entranced by the animal whisperer.

I knew how he felt.

Chapter Five

Tiber

I WAS BACK from the stables in time to make dinner for myself and my pack and get them all out for a walk before dark. We'd returned home, and I'd just changed into my comfy night-at-home clothes—as if I had any other kind of night—when there was a firm knock on my front door.

The dogs barked and bayed with alarm, and that told me it wasn't Gabriel. Which was weird. No one else ever visited me. Even delivery men came and went with alacrity, tossing boxes onto my porch thanks to my pointed *DO NOT KNOCK* signs.

I checked out of the window and saw a woman on my doorstep. She was wraith-thin under a tightly belted khaki raincoat. Wiry gray hair peeked out from under a matching khaki rain hat.

Yeah, I had no idea who she was. Maybe she was lost?

"Leo, Ferdinand, Gracie, Duke—get back." I pointed firmly down the hall to the living room.

With reluctance they moved back, and I opened the door.

"Hi," I said, more confused than friendly.

Intelligent green eyes studied me from a lively, wrinkled face. There wasn't a trace of make-up and the woman's energy was rock-solid, strong. "Tiber Russo?"

"Yes."

"I'm Libby Smith. I need a moment of your time."

It took a second for the name to register. *Libby Smith.* Wow! I'd seen her gorgeous paintings in the gallery on Main Street, and I knew her work was on US postal stamps and hung in national galleries, but I'd never met her. "Oh, hey. I mean, hi."

She raised an eyebrow. "May I come in?"

"If you don't mind animals. I have a lot."

A dismissive puff escaped her lips. "Mr. Russo, I make my living painting wildlife. There's no animal I haven't stalked, photographed, studied, and accidentally rolled in the shit of. Pardon my French."

I smiled as I stepped aside, and Libby walked in. The dogs crowded around her, sniffing her shoes, her legs, her thigh-length raincoat. She didn't pet them, but she didn't seem bothered by them either. She was all determination as she faced me. "I have one question for you."

"Okay."

"Do you believe wolves killed Billy Odette?"

I started to answer, stopped. It was a question I'd asked myself over the past few days since Billy had been found.

I'd studied wolf packs while getting my degree in Animal Behavior at UDub. They were an important species for a number of reasons. Since the common dog is descended from wolves, it was fascinating to see how the modern dog and wolf differed from each other. That was, the effects of domestication. For example, one study gave a wolf and a dog a problem to solve—such as a yummy treat inside a puzzle box— and had a person sit quietly in the room. The dog would try to open the box on his own once or twice, then go to the human for help. Every time. Even dogs who had not had a lot of human contact. On the other hand, a wolf would continue to attempt to solve the problem on his own indefinitely. He—or she—would ignore the human in the room. In another study, dogs were able to read the subtlest cues from humans—such as a glance at the fist that holds a treat. Wolves were oblivious to those signals.

I'd also had an entire class on pack behavior with wolves being one of the primary species studied.

I already had some knowledge about wolves, but because of what had happened to Billy, I'd done some googling in the past few days to brush up on the latest research. Since wolves had been reintroduced to the US almost thirty years ago, there'd been incidents of wolves attacking livestock, horses, dogs, sometimes barn cats. But not humans. And certainly not a human on a horse—not even in Yellowstone, where riders reported seeing wolves while out on the trail.

I looked Libby in the eye. "No. I don't believe it was wolves."

She let out a sigh of relief and deflated, as if she'd been puffed up and prepared to fight but was glad not to have to. "Good. Then you're coming with me. Right now, please."

"What?"

"There's a town meeting. I'll drive."

I felt a flutter of dread. "No. No, I don't do… people. Or big gatherings. Sorry, but no."

Libby placed her hands on her hips and glared at me. "Mr. Russo, I've had the privilege of observing the wolf pack that moved into this region. There are two males, three females, and three cubs. They're beautiful, and they're surviving, and they ask nothing of us except to leave some small part of this planet undisturbed so they can simply exist. And right now, they need someone to stand up for them. Are you going to make me stand alone?"

Fuck.

I closed my eyes but couldn't close myself off from the painful thudding of my heart. *Empathy mode engaged.*

"Fine," I snapped. "Let me get changed."

THERE WAS a big turnout for the town meeting. We had a hard time finding parking on Main Street around the community hall and ended up on a side street several blocks away. I wished I was anywhere else as I followed Libby down the sidewalk and up the steps to the hall. We arrived just as the meeting was getting started. The seats were all filled, and people stood in the back—which gave me an excuse to stand in the back too.

Libby glared at me when I refused to go down the aisle, but since there were no open seats, she couldn't protest too much.

"Well! Attention. Attention. Is this thing working?"

Mayor Alice Darnow, a plump woman with steely blue eyes, and beauty shop-red hair, stood at the podium and tapped the mic. "It is? Thank you. Goodness sake, we haven't had more than three or four people show up for our town meetings since the flood of '18. So, it's nice to see you all here."

If she was being sarcastic, it didn't show.

My gaze went to Gabriel. He was seated on the little stage in front along with Devin and another man I didn't know. Gabriel seemed surprised to see me. I shrugged and tilted my head toward Libby, who stood to my right. He raised his eyebrows as if to say *oh, really*? But it was half-hearted teasing. He looked tense.

Me? I had the uncomfortable feeling that I couldn't inhale deep enough and that the air was stale and foul. I hated crowds. Worse, I had a feeling this wasn't going to be a friendly exchange.

Mayor Darnow went over some business—the last meeting's minutes, a treasurer's report, and a report from a county utility representative. He was the other man sitting on the stage with Gabriel and Devin.

As soon as the utility man sat down, someone in the crowd spoke up. It was Dell, the white-haired guy who'd been with Gabriel and me when we found Billy. "Mayor— do we have to wait until the end of the agenda to bring up the killing? I think I speak for everyone here when I say we want to talk about it now. One of our own was murdered for the crime of being out on the trails. It could have been any one of us! And it could happen again. I wanna know what you and the sheriff are gonna do about it!"

There were murmurs of agreement and the atmosphere went from bored to upset in a heartbeat. The mayor glanced at Gabriel, then turned back to the mic. "As a point of order, any new business should be discussed under *new business*, but I suppose we can move that up on the agenda. I'll let Sheriff Thompson speak on the unfortunate, er tragedy that befell Billy Odette. Sheriff?"

Gabriel stood up and went to the mic while Mayor Darnow sat down. I felt nervous for him. It wasn't easy to face this crowd.

"As Mayor Darnow said, I'm Sheriff Thompson. Billy Odette went missing on Friday, September twenty-nineth while out on a trail ride alone. He was reported missing that evening when he didn't return to the stables, and the Sheriff's Department organized a search party that went out at first light on the thirtieth. I want to thank those folks who volunteered for the search party." His gaze moved around the room, and he nodded at several people.

"We know all that, Sheriff," Dell bellowed. "And we also know Billy was found dead!"

Gabriel glanced at Dell but went on as if he hadn't spoken. "The search party located Mr. Odette, who was deceased. He was removed to the Clallum County Morgue where a full investigation on the cause of death, along with an investigation opened by us here in Prophet, has commenced."

"What is there to investigate, Sheriff?" Big John, a Makah man from Neah Bay, stood. "I heard it was an animal attack. Is that true?"

Gabriel nodded. "Yes. The coroner has confirmed it was an animal attack. But we—"

"It was wolves!" Dell said. "That wolf pack that's been in the papers. We never had this kind of thing before they arrived. Are you gonna take care of those wolves, Sheriff? Or are you gonna issue us hunting permits and let us do it?"

"Yeah!" said another man.

"I'll go after them," said another. "They killed one of ours. I'd say they're fair game."

"What about hunting permits, Sheriff?"

The mood of the crowd swelled in favor of this sentiment. I saw fear and worry on the faces of men and women. I saw bloodlust too. Hunting was a popular sport around here, usually deer and duck, and I got the impression some of these guys would love to mount a wolf's head on their wall.

It made me feel sick. My head swam.

"It wasn't the wolves!" This was Libby, her voice loud and clear. She tried to drag me down the aisle towards the podium, but I froze in place, so she gave me a look I wasn't sure how to interpret and marched up to the podium by herself. She half-shoved Gabriel away from the mic.

The room was silent as she glared around. "A lot of you know me. I'm Libby Smith, and I've spent weeks out in the woods photographing the wolf pack for my paintings. I know for a fact at times they smelled me, but they ran away when they did. I never once felt I was in danger. I'm the only one in this town who knows that pack firsthand. And I can tell you for a fact, they didn't kill Billy Odette!"

There was hushed murmuring in the crowd and people consulted each other over Libby's words.

Dell spoke up, "Sorry, Libby, but I call bull! I saw Billy's body with my own two eyes—you didn't! He had bites all over him and his throat"—a woman next to Dell poked him with an elbow and Dell glanced at her and softened his tone a touch—"that is to say, his wounds sure looked like it had to be something like a wolf attack to me. Bears don't go for the throat like that."

Gabriel leaned past Libby to the mic. "Excuse me, but we're not jumping to conclusions. Fish and Wildlife is sending someone here to investigate too, and the coroner's submitted samples of saliva and hair and other evidence found on the body. Until we get those reports—"

"How many more will die while you're waiting on reports, Sheriff?" Dell insisted.

More arguing ensued, but Libby spoke forcefully into the mic. "Hold up. Hold up!"

The room quieted.

"We don't need to wait for reports. We have a scientist right here in this room that'll tell ya. Tiber Russo—he lives in Prophet and he's a trained expert in the field of animal behavior. Tiber, you tell them!"

Libby motioned to me and, like in a horror movie, everyone in the room turned their heads to stare at me.

Why does the floor never open up and swallow you when you really need it to?

"Tiber?" Libby repeated, waving a *come here* at me. "Get on up here and speak. We need some facts about now, don't you agree?"

What could I do? Turning tail and running from the hall would be more ridiculous than even I was willing to be. My feet were so hesitant I stumbled as I walked down the aisle to the podium. Go me.

Libby shifted aside and I stood at the mic. Every eye in the place was on me.

I clenched my fists at my sides and cleared my throat. "Libby's right. In fact, there has never been a recorded wolf attack on a human being in the lower forty-eight states. Not since wolves were reintroduced in 1995. And Billy was attacked while riding River. I was unable to find any cases of a wolf or a wolf pack attacking a man on horseback except for one incident in Europe in the 1800s."

There was more murmuring among the crowd. Some people looked relieved.

"Was it a bear then, Sheriff?" someone asked.

"Now hold up—" That was Dell again. The blowhard. "You said 'lower forty-eight.' That's kinda specific. What about Alaska?"

I swallowed. "There have been a couple of predatory wolf attacks in the wild in Alaska, but it's still extremely rare and there are around seventy-thousand wolves there. The pack near here is small and isolated. I'm sure the last thing they want is to have anything to do with people."

Which was exactly the way I felt at the moment.

Dell waved a dismissive hand. "Wolves are wolves, *Mr.* Russo. Not cute doggies or whatever it is you deal with. We all know wolves are dangerous. Hell, it's only logical. They're wild animals—predators! And we've seen it in the movies." He looked around for support. "Right?"

"I'd say you're more likely to get struck by lightning while blowing a kazoo than to be the victim of a wolf attack," I snapped.

"Well lightning didn't rip out Billy Odette's throat!" argued Dell, his voice booming compared to mine. "This isn't some case study or statistic. We have a dead body. It goddamn well happened!"

I felt Gabriel's hand on my arm, and I stepped back gratefully from the podium and let him take over. I'd said what I had to say. I shot an apologetic glance at Libby, but I hadn't asked to be dragged here. It wasn't my fault I wasn't the type of person who could argue in public with a bully like Dell Prosser.

I slipped off the stage and around the side of the room. I felt like a failure. And it mattered. It really fucking mattered. Libby was afraid for the wolf pack, and she was right. Dell and his kind—they wanted to destroy. They'd slaughter those wolves and consider themselves heroes. And I couldn't stop them. That made me angry, and it made me want to puke.

I prayed Gabriel could stop them. Or someone with more authority than me. But at the moment, I just had to get out of that hall.

Gabriel was speaking again, his voice louder and irritated. He was getting fed up. I heard him reiterating how no one was going to do a damned thing until Fish and Wildlife concluded their investigation, they got the lab results, and how, in the meantime, he suggested people hike in groups or stay off the trails.

I reached the door of the hall. I'd put my mental blinders on and ignored the people who stared at me as I passed. I think Hen was one of them. She said something sympathetic, but I moved past her, desperate for air.

I slipped outside and down the few steps to the

sidewalk and stood there, head back, eyes closed, taking deep gulps into my lungs. It was a chilly October night, and it was raining, naturally, but the cold drops felt good on my face. I was grateful for them.

That was the wonderful thing about rain. If a tear or two escapes, no one is the wiser.

Chapter Six

Gabriel

MY HEART SANK as I watched Tiber leave. I'd seen his panic, instinctively wanted to get him away from the stage and guide him out of there so he didn't have to deal with the chaos caused by fearmongering. Then I wanted to head back to his place and snuggle on his sofa for the rest of the night and offer him a safe haven for him to be quiet. In my official capacity I should be calming everyone down, but the impetus to just run out was so great I had to force myself to stay.

I wished we could have held this whole thing one day later so someone from Fish and Wildlife could have been here to back up what Tiber and Libby had both said. I hadn't felt this much out of my depth since joining the LAPD undercover team and finding out I knew nothing about anything. What if the wolves on the mountain *were* guilty of this? What if the DNA test results proved the killer was a wolf, and we had to trap them and relocate them, or worse, put them down? It didn't bear thinking about. I trusted Tiber's judgment, but I couldn't be entirely sure everyone would be safe, and it killed me that Tiber looked to me to be the one to make sense of all of this.

The Town Hall meeting had ended up giving the paranoid a forum to disseminate exaggerated claims. I'd come here ready to listen to residents' concerns, answer their questions, and provide an update, that was all—anything to foster trust and understanding and to keep the lines of communication open.

"What kind of measures are in place to keep us safe?" someone called, loud enough to be heard over the chaos.

"Build a wall!" someone shouted, and I had to try very hard to keep a straight face despite the anxiety in my chest.

"Until we know more—" I started.

"Electric fences keep critters off my land!" another voice chimed in.

"What about the children! Somebody needs to think of the children!"

Fuck. This was getting out of hand.

I shouted for quiet, and with one or two rumblings of discontent the room fell silent. "I'm here to advise you on the kind of precautions you can take to minimize potential encounters with wild animals—"

"Wild animals like the wolves that ripped out Billy's throat!" And we were back with Dell Prosser and his inability to stay quiet.

"That isn't what I said." I held up a hand to stop people talking. "Secure your garbage, making sure to remove anything that might attract wild animals, and keep your pets indoors at night."

"I'm not keeping my Missy in at night, she would hate that!"

"Or Snowy! But what would I do if they ate Snowy?"

I forged ahead. "The Clear Creek Falls area is closed for the time being. As for other trails, be aware of your surroundings and don't hike alone. My deputy will create a system for you to report any sightings or encounters with anything that concerns you, then we can make informed decisions."

"What about patrols? Are you going into the woods to track them down?"

"We have protocols in place, and we're seeking guidance on deterrents from—"

"Shoot 'em!" One of our more bloodthirsty residents shouted.

"Kill the wolves!" Dell said. "Kill them all!"

"Our park rangers will be running regular checks, coordinating efforts with the Sheriff's Department and—"

"Patrols won't stop them killing!"

I'd had my fill of hysteria now, and I shoved supportive-open Gabriel to one side.

"Enough! Everyone settle down!" I began with authority, then waited until everyone stopped talking and turned to me. "There is *no* conclusive evidence that this was a wolf attack, none. I'd like to remind you that our behavioral specialist has clearly said the wolf pack, which incidentally is some miles from here, is not dangerous. This matter is now complete until such time as we have more information. If you have questions, then you know where to find me, or my deputy. Goodnight."

With that I left, because if one more person suggested

deadly force, or told me I wasn't doing enough, then I might shoot them.

Or at least glare at them.

And if that didn't work I could always arrest them.

I couldn't see Tiber outside, nor his truck, but he'd arrived the same time as Libby and they'd been late so did that mean he was parked away from the hall? I jogged around the block—avoiding everyone pouring out of the hall by hiding in the shadows. It was amazing what a person could see when no one knew they were there, but when all I saw was people saying goodnight after hanging out in small cliques, I nearly gave up. Which was when Dell Prosser approached Devin. I'd left the kid in there—baptism by fire—and I could tell from his body language that Devin wasn't taking any shit from Dell. After a moment Dell gesticulated at Devin, and then turned on his heel and left, Devin staring after him. I stepped out of the shadows.

"What did Dell want?"

Devin jumped a mile, grabbing his chest. "Jesus, Gab—sir, you scared the living… jeez."

"Sorry."

He took a few breaths and then shook his head.

"Man was talking nonsense," he muttered, and I waited for him to realize that wasn't the PC way of explaining the situation, nor that respectful of his senior officer. "Sorry, sir, Dell Prosser demanded to know if we'd found anything else up with Billy's body, and began to explain at length that he used to hike up there and then he was rambling… I have no idea what point he was trying to make actually."

He pulled his shoulders back. "I should have been paying more attention."

"It's enough that Dell is on our radar. Let's get some sleep and meet the Fish and Wildlife rep with clear heads, yeah?"

"Yes, sir. Night, sir." He jogged over to his car then headed out of the parking toward his dad's place where I knew he had an apartment over the garage. I should head home myself—I wanted to be up early to run through my notes before speaking to the biologist in the morning, but good intentions went out of the window as soon as I started up my car and without thought I headed straight for Tiber's place.

I just knew if I went home and tried to sleep I wouldn't be able to forget the fear in his expression.

I'd seen fear like that before, the wide, panicked eyes at being trapped.

I'd felt that terror.

I'm just being a neighborly sheriff.

A security light sent a soft glow over the path from the gate, everywhere was silent but I could see his car. I headed up to his stoop and knocked, but apart from the pack kicking up a storm at first, there was no answer. I settled there, welcomed by barking, and reassuring the dogs in a low tone. They stopped their skittering around behind the closed door. I recognized Duke's low woof, and Leo's high-pitched yap, I swear I could hear Patch meowing. I loved it all. What would it be like to come back here every night, to sink into the pack and chill and just be with Tiber?

It would be my idea of heaven.

I heard a car long before I saw the lights bouncing down the road that rose and dipped with potholes, but I didn't move from my perch on the stoop to greet him. He would see my Department SUV, and I wanted to give him those few moments before he spoke to me.

Libby was dropping him off, and when he stepped out, he watched her turn and leave with a wave before staring at me. I could imagine he was contemplating what to do next and whether he wanted to see me. I should have gone over and checked that he was okay, told him I wasn't here to break our keep-it-casual rule, or ask for more kisses, or for anything else, come to think of it.

Finally, he opened the gate, stopping to talk to Frank who was positioned with one scaly claw on the paving stone. When Tiber straightened, the light from the porch illuminated his face, and I watched him tuck loose hair behind his ear, then tilted his chin to glance up as he took the few steps toward me.

"Gabriel," he murmured.

"Just here doing a welfare check," I said with a smile I hoped told him I wasn't here for anything else. I didn't move from the stoop, waiting for him to come to me, giving him space.

"My welfare?" He seemed surprised.

"Of course, yours, I didn't like what happened at the hall."

His lips thinned and he nodded. "I didn't like it either."

"No one was listening to anything rational." I sighed heavily.

"It was like my opinion meant nothing, as if I didn't know what I was talking about." He crossed his arms over his chest. "Then everyone stared at me, and Dell was shooting his mouth off." He let out a frustrated huff. "He's lying, you know."

"Dell is?"

Tiber nodded. "I'm not sure about what. But there's something fake in the way he's drumming all this hysteria up. I felt it the day we found Billy. It's as if he already had his mind made up that it was the wolves before we even found the body. I don't know. It's hard to explain but I don't get a good feeling about Dell."

I thought about that. Now that he'd pointed it out, Dell had been pretty quick off the mark, and I would never ignore Tiber's instincts. "Hmmm."

"I don't do well in arguments," Tiber said in a small voice. "I panicked."

"I get that. Hence me checking on you. Just wanted to make sure you're okay and that you didn't need anyone to…"

"To what?"

He went to a crouch in front of me, and he was so close I could reach for him and hold him close and kiss him until he melted in my arms.

"To talk to you, hug you, just be there for you."

"Is that maybe what *you* need?" He asked me, resting his palm on my knee.

"Me? No." *Maybe.* I'd love to fall asleep with him cuddled into me, because then the nightmares might not visit.

Frank approached from the side with his lopsided tiptoe gait, and it was enough of a distraction that Tiber stood and took the few steps to his front door, the animals inside crazy to see him. He stopped at the door and looked back at me.

"Do you want to come in?"

God yes. I'd caught the scent of him when he passed, of the outdoors, of petrichor and just that hint of citrus from his body wash or deodorant or whatever. It was enough to get me hard, and needy, but that was not how I wanted this to go. I'd be happy with a hug from him, along with a dose of canine and feline affection. Was he asking me because he felt as if he had to, though? Doubts assailed me—he shouldn't be forced to have mopey-me in his space when he'd had such a shit night.

"Do you *need* me to come in?" I asked as I stood, the emphasis on need rather than want.

"Do *you* need me?" he countered, and so we were at an impasse, neither able to vocalize what we wanted, and both worried about the other.

"I'm okay," I said after a pause.

"So am I," he reassured.

We stared at each other, and I wanted to push inside and curl up with him on the sofa, and love on him and… I did nothing like that.

"Okay then, I'm glad you're okay. Night." I turned to leave but then it occurred to me that I had the perfect excuse to see him again real soon. "Will you come to the meeting with the Fish and Wildlife rep tomorrow? Nine a.m., meeting at my office?"

He frowned again, and I was close to grabbing him to kiss away the worry. "Sure," he said after a pause.

"See you tomorrow then." I took a step back, checking

to see if Frank was behind me. There was no sign of him, so I turned and headed for the car.

"Wait. Sheriff?"

I stopped at the gate, and turned—was this the moment he told me he needed me to go inside? Was that the right thing to do after his panic attack?

Only it turned out having me in his house wasn't on his mind at all.

"Will there be muffins?" he joked.

"Always," I said, but couldn't help feeling disappointed that he wanted to talk muffins.

Oh well, there was always tomorrow.

Chapter Seven

Tiber

IT WAS POURING as we hiked up the trail to Clear Creek Falls. I led the way while Gabriel and Dr. Susan Mason chatted behind me about new Fish and Wildlife regulations.

Susan was unexpected. When Gabriel called to say an expert had arrived from the Washington Department of Fish and Wildlife, I'd expected some burly older man with a porn stash. But Susan could have been a model. She was maybe late twenties, with thick dark hair worn back in a plain bun, dark eyes, and a gorgeous face hinting at a Latina heritage. I might have been jealous of Gabriel's easy rapport with her if I hadn't known for a fact that he preferred men.

Jealous?

I couldn't deny it. Sure, I was the one who insisted we be friends only, who'd said I wasn't ready for, and maybe never would be ready for, another relationship after what had happened with Jeff. I still felt that way. Most of the time. Some of the time?

Sometimes it was hard to hold that line. Last night, for example, when Gabriel had stopped by after the town meeting to see if I was okay. What I'd wanted, more than anything, was to hold him, and be held, to find comfort in his kisses and let passion sweep me away from thoughts of what had been an uncomfortable and awkward night, from the memories of Billy's corpse, from the fear and futility.

That goddamn five o'clock shadow!

But giving in to a momentary weakness would make things awkward the next day. I had to stay strong.

We stopped to admire the falls, walking out onto the bridge.

"I love this park." Susan smiled at me and Gabriel. "Wish I got to spend more time over here. You guys live in a beautiful place."

The fact she was sincere, even while rain pelted us, made me like her a little more.

"Not a great day for it." Gabriel gazed up at the dark October sky. "I'm not sure how much evidence will be left."

"We'll find out soon enough," Susan said confidently.

And we went on.

Gabriel had asked me to come along today. He'd said I was "*our local animal expert.*" But I wondered if that was the full picture. Or if he wanted me to hear the conclusions Susan reached for myself, especially if it ended up being bad news about the wolves. That way, I couldn't blame him.

Yes, I was paranoid. Living for a few years with someone who gaslit you had that effect.

The trees were marked with yellow crime scene tape in the spot where we'd gone off-trail and into the woods to find Billy's body. We paused and Susan looked around.

"There were boot prints here." Gabriel indicated a spot on the trail. "We took photographs. But it's a public trail, so foot traffic is to be expected."

"Are you sure they weren't Billy's prints?" I asked. I remembered him taking the prints, but I'd been focused on Duke and, anyway, I had zero memory of what Billy had had on his feet.

Gabriel shook his head. "Billy was wearing cowboy boots. These were more like work boot prints or a hiking boot."

"So this trail sees a lot of traffic?" Susan asked.

Gabriel nodded. "Yeah. It's outside the national park, so it's free to park at the trailhead. And the falls are popular."

"What about animal tracks?" Susan moved aside a fern frond to check the soil.

"We found some dog prints on the trail. But again, lots of hikers bring their dogs."

"I had Duke with me, too," I added. "He's the one who sniffed out Billy's location. He's a yellow lab."

Susan gave Gabriel a sharp look. "I hope you got a record of all this."

He nodded. "We photographed everything we saw. I have the pictures back at the station."

She rose. "Can you show me where you found the body?"

"This way." Gabriel held up the crime scene tape and we ducked under and headed into the trees.

I hadn't said much so far. I wanted to wait and see what Susan had to say for herself before I raised my own opinion.

We reached the log where Billy had lain. Susan searched all around it carefully. She located a paw print in the mud up against the log. It had been sheltered from the rain by foliage. I leaned in. I was no expert on prints, but I recalled a little from a class I'd taken. Felines retract their claws when they walk, unlike dogs. The prints had clear, deep claw marks. Not any type of cat, then.

And it wasn't a hoofed animal. Or a bear. And it wasn't Duke's print either. His was considerably smaller. My stomach dropped.

"Canine," Susan pronounced. "Did you photograph this as well?"

Gabriel shook his head, frowning. "Didn't see it. We didn't do much of a search of this area. Right after we found the body, and it appeared to be an animal attack, I called your office. They said not to touch anything until you got here. So we just photographed the body and removed it. We took photos of the prints on the trail because, well, they were out in the open. And I didn't want rain to wash them away."

She nodded. "Good. That's the proper procedure." She took a small camera and took photos of the paw print from various angles. Then she squatted down, got a small kit out of her bag, mixed some powder and water, and poured the resultant white liquid into the print. She was making a cast.

She glanced at her watch then up at me. "You're an

animal behaviorist, Mr. Russo. What's your opinion on this?"

I didn't want to lead with *my gut says they didn't do it*. "If it was a wolf attack, it would be one for the record books. Wolf attacks on people are super rare, and attacking a man on horseback is practically unheard of. Seems unlikely to me. But I don't have a great alternative theory except bear or mountain lion, and there're no signs of either of those. And, of course, rabies can make any animal hyper aggressive."

She nodded. "That's pretty much where I'm at. I checked the database before I left the office. The last report of rabies in the Olympic National Park was from a bat found in a campground in 2008. Rabies was detected in another bat in 1975, and those two incidents are it as far as the historical records goes. But we may be looking at a new outbreak. Has anyone had eyes on the wolf pack to see if any of them are sick?"

I was doubtful. "We have a local wildlife painter, Libby Smith, who's observed the pack. She says they're all healthy."

"The coroner's testing the wounds for any trace of rabies," Gabriel said. "And she got a few hairs from the body too."

"Great." Susan checked her watch again and pried the cast up with a popsicle stick. She bagged it and rose to her feet. "Well, that's helpful. Think Libby Smith can lead us to the pack? I'd like to get a look at them myself."

"Sure." Susan was right. We needed to see the pack. But I wasn't satisfied. "You said the print was canine. Can you tell if it belongs to a wolf?"

She squatted down to examine the print again. It was still pretty much intact despite the casting procedure. She motioned me over and I moved close to her to get a better view.

"It's a big print, three-and-a-half, four inches. So it's definitely not coyote. And if it were a dog, it's a very big dog. It's the size of a wolf."

I nodded, though I didn't like it.

"And see these two claws here?" She pointed to the middle two claws, which were parallel and close together at the top of the print. "They're normally more spread apart in a dog's print. Close together like this is more indicative of a wolf. But then, some dog species are closer to wolves than others."

"Hound of the Baskervilles?" Gabriel put in wryly.

Susan tilted her head. "I'm not ruling out even that—yet. I'll consult with some colleagues on the prints. There's a guy in Montana who's our go-to wolf expert."

My heart sank further. This was not good. "But even if a wolf came around here, maybe lured by the scent of the body, that doesn't mean the wolves made the initial attack."

The look she gave me, her lips pressed together, said she thought I was being naive. Maybe I was. "I would never blame any animal for an attack like this without clear evidence. And believe me when I say that the last thing we want, at Fish and Wildlife, is for wolves to be involved in the death of a human. We've been watching their progress through Washington with excitement. But all we can do is gather the facts and see where they lead."

She turned to Gabriel. "You said the Clallum County

coroner has taken saliva and hair samples. If we can find the pack, we can get samples from them for comparison. Once we get all the test results back, along with our direct observation, that should give us a full picture. It's also possible that it's a lone wolf, a rogue, perhaps a sick one, that's wandered into the area. Normally, a lone wolf wouldn't encroach on a pack's territory, but the Olympic range is a big place."

I nodded again. There wasn't much more to say, but I was reassured by her words—and more by her tone. She really didn't want the killer to be a wolf any more than Libby or I did.

Gabriel folded his arms over his chest, his expression grim. "Time is of the essence. The people in Prophet have been stirred up against the wolves. I've told them we need to wait for the official report, but we have some rabble-rousers."

"That's unfortunate. I hope to God this doesn't make the press in Seattle or, God forbid, nationally. There are a number of wolf protection groups who'd be on this like ants on honey." Susan got to her feet, so I did too. She slung her pack over her back and dusted her hands. "I'm going to scout around some more. I may be awhile. Tiber, can you communicate with Libby about a time to go out and look for the pack? This afternoon, if possible. I'm staying at the motel in town."

"I'll call her."

Gabriel needed to wait on Susan before heading back, but he walked me out to the trail. His expression was worried.

"Are you okay?" he asked me.

"You keep asking me that. I'm not a child."

Gabriel blinked. "I know. Sorry. It's just with that paw print and everything… I mean, it's not looking good."

"The wolf pack did not kill Billy!" I said vehemently. And I hadn't realized until that moment that, despite everything, I still believed that. One hundred percent. I knew it in my bones. But that was no excuse to snap. "Sorry."

"No, I get it." But the doubt lingered in Gabriel's eyes —along with a hint of pity. "Okay. Well. Guess we'll see what Fish and Wildlife comes up with. It's good you guys are going to go see the pack."

I decided to ignore his doubt for now. Because it wasn't his fault he didn't share my inner conviction. Even I wasn't sure where it came from.

"You aren't going with us?" I asked.

He shook his head. "No. That's your thing, and Susan's and Libby's. I have some work to take care of at the station." He sighed. "What Susan said about the press is worrying. Hopefully we can get some answers before the news spreads."

"I hope so too. Well, guess I'll talk to you later then."

"Sure."

He shifted towards me, but hesitated. I could tell he wanted a hug or maybe something more, but it wasn't the time or the place. He was on duty, and the doubt in his eyes was too fresh so I turned and started the hike back to my car.

. . .

I HAD a cell phone signal at the trailhead, and I called Libby. We agreed to meet at the South Fork Trailhead at 3.00 p.m. That was the closest trailhead to the pack, Libby said. We'd have to hike for about an hour to reach them. She reminded me there was no guarantee we'd spot them, but it was worth a try.

I texted Gabriel and he must have a better provider than me or a satellite link, because he responded right away. He said he'd pass the message on to Susan.

With nothing to do until it was time to meet at the trailhead, I decided to pick up a sandwich. I drove back to the Mercantile in Prophet. The inside was cool and smelled of BBQ. Oh, right, they had a BBQ pork special on Tuesdays. I ate meat sparingly, and then, only fowl and fish, but the smell was tempting. I grabbed a hummus and veggie sandwich and a bag of chips, then headed to the checkout.

It was quiet in the store and One-Eyed Jack gave me a tired smile. "Hey, bruh."

"Hey. How are you?" I placed my items on the counter.

He shook his head. "Been better. Billy, man. That one hurts."

"Yeah," I agreed, my heart thudding in sympathy.

One-Eyed Jack rang me up. "Me and him, we went to school together."

"You did?"

"Yeah, bruh. From the time we were, like, five. All the way through high school."

"I'm sorry."

One-Eyed Jack put my items in a paper sack, glanced around as if to make sure no one was listening, then leaned in conspiratorially. "Hey—you know the sheriff pretty well, right?"

News certainly got around. I hoped I wasn't blushing. "We're friends."

He nodded. "So, listen, you didn't hear it from me, but he needs to look into Orson Travis."

"Orson Travis?"

"He runs the gift shop in Neah Bay. Him and Billy—there's major bad blood there."

I got a spike of adrenaline and leaned my elbows on the counter. "Go on."

One-Eyed Jack grimaced. "See, Orson married Jemma. She was Billy's wife before Billy went to prison. They divorced and she married Orson. But Orson, he's the type of man that'll never forgive any guy who ever laid a hand on his woman. Like, it eats at him. You feel me?"

I nodded.

"Word was, a while back, that Orson had gone to Stone Whiteplume to put a curse on Billy. And now Billy's dead." One-Eyed Jack gave me a knowing look. "You believe in magic, Tiber?"

I thought about my coming-of-age ceremony in the sweat lodge in Arizona. I thought about a lot of things I'd seen and heard on the rez. "Yes."

One-Eyed Jack nodded. "Thought so. You're not as thick as these *wasichu*. You know the score. I heard you speak at that meeting. You're right—it wasn't wolves that killed Billy. Not regular ones, anyway. You ask me, it was that curse. Maybe a shapeshifter or maybe a spirit wolf. So you tell that sheriff to look at Orson. Okay?"

I nodded. "Yeah. Definitely. Thanks for the tip."

I was deep in thought as I left the store with my lunch.

A curse? A shaman? Spirit wolves? The magic traditions of the Navajo had fascinated me as a boy, but it wasn't something I associated with the Makah. Clearly, I was wrong.

I was lost in thought as I opened my car door and tossed the bag onto the passenger seat.

"Tiber?"

I froze as I was about to get in the driver's seat. For a second, I thought the voice was in my head—an echo of a nightmare. But it came again.

"Tiber? Hey."

My blood ran cold as I turned my head. And saw Jeff. My ex.

Instinct took over. I scrambled into the car and tried to close the door, but Jeff held it open then blocked it with his body.

He was close. Too close. But I was cornered now. And like any cornered animal, I could only fight. "What the fuck are you doing here?" I spit out. "What do you want?"

He looked both surprised and hurt. And he looked good. He was wearing a navy jacket that was effortlessly cool and a gold T-shirt underneath. His thick, red-brown hair was perfectly styled in its long layered cut and rain glistened on the lashes of his gold-brown eyes—his very worried, pleading gold-brown eyes.

He appeared so normal, so harmless. My heart did a sickening lurch.

"I came to see you, of course. I needed—"

"It is *not cool* that you tracked me down."

"Ah, come on." He gave me a sheepish smile. "You didn't miss me? Even a little?"

I gaped at him. "No! Maybe me moving six hours away should have been a clue. This is called *stalking*, Jeff."

His mouth twisted. "Honey, come on. I wanted to let you know I was coming, but you changed your phone number *and* your email. You left me no choice. Look, let me buy you lunch and we can talk about it. There's got to be someplace around here to eat."

"No! Just… go away."

Jeff gasped and put a hand to his chest as if I'd struck him. "Do you know how long it took me to drive here? All I want is a chance to talk to you. One hour. Please, Tiber."

"I said—"

"Is there a problem here?" The deep voice startled me. It was as if everything in the world had disappeared except for Jeff, but the voice brought me back to the moment. I hadn't even noticed the sheriff's SUV pull up, but apparently it had, and Gabriel was standing there.

He gave Jeff an icy stare.

Jeff offered him a dazzling smile and held out his hand. "Hi! I'm Jeff Strickland. An old friend of Tiber's."

I could tell Gabriel recognized the name and knew exactly who Jeff was. He didn't shake. Instead, he looked at me, concern in his eyes. "Tiber, I was hoping you could come back to my office with me and give me a rundown on those statistics you were talking about."

The earth further solidified under my feet. Bless him. I took a deep breath. Then I glanced at the clock on the dash. "Umm. I'd love to, *Sheriff*," I emphasized the word, "but I need to go meet up with Libby and Susan right now, or I'll be late."

"Tiber," Jeff pleaded. "I'm sure that can wait. Give me one hour. Please."

A spark of anger flared inside my chest. "No, actually, it can't wait. I didn't ask you to drive all this way. And I don't want to talk to you. Or see you. Now I have to go."

"Like the man said," Gabriel growled to Jeff. He motioned with his hand for Jeff to move away.

Jeff's eyes filled with tears and his chin wobbled. He leaned closer to me. "I came to see you because I… there's no one else… it's my mom. My mom passed, Tiber. And I… I can't do this alone. Please. I need you."

My will shattered. It happened as easily and as completely as if someone had taken a baseball bat to a mirror. Oh.

Oh, hell.

Jeff had adored his mother. So much.

He had to be devastated.

"I'm sorry," I said, feeling, for the second time in recent days, like a failure as a human being. First, I couldn't defend the wolves at the town meeting. Now I'd kicked a man when he was down. "Really, I'm sorry."

Jeff took a deep breath, and tried to collect himself. "Can we grab a coffee or a drink and talk about it? Please?"

"I can't right now. It's not—I really do have to be somewhere. But we can meet tonight."

"At your place?" Jeff asked hopefully.

I shook my head. "The Western Winds Diner."

"But—"

I glared. I might feel sorry for Jeff, but I wasn't going to tell him where I lived. "The diner or nothing."

He did a shake-nod of his head. "Okay. Okay. Thank you." He sniffled. "What time?"

"Seven."

"Okay. Thanks, Tiber."

I gave Gabriel the same apologetic look I'd given Libby. His lip curled as if he'd just gotten a whiff of something rank, but he said nothing.

I shut them both out and headed for my date with the wolves.

Chapter Eight

Gabriel

OKAY. Jeff being here in town was a problem.

I wasn't concerned at having him anywhere near Tiber given what he'd told me about their toxic relationship, but I was consumed with a burning passion to pummel the asshole into the ground. My anger and focus must have shown on my face because he took a few steps away from me and held his hands out in front of him as if he was showing me he meant no harm. Fuck that. I'd been so proud of Tiber for shutting the door on his ex, and then seen for myself how Jeff's eyes had glittered with something as he'd manipulated Tiber's feelings. Yes, if the guy had lost his mom then that was sad for her, and for him, but Jeff knew how to word the announcement, with added tears for the most dramatic effect.

Of course he'd cry if his mom had *really* died—it was his mom, he was grieving, but when I watched the way the tears fell it was almost as if...

I shouldn't judge because it was clear having feelings for Tiber had made me an irrational mess.

I'd seen this kind of behavior before and in far too many cases it had ended bad for the partner being manipulated. At first witnessing the result of a skilled actor preying on vulnerabilities of those around them and winning, I'd never understood how someone could fall for their shit. But then I'd seen firsthand how clever they could be, horrifically so, and now I had the man who'd hurt Tiber right *there*. I stared at him. He confronted me, tilting his chin as if he had nothing to be concerned about —as if he dared me to say a thing to him.

"Tiber and I have known each other a long time," Jeff said, with what I assume was his best disarming grin.

"I know who you are," I said.

For a moment there was a twitch of fear in his expression. Then oily-Jeff was right back. One of the most disconcerting aspects of a gaslighter was how subtle they were, and there was no way I was letting him get to me. I'd just seen Jeff plant a seed of doubt in Tiber's thoughts, and my big-hearted compassionate man didn't have any idea what to do with that. It was bad enough that Jeff had dripped his slow poison when they were together, affecting Tiber's self-esteem and confidence, but to bring it to my town and try to start it up again? To do something in front of me as blatant as that? What was his end game here? Was he going to imply that if only Tiber was with him then his mom's loss would be easier to bear?

Would he win Tiber around?

Not happening on my watch.

"Then you have the advantage, Sheriff," Jeff

murmured, "because Tiber hasn't mentioned you at all." He said all of that with a disarming grin and a sympathetic vibe.

He was good. Even I could see that. I rested my hand on my weapon—just for somewhere to put it, no harm intended, no warning meant.

"Tiber hasn't contacted you since he arrived in town," I said, and wished I'd kept my mouth shut.

Jeff tilted his head, his eyes widening in surprise. "Is that what he told you?" He chuckled and smoothed the front of his jacket. "I guess you don't know him as well as I thought. Poor, sweet Tiber."

Fuck this shit. I wasn't falling for it. I could see *exactly* how confusion and doubt would creep into Tiber's mind and I knew that was why he'd agreed to see Jeff, but I would be there. Right next to him, or at least at a nearby table, and the minute I saw…

What?

What would I do if I saw Tiber wavering to go back to Jeff? We weren't exclusive, and yes there'd been a few kisses, and a lot of popcorn-eating, and quiet times with the rest of his little family, but that didn't make us boyfriends, and that meant Jeff could slide back in.

"I'm sorry for your loss."

"Thank you," he said, with damp eyes and a slight slump to his shoulders. "Tiber loved my mom so much. I knew he'd want me to interrupt his vacation to tell him. I need to be there for him now."

Well, that was a change from him implying he needed to see Tiber for comfort. Now it was the other way around?

"Tiber lives here; it's not a vacation," I said.

"It's only temporary, you and I both know that."

I didn't know that at all, but I'd go with the flow to see what other bullshit Jeff came out with.

"Was it a recent loss? Your mother I mean."

He paused, a calculating gleam in his eyes, and then he shook his head. "Grief never leaves us, Sheriff. Excuse me," he said, and then before I could ask him for more exact details he turned on his heel and walked around the corner. I wasn't sure where he thought he was going. That was a path to the park by the runoff down to the lake, but still, it seemed he'd decided his conversation with me was over.

I could follow him.

Intimidate him.

But instead I used my brains and not the instinct to pummel him, and headed straight into my office, stopping at the small side desk where Devin was doing paperwork. He glanced up, his eyes widening. Guess I wasn't hiding my temper very well.

"Is it the wolves? Did something happen, sir?"

"No, I need you to do something for me."

He pulled a notebook closer, and I shook my head, then I lifted an eyebrow that I hoped would indicate it was information that I needed on the down-low. He stared back at me with a confused expression.

"I need you to keep this between you and me," I explained, and he frowned. I'd given him the big speech on day one of his training—all about not abusing power—but every sheriff is entitled to search records if they have due cause. Jeff was out there messing with Tiber who lived in my town, so that gave me due cause. Right? After all, I'd done worse as a cop.

"Are you okay, sir?" Devin's frown hadn't slipped as I stood there like an idiot.

I was torn with indecision. Maybe I should leave well enough alone? Tiber was already on edge about the wolf situation, but... fuck it. What could go wrong? Tiber could hate me for interfering, but if me doing so kept him safe, then it was a non-decision.

"Track down everything you have on Jeff Strickland, Portland, dig into the results, socials of the driver, that kind of thing," I showed him a photo I'd taken of his flash BMW with its Portland plates, and even though he frowned at it, and then me, he took a note.

"Am I looking for anything in particular?"

"Family, work, relationships, the usual." That was loose enough.

"Sure thing. Is this something to do with the wolves?"

I blinked at him. *It's more to do with protecting the man that I have feelings for.* "Parking issue," I lied and if he thought to push me on more, he swallowed it and nodded. "I'll be in my office."

"Sheriff?" Hen called from the front desk, and at first I headed over with reluctance—only because I had a lot in my head that was focused on Tiber—but then pulled myself together and smiled at her.

Maybe it was too bright? Maybe I looked like I was manic? Either way she sat back in her chair and stared at me.

"Can I help?" I prompted.

"The records are here for Billy Odette. To summarize,

his time inside was exemplary, and he was released early."
It had been a matter of procedure to get that information
after Sam had told me, but it would also have come up in
any coroner's search on Billy's name. "It's logged under
the case for you. Also Jill at Grounds for Joy called about
Dell causing some problems and would like you to go and
get a coffee, if you know what I mean."

"What kind of problems?"

"She says he's running his mouth off about the wolves
to anyone who goes in there. Jill said she already had a
couple of tourists turn tail, and that's not good."

"I'll head over there now." Maybe I'd see Jeff hanging
around and ask him more questions. After all, there
weren't a lot of places to sit and wait in town, and it
wouldn't hurt for me to just wander around and check
every single one of them out.

I headed to the diner first, saw Dell nursing a coffee,
and dragged over a chair.

"Dell," I said.

He started and stared around him with that shifty
expression that screamed he knew he was in trouble.

"Sheriff."

"How's the coffee?" I asked as if that was all I was
here for, and he stared at anything but me. I leaned over to
touch the Bigfoot-emblazoned mug and tutted. "Seems like
it's ice-cold."

"I like it that way," he defended.

"I think you're done here, Dell."

"I'll get a new coffee." He made a move to go get a
refill, but I placed a gentle hand to his arm and he froze.

"I think Jill needs the table. I'd probably get the coffee

to go, and maybe stay away from here for a while. Y'know, give other people a chance to taste some of Jill's delicious drinks and pastries. You want that, right?"

He stared at me, confused, and I met his gaze head-on.

"Is that… are you… I ain't doing nothing wrong."

"Town bylaw ten-twelve, subsection K point one-five, amended 1993, would suggest otherwise."

That had him meeting my gaze, and he was worried by the bylaw I'd just this second made up. I hope I'd delivered it with enough authority for him to leave.

"There's a law about drinking cold coffee?" He blinked at me.

"Nope, loitering with intent," I took the cold coffee from him. "I'll take the mug to Jill. Best you go before I arrest you for staying here longer than an hour."

He left so fast it was as if his tail was on fire. I crossed to the counter, to soothe the ruffled feathers of Jill who shot an evil glance at the departing Dell.

"Idiot," she muttered, and smoothed her blue bangs from her eyes. "Thank you," she added. "Coffee? On the house."

I wasn't going to turn that down, nor the cruller that came with it, but I tipped more than enough to cover it all —as sheriff I couldn't be seen to take baked goods and caffeine as a bribe.

"Heard Tiber and Libby are heading up to see the wolves," Jill said as she made my coffee. I know she was only being conversational, but I hated the reminder I was missing out on going to see the pack myself.

It wasn't so much about seeing the wolves, and I

wasn't patient enough to be sitting around on the ground for hours at a time. It was all about looking out for Tiber.

Everything seemed to be about Tiber.

I wanted to see the wonder in a beautiful smile that lit up his eyes when he first saw the wolves. I was missing that moment and it hurt.

"They sure are," I answered, gave my excuses, and left before she got me spilling my heart out.

As I walked away from the counter, my phone dinged. I juggled my coffee and donut so I could dig it out of my pocket. My heart did a double beat when I saw it was from Tiber.

Hey—heads up. Forgot to say that One-Eyed Jack told me Billy had some major bad blood with Orson Travis. He runs the rez gift shop in Neah Bay. Said he went to see a Shaman about something?!? Weird. Thought you'd want to know ASAP.

I stared at the message. Tiber's message wasn't anything about being upset about Jeff, in fact he didn't say anything personal at all. What did that mean? Did it mean something?

It's not personal because this is about the case. Get your head in the game, Sheriff.

I confirmed the time. I needed to check in with Devin to see what he'd found on Jeff, but was it bad that I wondered if I had time to go talk to Orson Travis and be back in time to just happen to be at the cafe at 7 p.m.? If Tiber thought it was important I visit this Orson guy then I wasn't going to ignore him.

Jesus. I was such a goner for Tiber.

Devin turned his screen to me as soon as I walked into the office.

"This," he said without preamble. What he'd found was a lot of fluff on social media, pictures of Jeff's *supposedly* perfect life—no sign of grief for his mom, although people handled grief in different ways and I would never judge.

Okay, I was judging. Sue me.

It all seemed fake, as much of social media was, but one photo in particular stood out, or at least a series of them, all featuring Jeff in love with a tall blond guy called Martin. Did that mean I needn't worry about Jeff talking to Tiber? Surely if he was in a new relationship with this poor guy Martin, then Tiber would be in Jeff's rear view mirror.

"Meet Jeff Strickland. On the surface it's all normal— work, meetings, I'm-a-great-doctor-in-residency, I save lives but don't make a big thing about it, blah blah," Devin began, but I could tell from his tone he'd found something else.

"And?"

"Sources confirm that things aren't happy in Jeff and Martin land."

"You have sources already?" It didn't surprise me— Devin was tenacious as hell and networked with anyone he could get up close to.

He nodded, and blushed, then cleared his throat. "I found quite a lot, like, as of last Thursday, Martin Toride, Jeff's *former* partner, was granted a restraining order against Jeff."

"He what now?"

Devin pushed back from the desk and stared up at me.

"So, sir, I found something else that makes me think this isn't just a parking issue." He paused and tapped the screen. "Given the number of photos of Tiber that this Jeff guy had on his timeline from a few years back."

Busted. "No. Not just a parking thing." But that was all I was going to say because Tiber's secrets were his own.

I checked the clock on the wall to see it wasn't much past two. Five hours to go until I needed to be at the cafe. "Can you forward what you found?"

"I'll send you a link to the Instagram account and you can uh… check in there for more of whatever you're looking for," Devin finished, and I wanted to hug him for being so careful with me.

"Thank you, Devin."

"And now I'm deleting my history and pretending I never looked at anything except the official things."

I smiled at him then, relieved, and he nodded.

"I'm heading over to the rez."

"You want me to come with you?" he asked and brightened. I considered taking him, but I didn't want to arrive heavy-handed.

"Not this time. Next," I reassured him when his face fell. "I promise."

I sent a quick message to Will, my contact with the tribal police, explaining briefly that I was following up on Billy, and his connection with Orson. I suggested he meet me, and felt better that even if he didn't, at least he knew I was heading to the rez on informal business.

He contacted me straight back to say he'd meet me in the parking lot at the community hall.

At least if I was working I could stop thinking about

Tiber being out there with his wolves. Worrying about him. Wishing I was there with him.

And knowing for sure I'd *happen* to be in the Western Winds Diner at seven tonight.

Chapter Nine

Tiber

I WAS QUIETLY FREAKING out as I met up with Susan and Libby at the trailhead. The two women introduced themselves to each other and were instant mutual admirers, chatting about the wildlife in the Olympics as we donned hiking boots and backpacks and headed up the trail.

Libby seemed worried, though, and she gave Susan the hard sell about how harmless the wolf pack was as we hiked. Susan remained non-committal about the local pack, but she did wax lyrical about how the wolves in Yellowstone had benefited the park in expected and unexpected ways since they were introduced in 1995.

With the wolves keeping down the deer population, meadows and riverside vegetation had flourished, which meant beavers, birds, and small mammals had moved back into the area. Beavers built ponds and denser vegetation stabilized riverbanks, transforming even the geography of the park. It was clear Susan was a fan of wolf reintroduction in general.

It made me think about how many species we humans had caused to go extinct, and the ways in which their loss would have reverb effects we'd never understand.

I didn't add much to the conversation though. For one thing—my social skills sucked. But also, as interesting as the conversation was, my mind kept returning to my own worries.

Jeff had found me. He'd found Prophet. Which meant he could not only show up now but anytime he felt like it. I was no longer safe.

The idea was nauseating. A pit of despair opened low in my belly.

I told myself not to get worked up. I told myself I didn't need to hide from Jeff. He'd never physically hurt me. And I was stronger now, emotionally. I had his number. I could, and would, say no. He couldn't *make* me do anything.

Besides, Jeff lived in Portland and had an intensive medical internship at St. Vincent's. If there was one thing I knew about him, it was that he was ambitious as hell and that his ego was tied up in being a doctor. He wasn't going to abandon his career to hang out in Prophet and badger me. He must be on a break. Maybe bereavement leave? When had his mother passed, anyway? And how?

Madeline Strickland had never been a fan of mine. She was fifty-something cool blonde, rail-thin, and always immaculately dressed. She'd been Jeff's biggest cheerleader and fan, and they'd been super tight.

I'd been devastated when my dad died. So, I felt sorry for anyone losing a parent.

Maybe Jeff's words had been sincere. Maybe he did just need someone to talk to about his mother's death. After all, I knew he had a hard time making friends. His friends from childhood were distant and the atmosphere at his work was competitive. But was I really the only person he knew who had a sympathetic ear?

Anyway, his leave couldn't last indefinitely. He couldn't stay in Prophet long.

I felt guilty for wanting him gone when he must be hurting. But another part of my brain reminded me of what it'd been like living with him for two years. I recalled, viscerally, the many times I'd wanted to leave him after an argument or his hurtful digs. But he always dragged me back in.

I'd met Jeff at UDub when I was getting my masters in Animal Behavior and he was studying medicine. He was handsome, charismatic, and brilliant. The intense attention he paid to me was flattering. I fell for it hook, line, and sinker. And before I knew it, he'd talked me into moving in with him. Said it made sense since we were both busy students and wouldn't have time to see each other otherwise.

The thing about Jeff was, nothing was ever enough. It wasn't enough to have me as a boyfriend. He had to control everything. His easy charm became nagging. The list of things he wanted to change about me kept growing. He had an opinion about everything I did, from my career path right down to the number of minutes I brushed my teeth.

Whenever I tried to challenge him about it, he made excuses. He was only interested in my success and happiness. I shouldn't be so insecure that I couldn't take suggestions. And so on.

He wore me down. He made me small. He made me question my own judgement.

I'd finally left him after a nightmare incident in which his brother ran over two fawns on a road when we were all coming back from a concert. He did it on purpose, just to torture me, because he knew how much I loved animals. And Jeff stood up for his brother, told me to stop being so hysterical.

I'd packed my things, and vanished while he was in class the very next day.

I hadn't talked to him since. I was afraid if I let his voice into my ear again, he'd gaslight and debate and cajole until I went back to him. The thought terrified me.

But that was over a year ago. I was stronger now. I'd learned a lot about myself after I left Jeff. I learned my empathetic nature made me a target, and that I'd always be vulnerable to people like him. I could be manipulated because I cared. And the best solution was to avoid human entanglements entirely.

Ever.

Which was why I'd moved to the remote hinterlands of Prophet—or, at least, one reason.

And why I'd kept Gabriel Thompson firmly in the friend zone.

Or maybe not so firmly. Lately, there'd been toes over the line. Kisses. *Feelings.*

And now Jeff was here. But it was going to be okay. I

could handle it. I'd have one meet-up with him, offer him some sympathy about his mother, and he'd leave town.

So why did I feel like I was standing frozen in front of an oncoming train?

We hiked on, me lost in my own thoughts, for quite a while. Then Libby gathered us close and whispered. "Okay, listen. The pack is about a fifteen-minute walk into the woods from here. There's a stream and a huge fallen tree where they have their den."

"How did you find them?" Susan asked, her voice equally low.

"A ranger out of Hurricane Ridge told me they'd been spotted there. He gave me a map."

Susan looked at the GPS on her phone. "This isn't exactly close to where Billy Odette was found. Maybe thirty miles as the crow flies. Not outside the bounds of their potential range, but still."

"It's not them," Libby insisted. "You'll see."

"Let's go take a look," Susan replied.

"We have to be very quiet. I watch them from a little hilltop. But if they hear us, they'll vanish."

Susan nodded. "Can do."

Libby glowered at me. "Are you with us now, Tiber?"

I felt embarrassed. No doubt, I'd been a million miles away. I stiffened my spine and nodded. "Yep. I'm ready."

It suddenly struck me. We were going to view a wolf pack. In the wild. How amazing was that? I vowed to be present and not to give Jeff another moment of my thoughts.

When we reached Libby's hilltop, the wolves were not visible. We spread out, lying along the edge of a flat rock on our stomachs and peering down into a little glen.

The afternoon sun painted the woods gold. From the little hilltop there was a drop of only about ten feet and then a short slope. Below, and maybe twenty feet to the north, was a narrow stream. It was a trickle this time of year but the carved banks showed it got a decent amount of runoff in the spring.

The glen had formed when a huge old cedar had come down years ago, allowing sunlight to hit the ground from a part of the sky that had probably been blocked by the tree's canopy for decades. Moss and spots of grass made a green cushion and a flood of golden sunlight lit up the band of water still in the stream, making it sparkle. The ferns and lichen growing along the stream bank were emerald green.

It was a beautiful place. Very quiet. It could have been right out of *The Hobbit*. I thought I saw a flash of movement towards the far end of the massive fallen trunk. there was a dark area—a place where some animal— maybe the wolves—had dug under the tree to make a den.

A tingle of energy ran up my spine. The wolves were nearby. I could feel them.

Susan got out a pair of binoculars and put them to her eyes, resting on her elbows. Libby's face glowed with pleasure.

We stayed quiet. I wasn't sure how much time passed, but a wolf appeared. It was a male, young, limber, and lean. His gray fur was thick and shiny in shades from the palest gray to steel. His eyes were golden-brown. He jumped onto the fallen tree, a good five-foot leap, and stood there, alert, looking around.

He sensed us, but he didn't seem to be able to smell us. Libby had chosen a good spot. We were uphill and downwind from the den. The wolf scanned the forest—his kingdom. He turned to check behind him, showing us his bushy tail. A feeling of wonder broke over me. All my personal human drama melted away—small and unimportant compared to this. Compared to him.

I took a deep breath and let myself settle into the moment, feel gratitude for being allowed to be a witness here. I thought of how nice it would be if Gabriel were at my side, if I could share this moment with him.

The wolf relaxed and jumped down. He trotted over to the stream and took a drink. As if that was the signal, a trio of wolf cubs came out from under the tree and sniffed around. One of them pounced on something near a fern fond—maybe a bug. A young female adult came out of the den too and went to the stream. She stood next to the male and lapped water. Another young adult pair appeared from the forest, stretching out on the log for a rest. I noticed a third, smaller female lying near the tree trunk.

A bone-deep thrill of awe tinged with a prickle of fear washed through my body. Damn. It was a privilege to see them, and what a blessing that they existed here, so close to my home. These creatures had once been hunted to the threshold of extinction by men seeking pelts or out of sheer destructiveness, but they'd returned to the wilds of North America. I understood why Libby was so dedicated to them, and why there were many animals rights groups advocating for them.

If the wolves could return, maybe there was some hope for our planet. Some sign we wouldn't, in fact, use up the Earth to death. That nature could survive even the apocalypse that was humankind.

I watched them greedily for a long while, and then remembered why I was there, and tried to get a sense of their mindset. Could they have killed Billy Odette? Would they drag him off a horse?

It was an ugly image, and it felt wrong in this setting, with them, but I forced myself to consider it. After all, wolves were predators. They brought down deer. They could be aggressive, lethal.

But as I watched the alpha wolf repeat his survey of their area, his body tense, I knew that, should I stand up and shout, they would melt into the woods before I could blink.

What would it take to make him—or any of them—attack me? Threatening the cubs, maybe. Or getting the pack cornered somehow. Threatening them with a weapon. Being found inside their den, taking them by surprise when they entered.

I couldn't imagine Billy and River's situation coming close to anything like that. They'd been riding on an open trail. Watching the pack, I knew they'd not go anywhere near the man-horse smells and sounds. That was not their prey. And they all appeared healthy, just like Libby had said. Not starving. Not diseased. There was no reason for their behavior to deviate so dangerously from the norm.

I'd known this, in my gut. But, now, seeing them with my own two eyes, it wasn't merely instinct; it was conviction. I would fight to the death to hold back anyone who attempted to harm them. *Anyone.* My heart thrummed with it.

I glanced at Susan, wondering if she felt it too. She was studying the pack through her binoculars. She put them down and raised her camera, took photos. Fortunately the shutter didn't make a sound. I could tell nothing from her expression, but I hoped she could see what I saw.

Libby took some photos too, probably to use for her paintings. I was the only one without some gadget. Lucky me. I put my chin on my forearms and went back to watching the wolves. Drinking in every moment of this rare experience.

WE WATCHED the wolves for at least an hour. I could have stayed there all night, but Susan had other plans. She sat up and put her camera and binoculars back into her pack, no longer trying to be quiet.

Down below, the male perked his head from where he'd been lying by the stream. But he didn't stand.

Susan took out her phone and started blasting "Night Fever" by Bee Gees. Within seconds, the entire pack had vanished into the woods.

Libby was incensed. "What'd you do that for?"

Susan grimaced. "I need to get down there to gather samples. Music is a good method for scaring them away. Studies show they'll come back to the spot later on when music is used. I could have fired my gun into the air, but that is more likely to chase the pack away from this spot permanently."

Libby didn't look happy about it, but she stopped complaining.

"Give me a hand, Tiber." Susan backed up to the edge of the rock and I held her hands while she lowered herself then dropped to the forest floor. She glanced at me. I figured she'd be just as glad to have company down there in case the wolves came back, so I clambered over the edge and did a little scrambling to join her.

"I'd like to get casts of prints for all the wolves in the pack," Susan said. "So scout around and see what you can find. Try not to step on any. I'll need samples of their fur as well. And we might as well take droppings if we find them. We can see what their diet's been."

"Got it."

Susan turned the music back on and set her phone near the stream to play while we worked—hopefully that would keep the wolves at a good distance. Susan made print casts from the soft earth along the stream bed and near the den, I scouted around for hair and wolf poop. Susan gave me a pair of gloves and a bunch of collection baggies, and I bagged everything I found.

It was unnerving. As much as the *sight* of the wolves had inspired awe, and as much as I was sure they wouldn't attack a man unless provoked, my primal instinct did not enjoy trespassing near their den. I kept a nervous eye on the woods as we worked. Would the Bee Gees keep them at bay indefinitely? I hoped so. My canines at home would come back sniffing, curious. But they were used to humans and human sounds.

We gathered everything we could. Susan put the samples in a waterproof stuff sack, put that into her bag, picked up her phone, and turned off the music. She searched for a way to get back to the top of the rock, and I motioned to a lower section a short ways south that should let us climb more easily.

When we rejoined Libby, her eyes were bright with worry. "So what do you think?"

Susan gave her a guarded smile. "Like you said, the pack is healthy. There's no reason why they'd go after anything but their usual prey. But we won't know for certain until the test results come back. We can't even initiate a hunt for an animal until we know what it is." She turned to me. "I'll call the sheriff when I get a chance, but, for now, we need to keep that whole trail network at Clear Creek Falls closed. The DNA tests should be back in a few days. I'll examine the paw prints tonight."

"I'll tell him," I agreed.

As we left the glen, I glanced back. There was still no sign of the wolves. I hoped Susan was right, and that we hadn't ruined this beautiful place for them. They deserved to live in peace. I sent them a prayer in my mind. *We're going. We mean you no harm. You're safe here.*

But a pain in my gut said that was a lie. The wolves weren't safe. Not as long as the people of Prophet thought they'd killed Billy Odette.

Chapter Ten

Gabriel

WILL Abraham was waiting for me when I parked, and as I expected he wasn't alone. Tribal elder Charlie Bowie, was with him, suspicious of me and the office of sheriff. I was aware of the respect he garnered from all of the Makah here, and with Will representing the Makah Tribal Police they were a difficult pair to walk up to. I held out a hand to Charlie first, and he shook it without comment, then to Will.

"So what's the situation?" Will asked before we even got to hellos. He was always straight to the point, focusing on the rez, and there might be professional respect between us, but the Makah would always come first with him.

"There isn't a situation as such," I hedged. "I wanted to catch up with Billy's family for a welfare check."

Will narrowed his dark eyes, Charlie remained in suspicious mode, and for the first time I wondered what I was actually doing here.

Because Tiber has a feeling.

Tiber had messaged me about a shaman, and I'd understood he felt unsettled by it, add in what my brother had said about Billy feeling off-center and wearing a talisman, and it was enough for me just to poke around. As far as I was aware Billy's death was caused by a random animal attack, but… there was something, and I wondered if I was channeling Tiber.

"Let's get a coffee," Will suggested.

We walked over to the small cafe and gift shop, which was in a prime location right next to a burger and seafood shack, front and center with views over the rugged coastline of Neah Bay. The wooden structure was old, embedded into the rocks behind, with parking out front, the windows letting light flood onto the groups of tables. One side was a cafe, the other was a collection of souvenirs and gifts ready to tempt the casual visitor. Just like the mercantile in Prophet with its Big Foot merchandise, there were a lot of stereotypical gifts someone who thought the Makah were quaint would want —native American tattoos, tiny headdresses on keychains, and posters with spirit animal information. It was all as inappropriate as anyone in Prophet hawking Bigfoot, but it was an economy that kept on rolling.

We were the only ones in the cafe area as Will took a chair at the table nearest the counter. Charlie sat next to him, which left me opposite—at which point I swear a hundred interview nightmares flooded my thoughts.

Will picked up a menu, but he wasn't reading it. "And the real reason you're here?"

"Like I said, just a few questions to close the file."

Charlie huffed and leaned forward in his chair. "Billy wasn't murdered, so why are you still sniffing around?"

I copied his stance. "Nothing is conclusive at this point," I reminded him, which stopped him in his tracks.

He stared at me for a while, but the impasse was broken by the arrival of a Makah woman with braided hair who I recognized as Jemma Travis, Billy's ex-wife.

"Mrs. Travis." I stood, and offered my hand, which she shook after a pause. She was wide-eyed, and cautious, as if she'd flee at the slightest sound. "How're you doing?"

"Fine," she responded, then glanced over her shoulder. "This is my husband, Orson."

We shook hands. "Orson Travis," he said. In his early fifties and older than Jemma, his features were weathered by whatever storms had hit his life, and he stared at me, then his wife, then back at me.

I wanted to blurt out the question I had—was it true that Travis had approached a shaman and why—but that would tip my hand and come over as madness if not handled the right way.

"Nice place you have here," I said.

She gave me a little smile. "Thank you."

"Used to be yours and Billy's place before…" I left it hanging because silence was the most effective weapon in the arsenal for investigation. People liked to fill silences, and I waited.

She nodded, the smile falling. "Can I take your order?"

"My usual," Will said.

"And mine," Charlie added.

"Coffee, black, please." I said, feeling like an outsider.

She left us then, along with Orson, and both Will and Charlie eyed me with suspicion.

"What was that about?" Will asked. "What are you really doing here, and don't give me bullshit about a welfare check."

I lowered my voice, wishing we weren't quite so close to the counter. "It was suggested to me there was bad blood between Billy and Orson, and that it might have led to a consultation with a shaman for a curse." I watched the two men for a reaction. Will was puzzled but Charlie's eyes widened.

"You're saying he did what now?" Charlie asked in as soft a voice as I'd used.

"What I'm saying is that, until the cause of Billy's death has been proven—conclusively—it's my job to look into anyone who hated him enough to wish him harm."

Silence.

Then Will sat back in his chair glancing at Orson, an unsettled expression on his face. He straddled two worlds, the Makah, and the town of Prophet, and it struck me that while he was one hundred percent Makah he wasn't as entrenched into local gossip as Charlie was. Charlie was very quiet, and then in, a flurry of motion, he stalked around the counter, grabbing Orson by the collar, and dragging him out of the preparation area. I made a move to follow but Will grasped my arm and stopped me.

"Give them a moment."

"What is Charlie doing?"

Will sighed with feeling. "Being the tribal elder he was born to be."

The coffee arrived then, and Jemma sat in Charlie's

chair. "What happened?" she asked Will, ignoring me. "Why did Charlie drag out my husband, Will?"

"Tribal business," Will said, as if that explained everything.

I wanted to explain that it was because her new husband had an issue with her ex, but that was major overstepping.

"Sheriff?" Charlie called from the back of the cafe, and I went over to him as he pointed at a door from the kitchen leading to a small room filled with shelving and supplies. Orson stood in the middle, his arms folded over his chest, belligerent and flushed with temper. "You have ten minutes, no more, no less, and you will respect him."

"Okay—"

"And, Will, you're in there with them. " I felt as if he was poking at me with each word, but ignored the feeling of being warned off.

Will hurried over and the two of us went into the small space, Charlie shutting the door. The last image I had was of Jemma, stricken and about to cry.

"I ain't got nothing to say to you," Orson snapped. "Billy was bad for Jemma, I was just looking out for her." He snarled the words, temper flashing in his eyes. "No one is getting Jemma, not even Billy with all his pretty words of being sorry, and not if she even loved him still."

I didn't recall Billy having pretty words, I recalled him as quiet, but Orson was forging ahead so I shelved that observation for later. The tension was thick in here, there was no air, and it was warm despite the cooler day outside.

"Sent her cards for her birthday, like he didn't do time, like he deserved to be in her life, so yeah I went out and got some backup." He tilted his chin, stubborn, determined not to see how suspicion might fall on him for anything at all. Okay, so he hadn't told us he'd consulted a shaman, but there was threat in his tone, and what was the legal standing for attempting to invoke a mythical creature to kill your wife's ex?

My brain hurt.

"Did you ask someone to kill Billy?" I asked.

Orson shot me a furious glance, incandescent with rage as if he were about to explode, and this was a tiny space for so much temper. If he wasn't already a suspect in whatever case we might end up having, then after this he was top of my list. I glanced at his feet. He was wearing boots, but I couldn't tell anything from one visual of scuffed dark leather under wide-legged jeans.

"No. I went to a shaman to get him to scare the hell out of Billy so he'd stay away from my wife, that's all. And I'd do it again." Something about Orson made the hairs on the back of my neck stand up, a tension in him that might snap at any moment—or was that just me?

What if the shaman had taken him literally? What if this shaman didn't do shaman-type stuff and instead put a contract out on Billy? And then what? Said shaman paid a wild animal to kill the guy?

I swear none of this made sense.

"Where were you on Friday?" I asked.

"I was in Wenatchee with my sister's family, only got back yesterday."

"And someone can vouch for that?" I insisted.

"My niece had a baby, I'm in the photos." He sounded

smug, and my instinct that he was lying about *something* moved front and center.

"You spend a lot of time with your sister's family in Wenatchee?" I asked, as innocently as I could manage.

"Sure, all the time." He wrinkled his nose, and wouldn't quite meet my eyes.

"And you're happy to show me the photos proving that?"

Will touched my arm. "Now, hang on, Sheriff—"

"What is this about?" Orson blurted. "I didn't do nothing to Billy!"

Apart from try to magic up a curse to kill him, but that wasn't occurring to Orson. The room grew even hotter as if Orson's anger had heat, and a familiar dread gripped my chest. There was no air, and if I didn't get out soon then the panic might well take over.

"And you'll be able to show me the photos?" I asked.

"You don't have to," Will interjected. "Not without a warrant."

"I've got nothing to hide!" Orson dug out his cell and scrolled to photos then stuck the phone in my face with triumph. The picture was of Orson with a tiny baby and a smiling but exhausted younger woman. I checked the photo's properties to get the location, date, and time stamps—Wenatchee, Washington, on Friday afternoon. That was a good seven-hour drive away. Of course that didn't exclude Orson, after all he'd shown intent to want to harm, but I knew I was clutching at straws over Orson talking to a shaman. I handed back the phone.

The door opened and daylight filtered in. "That's enough." Charlie wasn't suggesting, he was telling. I didn't want to stay in the room, but I had questions, and I was torn as Orson sidled past me and out into the main cafe.

"Now what?" Will asked me.

I wish I knew.

"Orson just admitted to wanting to hurt Billy, and hiring someone to do it."

Will shot me a look. "Whatever you believe he may or may not have done, you currently have a wild animal as your main suspect. Or did I hear it wrong?"

He had me there.

Then to round off the situation he leaned into me. "Watch your step, Sheriff."

I could have asked him what he was threatening me about, but I got the sense he was drawing a line in the sand to protect his people—to do his job.

When we were all out of the cafe, Will and Charlie left the parking lot, but I took a moment to gather my thoughts in my car, startled when someone tapped on the window. Someone I'd never noticed approaching the car. Jemma.

I climbed back out.

"Ma'am," I acknowledged.

She stood in silence, her hands laced together, and her eyes bright with emotion.

"Is everything okay?" I asked, though it was obvious that it wasn't. "Can I help at all?" Maybe she was going to demand an apology from me for coming into her workplace and talking to her husband.

"Did he suffer?" she asked in a small voice.

I took a moment to think about what she was asking.

"Billy?" I clarified, in case she was referring to what had happened just now.

"When Billy was in prison he insisted we divorce, said he wanted me to remarry and live my life, but I still..." She wiped away a tear, and struggled to get her emotions together. "Did my Billy suffer?"

"No, he didn't suffer," I lied. I didn't know if he'd suffered before, but the throat wound had been quick. He'd been terrified I was sure, and had tried to fight off whatever attacked him, but I silently hoped that the final bite had brought instant death.

She swallowed and then after a pause, nodded, wiping the last tears from her cheeks, her shoulders back.

"Thank you."

I should use this moment to ask questions, poke a little about Orson, but compassion stilled my tongue. She seemed to be on the edge, and I wasn't going to be the one to push her over.

When I left the rez I felt shaken and confused. Partly from the rush of adrenalin that kept me in the small room, and partly because this whole shaman thing had me second-guessing everything. I drove for a while before stopping the SUV in the first sensible place off the road, right outside the Prophet kindergarten, which was of course empty at this time of the day.

I glanced at the clock: Six-thirty. I had plenty of time to get to the diner and be there for Tiber, but for now I worked my way through all of my breathing exercises and calmed myself down. The dread that had curled inside me was still there, but it became a small thing and something I could handle.

If there was one thing I'd learned working undercover it was to pull up a shield that made everyone else think I was okay.

Tiber needed me to be okay.

For him.

Chapter Eleven

Tiber

I PULLED up in front of the diner and stopped the car. My palms were sweating, and I felt the first twinge of panic. I closed my eyes and thunked my head on the steering wheel.

It hadn't seemed so scary to agree to meet Jeff *later*. But now *later* was here, and my ex was sitting in the Prophet diner, waiting for me.

I didn't want to do this. I wanted to go home to Leo and Duke and all the rest. I wanted to shut out the world, as I had been doing. Because Jeff was out there in the world, and other people like Jeff, and that meant the world was not a place I wanted to be. But that was no longer possible. I had to face him, or he'd never go away. He'd find my house somehow. It was hopeless.

Besides. His mother had died. I couldn't just tell him to fuck off.

I had no idea what I was going to say. Or what *he* was

going to say. Or how this was going to go. Not the slightest clue. I could only open the door, get out, and walk to the diner. My legs were weak. My hands felt as though they belonged to someone else as I opened the diner door. The tingling bell above sounded a mile away.

"Tiber!" Jeff stood at a booth, smiling.

I smiled back, though it, too, felt unreal. I walked over and almost fell onto the side of the booth opposite him.

"Hey, watch it. Everything okay?" he asked with concern as he slipped back into his own seat.

"Mm-hm. Yeah." I nodded. I gripped the red leather booth seat.

He kept smiling, but his eyes were worried. "Good. Thanks for coming. You don't know what it means to me to see you again. God, I missed you."

My rictus of a smile felt plastered to my face as I grabbed the plastic menu and glanced at it. There was an awkward silence.

"I thought you'd like the grilled cheese," Jeff said. "So I ordered it for you. But if you want something else, get it. I don't want to presume."

He didn't want to *presume*? That was new.

For the first time, I truly looked at Jeff. In the year since I'd seen him last, he'd taken on near mythic proportions in my head. So there was a disconnect now, seeing him in the flesh. He was just an ordinary man. Handsome, yes. He'd gone all out for this meeting— freshly showered and shaved, blow-dried dirty blond hair, a crisp, ironed button-down shirt in cornflower blue. The scent of lemon aftershave wafted from him.

Good-looking? Definitely. But he seemed smaller than

I remembered. Something in his eyes was less arrogant, more desperate.

"How's your internship going?" I asked him.

His smile broadened. "Great! Really good. Everyone at St. Vincent's says I'm the best in this year's group."

I nodded politely. Jeff had always had a tendency to exaggerate. "Good. You've got time off?"

"A week. I've been wanting to come see you for a long time. Finally got a chance. I wish it'd been sooner, but you know how it is at the hospital. I barely have time to breathe."

I nodded and tried to sound casual. "How did you find me?"

Jeff stared at me for a moment, then opened up the messenger bag on the seat next to him and took out a small pile of mail. He put it on the table. On the top was a letter —it was from Leo's vet. It had been sent to the condo that Jeff and I had rented together in Portland, but there was a yellow forwarding sticker on it with my PO box in Prophet, then it had somehow been bounced back from here and returned to Jeff's house. Probably because I'd closed the PO box once I'd bought my home.

Thanks for that, USPS. Good thing I hadn't been in witness protection.

I didn't touch the mail. I didn't say anything.

Annoyance crossed Jeff's face. "You know, it's not right that you left without even saying goodbye, and that I spent a year not having a clue where you were. You shouldn't treat the people in your life like that. I loved you, Tiber. I still do. I only ever wanted the best for you. I didn't deserve to be ghosted."

He reached across the booth towards me, but I was clutching the bench seat and there was nothing for him to grab onto. He slowly retracted his hand. "What did I do? I thought we were happy. I know you were pissed at my brother, but why did you have to take it out on me?"

"Jeff—" I tried very hard to stay calm, "—your brother deliberately drove over and killed two fawns just to hurt me. And then you stood up for him."

Jeff grimaced. "I know. I know. I shouldn't let him get away with things. But I—"

"*Things?*"

Jeff flushed. "I was embarrassed! If you want to know the truth. I didn't know what to say to you about it. It was humiliating. And, yes, he was a total jerk that night. All right? And I'm sorry. I am. But *he* did that, not me. I don't understand how that negates how perfect we were together, or—"

"'Perfect'? You complained about everything I was, said, or did!"

Jeff blinked in confusion. "What? That's not even remotely true. Maybe I offered suggestions now and then —because I loved you! If you weren't so... so self-conscious and timid, it wouldn't have been a big deal. Name one thing that I..."

As Jeff went on, the panic came back and my chest grew tight. This argument was as old as the moon and stars, a déjà vu conversation from hell. I'd never won this argument before, and I wouldn't win it now. Didn't want to try. Didn't want to be here. Didn't want to exist, even. As in, on this planet. I wanted to crawl into a hole and die.

And that feeling, too, was familiar. Jeff made me feel

like that. Trapped. Like a fly in honey, overwhelmed by his dominant personality, his constant excuses and gaslighting. He made me feel like I'd never get away. He made me want to retreat from the entire human race.

The bell on the diner's front door sounded, and my gaze snapped to it as if it were a rope thrown to a drowning man. Gabriel walked in. He was in his sheriff's uniform still, and he had that tired vibe he got after a long day. The tightness on his forehead was accompanied by the dark stubble on his jaw that made my stomach do a slow roll.

His hazel eyes found me, and a small, involuntary smile tugged at his lips, as if the mere sight of me lit him up. Then he glanced at Jeff and the smile turned to a scowl. He ducked his head. I thought he might approach. Hoped he would. But no, he slid into a booth across the room. A booth where he could see me.

I turned back around. My pulse was racing.

I knew Gabriel didn't eat at the diner often. I also remembered that he'd overheard me agreeing to meet Jeff here at seven.

I glanced back at him. The waitress was taking his order. She walked away. He offered me an encouraging smile, then began typing something on his phone.

The warmth spread from my stomach to my chest. He was telling me he was here for me, if I should need him, but he wasn't going to interfere. The heat moved up to prickle my eyes.

"*Tiber*." Jeff sounded annoyed.

"Hmm?" I shook my head to clear it and focused back on the man sitting across from me.

"I said we can pick up a U-Haul in Port Angeles tomorrow and get you the hell out of this dump. Have you bought a lot of furniture since you came? Because if we can rent a smaller one, maybe we can stop at Rainier on the way down and—"

I sat straighter in the booth and folded my arms on the table. "I bought a house."

Jeff stopped talking and frowned. "You bought a house?"

I nodded. "Yup. I love it. And I have animals. Leo's still going strong, fortunately, and I have three other dogs now, two cats, a rabbit, and a giant tortoise. Oh, and Sid, the spider."

Jeff struggled to speak. I could see the calculation in his eyes. As if he knew that if he said what he wanted to say, I'd be pissed off, and he was still trying to charm me into going back to him.

Huh. It was so easy to read all that in his face, his eyes. For so long, I hadn't been able to read Jeff. Or maybe I hadn't wanted to see the truth.

I waited to see what he'd come up with. Giddy amusement rose inside me from nowhere. I glanced over at Gabriel. I caught him watching me, but he immediately went back to his phone.

God, he was handsome. What had he ordered? A hamburger and fries, probably. Maybe a piece of pie. That man did have a sweet tooth. He kept a stash of sour fish at my place in case the need hit.

I wished I was sitting with Gabriel right now. We'd talk about Billy, and the case, and Hen, and Devin, and the townspeople, and my pack, and hiking trails, and the fall colors, and a dozen other things. I'd tell him all about the wolves—about the wonder of seeing them, about how I knew they were not responsible for Billy's death. And he'd listen because he always listened. It would be easy. So easy.

And none of what we discussed, even if we talked for a year, would ever be what was wrong with me, or how I should change, or how my feelings for animals were stupid. I got a lump in my throat.

"I'm still in our old condo..." Jeff began haltingly. "You know we can't have pets. The owner made an exception for Leo, but there's no way..."

I glanced back at him, raised one eyebrow. *Do go on.*

"Well. We can... I mean. Why did you get so many animals? Can you rehome them?"

I smiled. "The new dogs are named Ferdinand, Gracie, and Duke. My cats are Patch and Fudge. Renfield is the rabbit—pure white and soft as down. Frank is the tortoise. And, to be perfectly honest, Jeff, I'd rehome *you* before I'd rehome a single flea from a single one of their heads." I laughed, it was so funny and so true.

Maybe I was getting a little hysterical.

"Tiber!" Jeff gasped. I saw him quickly recalculating. "Listen, I'm here for a few days. Let's just enjoy a date night, okay? I want to be with you. I missed you. We can discuss next steps later. If you need to take some time to figure it all out, it's fine."

"Really?" I feigned surprise. "It's okay to take some time to reconfigure my entire life to suit you? Wow. That's big of you."

For a moment, he looked confused. Then his

expression crumpled. "Tiber, please. Don't be cruel. I've thought of nothing but you since the day you left. And then losing Mom on top of it. It's too much. I'm… I'm not sure I can handle it. Please. You've always been so nice, so sweet. And I need your kindness now. I'm suffering here."

A flash of sympathy sparked inside me. It was true, I was being a brat. And I had come here tonight because he'd lost his mom. But the flash was only a flash. And, gazing at him, I felt sorry for him. But not in a way that necessitated my being here for a minute longer.

And I realized this psychopathically brilliant, gaslighting demon I'd built up in my mind just… didn't matter to me anymore.

He couldn't talk me into anything.

His hold on me was gone.

I took out my wallet and tossed down a twenty. "I'm sorry about your mom, Jeff. But I'm not going back with you. I'm never leaving Prophet, and I don't have anything more to say. Except that the quickest way to get back to Portland is to head south and pick up the 101 in Sappho. Oh, and have a nice life. Now I do, in fact, have a date night to get to."

I left him spluttering as I got out of the booth. The waitress was just walking up with a plate in each hand. I took my grilled cheese and fries from her with a *"thanks"* and walked over to Gabriel's table. I put the plate down and slid into the booth.

"Hi, honey," I said. I leaned over the table to give him a quick kiss before plopping back in my seat.

Gabriel's cheeks pinkened, his eyes sparkled as he glanced around shyly, and I swear, he smiled with his whole soul. "Tiber," he said with a deep, sexy voice that made my toes curl.

"Gabriel."

We looked at each other for a long moment, both of us smiling so hard, we were lucky not to break anything.

He reached over and touched my hand. "You okay?"

I nodded. "Yeah. Very much okay."

He sighed out a deep breath as if he'd been holding it for ages. "Good."

"Good." I picked up a French fry and began to eat.

Chapter Twelve

Gabriel

IF LOOKS COULD KILL, I'd be dead. Jeff didn't hang around long, cursing when his foot caught under the table leg, pissed when his wallet got stuck in his pants, and then he exited the diner muttering something about hick fucking towns, and then he was gone. I couldn't see his car where it was parked, but I sure saw it fly past the window as Jeff left. I couldn't hear what had been said between Tiber and Jeff, but I'd stared long enough to know there'd been a shift in their dynamic. I had things I'd been ready to throw at Jeff, things Devin had found out and sent onto me, and I was ready at the drop of a hat to launch myself over there and demand that Jeff leave Tiber alone because I had evidence proving Jeff was a lying asshole.

"His mom isn't dead, is she," Tiber murmured as he licked ketchup from his index finger. I was immediately half hard—who'd have thought that a simple lick of a finger would turn me on, but it was Tiber and it did. How should I respond to the statement? Was it creepy that I'd dug into Jeff? Was I just as bad as him? Had I overstepped—

"It's okay you checked him out," Tiber interrupted my spiral, and I glanced up to find a reassuring smile, that didn't quite reach his eyes.

"Is it?" God, I wanted to lean over the table and kiss him until we couldn't breathe, but I got the feeling I might fuck everything up.

After a while he seemed to relax and his smile widened and the relief I felt that he wasn't pissed was enormous. "My boyfriend is a cop, he's looking out for me."

I swallowed, and he met my steady gaze with one of his own, and I knew he was waiting for more. "Is that what we are? Boyfriends?" I knew I sounded like a teenager, but it was a huge step to go from friends, to boyfriends, for him with his past, and for me with mine.

"If you'd be happy to take on a weird animal whisperer with baggage." There was no uncertainty in his tone. He smiled again—god, I loved his smile—and then wrinkled his nose. So cute, so freaking adorable, so… mine.

"What about the burned-out LA cop with nightmares and issues fitting back in with his family?" I half joked.

"Not so much dysfunction now, I think you and Sam are getting closer, I see it every time you're together. He understands more of you, and you're slowly forgiving yourself. It's all good."

"You see all of that?" I loved what he was saying—I put a lot of store in what he thought and his sweet, then hot as hell, intuition.

"Yep, I do." He sipped his drink and turned shy for a moment. "So... boyfriends? Officially? Holding hands and talking about our feelings and more kissing and... stuff?"

"I'd like that."

We grinned at each other for a while, and all around us the world kept turning. Wesley chatted on his phone, and the waitress hummed an old country song as she cleaned tables, and yet the two of us had taken the first step toward something real. I was excited, nervous, worried, but most of all I understood that we fit and hoped that our journey was going to be a special thing.

It was Tiber who pulled us back to the here and now. "So yeah, did you get my message about the rez and shaman? I don't know if it means anything, but I wanted to tell you."

"Wait, first of all, do you want to talk?"

"What about? Jeff? No." Then he sighed. "But I get the feeling you have things to tell me about him, so let's get that done first, then we can talk about the case. First up, I'm guessing he lied about his mom being dead. Am I right?"

"Devin sent me a link to an Instagram account, and I clicked around, and as of a few days ago she was very much alive and posting photos of her vacation in the Bahamas."

He nodded and seemed relieved. "Okay. Good. She didn't much like me, nor I her, but I wouldn't wish a son like Jeff on anyone." He ate another fry and nudged the plate toward me but I shook my head. He needed to eat, and I was worried about him, and it was okay, because he was my *boyfriend* and I was allowed to worry.

"What else do you have to tell me?" he asked, and I poked at my burger, because if I looked at it for long enough I could forget he asked a question. "Gabriel?"

This was going to be the hard part, only because Tiber's heart was so open and he'd be devastated for the current, or rather ex, guy in Jeff's life. "His latest partner has a restraining order out on him."

Silence, and I glanced up to see Tiber staring out of the window as a heavy cloudburst hit town and shook the glass.

"Jeff said he'd thought of nothing but me since I left." Tiber huffed a laugh. "I should have known he showed up here because someone else dumped him. Well, whoever the new guy was, it sounds like he was a stronger man than me."

I detected a hint of self-recrimination that I instantly wanted to shut down, but he didn't give me a chance. "I'm done with Jeff, it's finished. I hope his new partner gets the same kind of closure I got, and I hope he's lucky enough to meet someone worthy of his time." Our gazes locked and I laced my fingers with his. "Like I did."

Suddenly, I wasn't hungry. I wanted to be back at Tiber's place where we could investigate this new relationship status with kissing, and snuggling, and maybe more, although right now I'd be happy just to be close to him. By unspoken agreement we left the cafe, and headed to my SUV, and he climbed in as if that was exactly where he was meant to be.

"I'm too amped up to drive. We'll pick up the car tomorrow," he explained, and I didn't argue.

"How was the visit to the rez?" he asked me again as soon as we started driving.

I shrugged. "Confusing. I need to get my head straight about it all, and then maybe we can talk?"

"Sure."

"So, your turn; how did it go today with the wolves?"

He was so quiet I wondered if he'd heard my question, "Beautiful, the most incredible experience... there were pups, and everything was so... real. They were all healthy, Gabriel. No sign of rabies or any unusual aggression. I swear, I could have watched them forever."

"I wish I'd been there to see *you* see *them*."

"I thought about you. I wished you were there to share it with." He smiled at me, then his smile slipped a little. "Please don't let anyone hurt them," Tiber whispered, and I wondered if that was a plea for me or for any spirits out there who might be listening.

"I will do everything I can to protect them," I whispered back.

He threw me a thoughtful smile. "I know you will. " He squeezed my hand. "Susan took casts of prints and some fur samples. She's going to compare them to the one she found where Billy was killed. But I know in my bones that it wasn't them who killed him."

I flicked my signal, although there was no one behind us to see it, turning onto the bumpy road leading to Tiber's place. I already felt peace building inside me, and could imagine Patch curling up on my shoulder and purring in my ear. I hoped Tiber would be as interested in sitting with me, but maybe after today he'd want me to leave.

"When One-Eyed Jack was telling me about Orson and his connection to Billy and the shaman, he asked me if I believed in magic," Tiber said. "I told him that I did."

I parked and cut the engine, turning to Tiber who was watching me carefully.

"Of course you do," I murmured, and reached for his hand, lacing our fingers, and tugging him toward me for a kiss. "After all, what is this between us?"

I walked him up the path, the barking and whining—a background chorus of happy animals—reached us and I felt a million times lighter. I stopped on the steps as he walked up them, and then he came back down and straight into my arms. I kissed him, and he squeezed my hand before he tugged himself free and opened the door, stopping at the last moment. "Aren't you coming in, *boyfriend*?"

"Are you sure you want me to? It's been a rough night."

"I'd like you to come in." Maybe he caught my hesitation, maybe it was nerves, but he dipped his gaze. "I mean, Duke will want to see you."

I was up those steps so fast I tripped and only just caught myself at the last moment, but then I was in with the dogs, and cats, and Tiber. The thing I loved the most about this home was that it took ten minutes to say hello to everyone, pats and scratches, and conversations with the more vocal members of the pack. Patch balanced on my shoulder, Duke was at my side, and they all wanted a piece of me and Tiber.

After giving Leo a cuddle, Tiber put him down and Leo barked at his feet while Ferdinand made a grumbling sound.

"I told you guys not to fight over that stuffed squirrel," Tiber scolded. "Leo, Ferdinand has equal custody, and that's it. No complaining when he plays with it."

Leo ducked his head, and Ferdinand stuck out his tongue and panted in what sure looked like a doggie grin.

I loved every moment. It was a family. And maybe I was a part of it now.

Tiber moved into the kitchen, and I could hear the clatter of mugs as Duke pawed at my leg and then mouthed my hand when I'd stopped stroking him for a second. He'd brought me a gift—a damp, half chewed stuffed carrot—and we played a short game of fetch, which involved all of the dogs, plus one very interested rabbit, diving for what was left of the orange toy.

It was only after this happened a couple of times that I realized Tiber hadn't come back, and a prickle of worry traveled my spine. I extricated myself from the canine bundle— Patch still on my shoulder and unhappy to be removed—then I went into the kitchen and faced a sight that broke my heart.

Tiber was sitting on the floor, his arms around his knees, his head bowed.

I shooed everyone out, even Patch, and shut the door, then sat down next to him, removing the empty mug from his hand with gentle care.

"Tiber? Sweetheart?"

"I don't want Jeff here," Tiber mumbled.

"I don't think he's staying." *I'll make sure he doesn't stay.*

I wriggled closer so our thighs touched and for a

moment I didn't breathe, waiting for him to tell me to leave him alone, but instead he leaned on me.

"It's shit, the way he makes me feel, it's like poison. I thought I'd broken the back of this thing, telling him to leave, seeing through his shit, understanding what he did. Then, just now, all I did was spill milk on the counter and it hit me so hard how he used to berate me, call me clumsy, making me feel like I was all wrong. I don't want him anywhere near me or Prophet."

"I'll make him leave." It was the least I could do as sheriff.

"You can't do that." Tiber sounded worried. "I should be able to deal with him on my own."

"It's what boyfriends do best, and I think you've handled enough today. I'm here for you," I kept my tone soft and reassuring, and he nodded. I'd bet my life that he'd seen that kind of empty promise before with Jeff, but I wanted him to know that I meant it. "I'll never hurt you."

"I want to believe that. I want to. I want to be a boyfriend who is flirty and sexy and fun, but all you're getting is me." He said it so fierce that I was startled. "And some days I don't know which way is up and which is down."

I had to make him see how I felt.

"What I want is a boyfriend who loves animals, whose heart is so big I'm in awe, and who argues with me over what goes on popcorn, and who would never turn a person away who needed help. That's you, Tiber." The unspoken *I love you* was right on the tip of my tongue, but saying it now might sound as if I were putting a Band-Aid over today's stress, and Tiber needed to hear it when he was sure of me, and himself, and when I was sure I could be the best man for him.

One of the dogs scratched at the door and whined— they knew we were in here, and they must sense Tiber's distress. "It's okay, guys," I called, for what it was worth. Tiber's little family loved him and there was some whining, but for the most part they settled down. Yet again I got the uncanny sense that they understood me, or maybe responded to the gentle tone of my voice.

"I wish I could undo the past you had with Jeff," I murmured and tugged him in for a sideways hug.

"I was so stupid over that asshole."

"Hey. No boyfriend of mine is stupid."

He snorted in self-derision, and it wasn't a sound I liked at all. I hated that he doubted himself. I hated Jeff for doing that to him.

"I'm not like him," I reassured, "but I'm not perfect either. I have my ghosts, and my bad parts."

"I know." He lifted his head to glance at me. "I sometimes feel…" He rubbed at his chest. "There's grief in you that I'm trying to understand." I blinked at him, unsure of how to take what he said. "We'll work through it together."

I was shocked that he could see the pain in me. I didn't want him to see the failing parts of me, I wanted him to focus on how I could be his strength if he needed me, so I ignored his insight which was far too accurate for me to handle. Then I focused on how I could understand him and help.

"Tiber?"

"Hmm?"

"I'll never belittle your emotions or dismiss your concerns, because every single one of them is valid. I'll always listen to you." I wanted to throw a thousand promises at him, but he didn't need empty words, he needed me to prove I could be trusted, and I wanted to start showing him that tonight.

He rested his head on my chest. "What if I just start distrusting myself again? What if I can't tell what's real and what's not? He made me doubt everything I did, made me feel... less. I thought I'd put all that to rest at the diner, but then you told me about his lies and everything got all fragile again. Like, I believed him when he said his mom died, when he said he'd been pining for me all this time. Why did I believe him about anything? It makes me angry that I'm so gullible. And that makes me afraid to trust anything anyone says, ever again." He added the last bit sounding so angry that it hurt.

I wished what had happened to him had an easy fix, that me promising him everything would be okay would make it so. But I couldn't guarantee that his wolves would be safe, let alone carry through on the promise I would never hurt him. I'd try to my dying breath, but what if we fell asleep together and the nightmares visited in the deep of night, and he had to deal with all of that in me? I'd only ever had surface sleep on his sofa, was only ever one lick or snuffle against my skin away from being woken up. Never going so deep that the horrors I'd seen visited me. I shoved that thought away—this wasn't about me.

"How about this?" I cradled his face, and he met my gaze. "Question every little thing I do or say to you. I don't care how many times you need me to reassure you, or explain what I'm saying, or hug you and not let you go. I will never judge you for doubting me, or us, and we can talk about everything, even the bits I'm sitting here thinking I never want you to know. I want to make this work, but it has to be because you're safe and happy."

He reached out to touch my knee. "You're a good man, Gabriel."

I could work with that even if it wasn't a hundred percent true. "I'll never *intentionally* hurt you, or deceive you, or try to manipulate you. But I have nightmares, and I have things in my past as a cop that I can't share yet, or maybe ever? Please believe me when I say I'll do everything I can, I mean, I'm seeing a therapist, I'm working on self-care..." I scrubbed a hand through my hair. "I'm doing everything and anything to be the best man I can for you. And it might not be all roses, but with mutual respect and understanding, and sharing everything, we can make this work, and you will always be safe with me."

"And you're okay taking it slow," he murmured.

"Yes."

He turned and buried his face in my neck, and I could feel the gentle kiss he placed there. "What if it takes me too long to get my head straight?"

Was it too soon to say we had forever to try?

"I'm not going anywhere."

"Me neither," he said into a kiss.

When I left, just after midnight, he hugged me for the longest time.

"Gabriel?" He lifted his face and I saw his eyes were bright with emotion.

"Yeah?"

"Don't give up on us."

Well, this was an easy promise to make. "Never."

Chapter Thirteen

Tiber

STONE WHITEPLUME LIVED north of Prophet. It was an eleven-mile drive—the last seven of it on a pitted gravel road. I could only hope my GPS wasn't hopelessly confused. But when I arrived, I knew I'd found the right place.

The gravel driveway was set on either side with posts topped with large, flat rocks. The rock on the left was painted with a sun symbol in red and the one on the right with an eye in black. I paused my car at the driveway. I'd always found the shamanistic traditions on the Navajo rez fascinating—but also a little frightening. I recalled one man, a Navajo witch, who my grandmother feared so much that she would not allow his name to be spoken in her house.

And this cabin was way the hell out here, as the saying goes, *"no one would hear you scream."* Mr. Whiteplume might not take too kindly to inquisitive strangers. Especially if he had a murder to hide.

Why had I come? And why had I come *alone*?

From what Gabriel had told me about his visit to the rez yesterday, he hadn't gotten anything meaningful from Orson Travis—other than an admission he *had* hired a shaman. It didn't sound as though Gabriel had the authority to probe any deeper into the matter. Yet the unease in my gut said there was something here, that the attack on Billy hadn't been purely random. And, unless we could prove it, the wolves were in danger.

I also couldn't deny I'd driven out here this morning because of Jeff. I'd felt itchy in my skin since waking up. Even the animals hadn't been able to snap me out of it. Had Jeff left town? What if he hadn't? What if he came knocking at my door? The safe haven of my little house no longer felt secure. And I hadn't wanted to go into town and run into him there. So checking out Stone Whiteplume had appealed.

Frying pan? Fire?

I shook my head. Screw that. Mr. Whiteplume was just a man, an elder. And maybe I'd learn something that could help Gabriel. Help the wolves. How much of a coward would I be if I didn't try?

I drove my car between the sun and the eye.

The trees cleared after a few yards, and the driveway ended at a small log cabin. It was old but well-maintained, with a narrow porch holding two rocking chairs and a round table. There were four sturdy pine steps leading up to it and a satellite antenna on the roof. A small garden of herbs and vegetables was positioned to the left of the cabin, in an area cleared to get full sun. On the other side was a penned area with a dozen chickens and a chicken coop. Smoke drifted from the chimney on this cool October morning.

I stopped the car and got out. It wasn't until I approached the porch that I noticed other things—bundles of herbs, feathers, and bits that might be horn or shell tied all along the roof over the porch. A triangle filled with symbols was drawn in chalk on the door. Red paint and a white powder were drawn across the bottom step like a barrier. I hesitated to step over it.

As I was studying the paint, I heard the screen door squeak. I looked up to see a man in the doorway. He had an ageless face but his long dark hair was threaded with gray. His body was lean in dark blue, still-new Wranglers and a long-sleeved green T-shirt. The belt around his waist had a large turquoise-and-silver buckle of the sort you'd see on the rez in Arizona. Worn work boots were on his feet.

"Mr. Whiteplume?"

"That's me. Want some coffee?" He didn't seem surprised to see me.

"Uh… sure. Thank you."

"I'm out of milk, so it'll be black." He went back inside and the screen door banged behind him.

This was the shaman who made One-Eyed Jack nervous? He seemed pleasant enough. Not a scary *yee naaldlooshii*—a witch. I relaxed a little but I stayed at the bottom of the steps and waited, not wanting to cross the red line. When he came out with a green-speckled tin camping cup in each hand, he didn't go to the rocking chairs. Instead, he sat on the top porch step and put one of the cups next to him. "Come on, then."

I stepped over the paint and powder, walked up the stairs, and sat next to him, leaving a few feet between us. I took a sip.

Yikes. Strong as tar. Chewy, even. I fought not to make a face.

"It's been a nice autumn, huh?" he said conversationally.

"Sure has. I've really been enjoying it."

We both sipped our coffee.

"Where abouts you live? Got some nice, colorful trees around you ?" he asked.

"I'm about a mile from downtown Prophet, towards the lake. There's a big oak in my yard that's yellow right now. Gorgeous."

"That's good." Stone nodded towards the woods to the left. "The berries are starting to go bad, but I have a freezer full already."

"I froze some too."

We continued to talk about the season. I knew from my grandmother's house that we'd get around to business eventually. But first you had to feel each other out.

I could sense Stone Whiteplume wasn't sure why I was there, but he didn't seem worried about it. After a while, he broached the subject. "I have medicine pouches for just about anything. Different types of healing. Protection against bad spirits. To bring good luck. There's a discount if you pay cash."

I almost laughed because it was so ordinary. He might have been selling produce from his garden. But I managed to keep my face blank. "I actually came to talk to you, if that's okay."

"Huh." He took out a cigarette and offered me one. I declined. He lit up and held the cigarette in one hand, the coffee cup in the other. He turned his head to study me. "You're not Makah."

"No. My grandmother on my mom's side was Navajo." I said it a bit too fast. Even all grown up, I was still nervous about being accepted, maybe because of the teasing I got on the rez about having mixed blood.

He nodded. "It is hard for a man to know which way to go when his two feet do not agree. Then again you don't have to be part *bilagáana* to have that problem. Just live in the modern world."

He'd used the Navajo word for white man. Which made me curious. "What about you? Are you Makah? Navajo?"

"Arapaho."

Arapaho weren't indigenous to this area. More like Montana, I thought. "So what brought you to Prophet?"

Stone smoked for a few minutes. Just when I thought he wasn't going to answer, he said, "This place here is like the dark cave you enter in the first stage of the afterlife. Only you don't have to die in the body to reach it. It is a place to run to when you want to leave your old life behind, when you don't want to be who you were anymore. A rebirth in spirit. That's why you came here, isn't it?"

The metaphor struck me viscerally. Had I died, in a

sense, when I'd moved to Prophet? I didn't like the word. But rebirth sounded about right.

"I guess it is. But what do you do when your old life follows you?"

Stone gave me a sideways glance. "Tell it to fuck off."

I barked a laugh.

"Or, you can buy a medicine pouch. I have a good *fuck off* one. Half price for you."

"Maybe I will."

I wanted to ask him what he'd been running from when he came to Prophet, but I knew he wouldn't tell me. And it was none of my business.

I figured by now we'd had our warm-up conversation. As much as I wouldn't mind continuing to chat with Stone —a surprise, since I didn't like chatting with most people —I'd come here for a reason.

"Did you hear about Billy Odette?" I asked.

Stone continued to smoke, staring straight ahead. "I heard."

"I was told Billy had enemies. Or *an* enemy at least."

"Few men get far in life without making enemies."

"But there are people who dislike you. And then there are people who will pay to do you harm."

Stone finished his coffee and stood. "I'm gonna refill. Want more?"

"No. I had some before I came. Thanks."

He went back inside with another bang of the screen door.

I wondered what I was doing there. Did I really think Stone could send a spirit wolf to kill Billy? As much as his cabin, his talismans, and even his persona, created a certain mystique, the logical side of my brain wasn't ready to go there.

Or, if not a spirit wolf, could the power of a malevolent mind, or a curse, cause an otherwise normal animal to be temporarily overtaken by aggression and used in an attack? I believed a man could train an animal to be vicious. But possess the mind of a wild wolf? I didn't believe that either.

I felt a surge of discouragement. I was wasting his time and mine. All because I was still running from Jeff.

I shouldn't be thinking about him at all. I should be thinking about Gabriel. Last night, we'd moved out of the friend zone. Well, to be fair, I'd been the only one keeping us there. And not because I didn't want him. I wanted him badly. Not just physically, but his arms, his warmth. I wanted him in my life. And once I knew for sure Jeff was gone, I'd be able to finally give us a chance.

I hoped.

Stone came out and sat back down on the step with a sigh. "You know, when I was young, I was full of myself. I thought I was special because of my gift." He turned his head and studied my face. "You have a gift too."

"Me? Not really."

He raised an eyebrow. "It's not bragging if I asked you. So, tell me. What is it?"

I felt embarrassed, like I always did admitting it out loud. "Well… I can understand animals. Sort of. But I have a degree in animal behavior, so it's as much education as a gift."

"It's a gift." He huffed. "I should have known." He waved his coffee cup to the right, and I saw three crows sitting on the wire fence around the veggie garden. They were watching us. I felt a spark of awe the way I always did when they appeared.

"Crows are go-betweens," said Stone. "Back in the bad days, when whites were overrunning all the tribes, Arapaho with crow totems were the ones to try to negotiate between the people and the whites."

"They were?"

He nodded. "A thankless task, right? Also—those who speak to the dead—they are go-betweens too. They are of the crow family. You are a go-between. Only with you, it's between the animal world and the human."

The way he put it touched me. A *go-between*. I took a sip of my coffee and looked at the morning sky. I wanted to believe that was true.

"Seems like a useful gift," Stone continued. "Especially to a farmer. Are you a farmer?"

"Nope."

He grunted. "Too bad. Anyway. To get back to my story, my gift was power. And when I was young, I misused it. I did bad things. And I lost the gift. I made enemies too. Bad enemies. That is why I had to run away and come here. It took me a year of praying and making offerings to the ancestors to get the gift back."

There was a lot there to unpack, but I thought I understood what he was saying. "So... if you cursed someone for money, that would be misusing your gift?"

He smiled. "It is nice to talk to someone who doesn't have cotton between their ears."

I thought about what he was trying to tell me. I was still

working on a reply when Stone spoke again. "See, it's not so much the curse, it's the intent. These days, before I do anything, I work spells of intent so that a person will be harmed only to the degree that they have harmed others. If they are innocent, they have nothing to fear from such a ritual. If they have done a little bad, a little bad will be done to them. If the person who seeks the curse is the one in the wrong, the curse will turn back around and bite them in the ass. When you work this way, you go along with the flow of the universe instead of against it. That is the right way."

I took a sip of my coffee. The bitter taste was growing on me. "One-Eyed Jack said Orson Travis paid you to curse Billy."

"One-Eyed Jack makes a lot of smoke," Stone said flatly.

I waited.

"*If* someone paid me to put a curse on Billy Odette," Stone said in a dismissive tone, "it would have been a long time ago. Maybe a year. It is true, a curse can take a long time to come about, but if something happened to Billy, it would only be what he deserved, because that is the intent I laid."

"Billy didn't deserve to die like that," I said, vehemently.

Stone only shrugged. "Then my curse was not responsible. Sometimes shit just happens."

We sat there for a while more. The sun came out and it got hot on the steps. Stone lit another cigarette.

"Some assholes in town are trying to blame a wolf pack that's just moved into the area." Anger crept into my voice. "They want to kill those wolves, and the wolves aren't guilty."

"Maybe, maybe not," said Stone. "That's up to you to figure out. You're the one who talks to animals, Tiber Russo. Not me."

Chapter Fourteen

Tiber

THAT AFTERNOON, I broke up a dispute between Leo and Fudge over a super-important squeaker toy, made a fresh batch of dog food, and fed the troops. Then I took them all down the trail to the lake for a long walk. The day that had been perfect earlier had turned overcast and windy. The lake was a sullen gray-green studded with whitecaps, but the dogs didn't mind the weather, and neither did I.

I threw the ball for Duke, who'd been pent up all day. He raced after it like a demon. While he chased it, I played tug-of-war with Leo over a stick while Gracie and Ferdinand explored fascinating smells near the water. With all of us together like this, happy to merely exist in each other's company, it reminded me of what Jeff had said. *Can't you just rehome them?*

I laughed out loud. It startled Gracie, who trotted over to sniff at me and make sure I was okay.

"Can you believe that?" I asked her. "That would never

happen. Not in a million years. If he understood the first thing about me, he would have known that."

Gracie yawned.

"I know, I know. That's all old news, and I shouldn't waste time thinking about Jeff."

Duke returned and dropped the ball at my feet. He danced around expectantly, staring at it. Subtle, dude. I threw it again.

It was getting dark by the time we got home. I'd just ushered everyone inside when I got a text alert. It was from Gabriel saying he was going to stop by. That sent me on a race to pick up dog toys, straighten couch cushions, brush my teeth, and run a brush through my wind-blown hair.

There was a knock on the door a few minutes later. When I opened it and slipped outside to foil the anxious hounds, Gabriel stood on the stoop with his hands in the front pockets of his uniform pants. He looked shy. "I don't want to intrude on your evening, but I have some news."

"Don't be ridiculous. You can come anytime." I almost added, *I'm always happy to see you.* Because I was. And the idea surprised me a little. I couldn't think of another person I felt that way about. Hell, I had to work myself up to even a visit from my mother.

We stood on the stoop awkwardly. Although we'd *said* we were boyfriends now, it still felt a little uncertain how to make that transition.

He cleared his throat. "I came to let you know that I followed up on Jeff. Daisy said he checked out of the hotel at nine this morning. She had choice words about some kind of styling goop he left on the towels."

"Sounds about right."

"I also drove around town and didn't see any sign of his car. I think he's gone."

Relief broke over me like a wave of cool water. And then, I couldn't help myself, I hugged Gabriel tight. "Thank you. Thanks for checking on that."

"No problem." His deep voice rumbled in my ear and his warm hands cupped my back. It felt wonderful. "If he shows up again, I can help you get a restraining order. Since he already has one on his record, it'd be an easy sell."

"He won't be back," I said, and I thought it was true. Though the me in this moment, the Tiber wrapped in the strong arms of Sheriff Thompson, was not the same me who might wake up worried in the middle of the night. But for now, I'd take it.

"I have some news for you too," I said. "Come inside."

I took his hand and pulled him into the house. Of course, the entire pack had to greet him. Even Renfield came hopping over to wriggle his pink nose inquisitively up at Gabriel. And Gabriel had treats in his pockets for all of them, including a baby carrot for the rabbit.

Such a good guy.

We sat on the couch and Leo ended up on Gabriel's lap, Patch on the back of the couch by his shoulder, and Duke lay between us on the floor with Gracie. Fudge, the kitten who was no longer so small, played her favorite game with Duke's tail.

"You have news?" Gabriel prompted.

"Mmm. I went to see the shaman today—Stone Whiteplume."

"You did?" Gabriel scowled. "You should have told me you were doing that. If he had anything to do with Billy's death, he could have reacted violently to your sniffing around."

"He doesn't," I said. "Or, actually, he does. But not in an I'll-kill-you-to-silence-you kind of way."

Gabriel barked a laugh but shook his head. "Go on. Tell me about it."

So I told him about Stone's cabin and about his business selling medicine pouches—and what he'd vaguely admitted about Orson Travis. "The bottom line is, I think Orson did hire Stone to put a curse on Billy. But not recently. I got the impression from Stone it was about a year ago. Anyway, I suppose you can't arrest someone for that."

Gabriel looked regretful. "No. But it's not the curse that concerns me. It's the fact that Orson wanted it made in the first place. What else might he have done when the curse didn't work? Unfortunately, I've got nothing that ties Orson to Billy's death. He's got an airtight alibi and he doesn't even own a dog. I doubt he's a wolf whisperer."

"No." I didn't know Orson, so I had no opinion about him or his motives. But the itch in my brain saying *someone* did *something*, continued to nag at me. But maybe I just wanted that to be true? Maybe it was my own blind spot. Not that I didn't understand that wild animals could be dangerous. But, barring rabies, this didn't fit any pattern I could understand.

Gabriel put a hand on my knee and rubbed his thumb over the denim. "Listen, I'm all for checking out Billy's enemies. If you hear anything more, let me know. But for right now, my priority is to find this damn animal."

"I get that." I sighed.

Gabriel pulled out his phone. "I got notification of an email from Susan with Fish and Wildlife before I got here. I thought we might take a look at it together."

"Yeah, definitely." I leaned closer and put my hand over his on my thigh while he brought up the message.

Gabriel didn't have to share this information with me. Maybe he shouldn't since I was a private citizen. But, studying his face, I thought I knew why he wanted to. He didn't want to upset me if he had to go after the wolves— or any other animal. Including me in what was going on was a way to get me on his side, perhaps. That he even cared what I thought caused a flood of affection. I'd been right to let him in. Into my house. Into my heart.

Gabriel tilted the phone so I could see better. "She says: From Libby Smith's repeated observations, there are five adults and three cubs in the Olympic pack. I was able to take eight unique prints at their den, indicating that I have prints for the entire pack. None of the prints are a match for the one found near the body of Billy Odette. This is a strong indicator that the wolves from the Olympic pack were not involved in Odette's death."

He glanced up at me and smiled. "That's good."

I nodded eagerly. "Yes. Thank God."

He went back to the message. "She continued: My own direct observation of the wolf pack confirmed that they are all healthy and well-fed; therefore, sickness and malnutrition, two factors that can cause animal aggression, can be ruled out. However, there remains the possibility that there is a lone wolf in the area, and that it is the animal responsible for the attack on Billy Odette. Another possibility is that the attack was made by a large dog. Some breeds have more wolf characteristics than others. For example the Alaskan Malamute, Alaskan Klee Kai, the Northern Inuit Dog, the Saarloos Wolfdog, and Czechoslovakian Vlcak.

"In addition to the paw prints, we are currently running DNA tests on fur found in the wolves' den along with two strands of gray hair, approx. two centimeters, that were found on Billy Odette's body, and also on blood and tissue taken from his wounds, which should include traces of the attacker's saliva. These DNA results should provide a definitive identification of the animal responsible for his death as well as either confirming or ruling out rabies as a factor."

Gabriel finished reading and put his phone down. Our gazes held.

"Thank God," I said.

"It is good news. For the wolf pack, anyway."

"But not for you?"

Gabriel grimaced. "Do I wish there was an easy answer and that I had it right now? Yes. I have a town to protect. Tourists. I'm meeting with the town board first thing in the morning. I'm going to request that we shut off the Clear Creek Falls Trails indefinitely, and I think they'll agree. But what if this animal—whatever it is—just moves to another area? They have wide territories, don't they?"

"Well, wolves do. Their territory can range from fifty square miles to a thousand. But a dog? I don't know."

Gabriel sighed and rubbed his face. "Fuck. We can't

close up the national park let alone the entire mountain range. What do you think? I know you've eliminated the wolf pack to your own satisfaction. But if not them, what is it? And how do I find it? Can we lure it out? Find its den? Do you have any sense of it at all?"

I checked in with my Spidey senses. I thought again about the flash I'd gotten from River, that feeling-vision of Billy being dragged off her back. But the vision had been so brief and full of panic. I couldn't get a handle on *what* had done it.

I tried to calm my mind and get some intuition about what Billy might have seen and then I tried to get a sense of what might be lurking out there, in the woods, in the night. Anything. Anything at all.

But the crows were silent.

"I don't know," I admitted. "I don't know what it is. Or how to find it. I'm sorry."

"Hey, no worries. We'll figure it out." Gabriel gave me a reassuring smile and squeezed my leg. "Anyway, I didn't mean to take over your night. We can touch base again in the morning." Gabriel shifted Leo off his lap, brushed off his pants, and stood.

Abruptly I didn't want him to leave. Like, really didn't want him to.

"Uh. Sure." My stupid mouth was not in sync with my brain.

I followed him to the front door. He opened it, shooing back Fudge who was making an escape attempt. I shifted from one foot to the other. Every part of me was sure I wanted him to stay, wanted, no *needed*, to kiss him, and more.

Was it okay? Was it time? We'd said we were dating now. Or I think we had? *Stop being so damn awkward.*

My hand darted out and grabbed his arm just as he was about to close the door.

He stopped, a question in his eyes. What now? What did I say?

"Don't go."

Chapter Fifteen

Gabriel

"Is everything okay?" I asked as soon as I saw the confusion in Tiber's gaze.

"Please stay," he repeated.

I closed the door again to stop Fudge from getting past me. "Tiber?"

"I want you to stay. I... want you. Do you want to ...?" Tiber worried at his lower lip, looking uncertain.

He was the one who'd stopped *me* from leaving, and this was *his* show, but I reached for him and slipped a hand behind his head, loosened the tie holding his hair, and carded my fingers through the silky length of it, holding him still for a moment as he caught his breath. Was he sorry for what he'd asked? Did he *really* want me to stay?

Was it a moment of madness he would regret?

"Do I want to, what?"

"Make love? I know that I've been..."

"Yes," I said when he ran out of words. "I've wanted you for so long, but we don't have to—"

He cradled my face and I stopped. Then he wet his lips, the tip of his tongue *right there*, and he went up on tiptoe, as I bent my head, and we met in a heated kiss. I could've stood there like that forever, kissing my affection and need into his warm skin from the tip of his nose to his lips, and right back up again. He moved me, tugging me back toward the sofa, where I imagined a curious menagerie was wondering what the hell was going on.

Only he didn't stop there, as my ass met a wall, then a handle, and then we were in his room. He shoved the door shut with his hip and not once did we stop kissing or touching.

A loud miaow indicated we had a random guest, and probably one that didn't need to be traumatized. In a clean scoop, Tiber picked up Patch and shooed the very vocal cat out of his room, then shut the door again. I glimpsed the crowd of animals by the sofa, a couple of them staring at the door, and it made me smile—even now they were standing sentry and that was okay as long as they were *that* side of the door. I did consider for one moment that the feline interruption might stop what we were doing, but Tiber was on a roll, going straight back in for kissing, then walking me in reverse until my legs hit his bed.

I fell, taking him with me, and we sprawled on the covers, him draped over me, the weight of him nothing, but the feel of him everything. I curled my fingers around the nape of his neck, tugging him in for another kiss, which started soft, a continuation of the goodbye we'd tried to have. But there was no way it was staying so gentle when all I wanted was to taste every inch of him, not when it was Tiber who'd tugged me inside, causing my libido to go from zero to a hundred in seconds.

And there was no doubting how much he was into this, his cock hard against mine, as he slotted between my legs, and we exchanged deep kisses that were a promise of so much more.

"Your uniform is the sexiest thing I've ever seen," Tiber murmured, "but we need it off now."

He sat up, straddling my cock, and began loosening buttons, as I tried to help. I gave up after we fumbled at the same one, and instead pulled at Tiber's T-shirt until he got the message and took it off before going right back to my buttons.

He was beautiful, the soft glow of the bedside lamp threw his features into sharp relief, his hairless chest, the dimples near his waistband, the V there that I wanted to taste. I inhaled sharply because I had this man in my arms, and we were about to—

He'd stopped, frozen, with half my buttons undone, my shirt tangled up under my arms, staring at me, his eyes wide.

"What?" I said with a smile of encouragement, but he was staring at me. "Don't stop," I said, and rotated my hips, showing him what I needed.

"I'm sorry," he murmured, and picked up his discarded T-shirt, "I know I'm not built like—"

"Tiber?"

"Sorry. I'm—fuck. I'm not good at this. Can we forget this ever happened?" He tried to wriggle away, and just like that his yes had turned into a no. I wasn't disappointed

—well I was, but I was all about consent, and I respected his decision. I was also concerned at the confusion in his expression.

"Okay, it's okay, we don't have to do anything. Is it okay to just get a hug?" I sat up as best I could and pulled him close, at last able to cradle him against me and trace a pattern of love on his skin with soft kisses.

"Fuck, I'm sorry." Emotion was choking him.

"It can wait," I said softly. "We have forever to work this out." I buried my face in his neck, and kissed him under the curtain of his hair, hoping I hadn't given away how I felt. *Way to scare a man off.* God, he tasted good everywhere, but this was me stopping. I leaned back a little and tucked his hair behind his ears one side at a time, staring into his eyes and the face that was so dear to me.

He was everything I wanted, and I *would* wait. Forever if needed.

He screwed his eyes shut and when he opened them again they were bright with emotion. "I thought I was ready, only I forgot…"

"'Forgot'?" I bet this was something to do with Jeff—I swear one day I would hunt the man down and arrest him. For what I didn't know, but I'd find something.

"That I don't look so good… y'know… when I'm naked… that I'm too skinny." He was barely audible on the last part, as though it was hard for him to even say that out loud.

What? "Tiber, you're perfect." He clutched the T-shirt and frowned at me, as if he didn't believe a single word. "I'm not saying that just to do this… look, we don't have to do anything."

He worried at his lip, then closed his eyes and pulled his T-shirt back on over his head, but I snuck in one last taste, pressing a quick kiss near one of his nipples, and then smiling up at him.

"Your pace," I promised, and then touched the tip of my nose to his.

I expected him to move away, but I realized he wasn't moving, around the same time as he reached out and pressed a hand to my shirt, which was still stuck up and under one arm.

"You sighed," he said. "When I took off my top, you sighed, but then you just kissed me there so you must want what I am, and my mind is playing tricks."

I took a careful moment to consider what he'd said— he thought my sigh was disappointment because I didn't like what I saw? That was impossible. Tiber was gorgeous, toned, and strong, and I needed to show him.

"That wasn't disappointment, that was me taking a breath because I had you in my arms and I couldn't believe how lucky I was."

"Oh."

"Hey, can I show you all the parts I love?" I asked with caution.

He still hadn't moved from my lap.

"Give me a minute." He closed his eyes again, his lips pressed in a thin line, and I didn't move, waiting for him to come to me if that was what he wanted, wondering what voices he was fighting in his head. Jeff had destroyed his confidence, and I needed to show him he could trust me and feel safe and secure that I wouldn't hurt him. I rubbed circles on his thigh with a thumb, just to remind him I was there, to anchor him to the here and now. "Okay," he finished.

"Okay?"

"Okay, I think I'm done panicking."

I kissed his reluctant smile. "How about you lie back?"

I let him gather himself enough to slip off me and fall back on the covers. He began to remove his shirt, but I stilled his hand.

"I want to start somewhere else," I murmured, facing him then pressing my fingers to his forehead. "I love this part."

"My forehead?"

"Well yeah, it's a very nice forehead, but it's the brain inside I love. All of your empathy and compassion is like this glow."

"Jesus, Gabriel," he murmured, and his voice cracked.

"You want me to stop, sweetheart?"

He shook his head.

I pressed my fingers to his lips. "I can't understand how it works, but when you talk to me, I instantly settle inside, and I swear it must be a charm you've conjured." I traced my finger down his neck to his chest, flattening my hand over his heart. "This is where all of your magic lives." I traced the shape of a circle there and kissed there over his top. "Did you know that having you in my life makes every day brighter?"

"It does?"

"Every second I'm away from you I feel untethered, stressed, like the nightmares are just waiting in the wings, but you make them fall away just by being you."

"I don't mean to," he murmured. "I don't know I'm doing it."

"That's just you. Every day since the moment I knocked on your door, you've made me feel safe and strong."

"I have?" He sounded so wondering, as if no one had ever told him what kind of man he was.

"Yes, sweetheart, you have."

"What about this part?" He raised his eyebrow in a challenge—a glint of his usual feistiness—and lifted the bottom of his top so I could see his belly, the tip of his happy trail, and the softness of his warm-toned skin.

I kissed him there, traced a path with my lips to his left hip and then back. "I've dreamed of this. Of having you in my bed and kissing you."

He reached for my hand, drew it up so it took the material with it, and closed his eyes tight.

"And here?" he asked.

"I want to spend forever kissing you there." He squirmed a little as I licked and sucked at the left nipple then paused. "Okay?"

"Don't stop."

I gave equal attention to the right, then mouthed a trail back down to his belly. "Your skin tastes like sunshine." I knew I was talking nonsense, but he was warm, and smelled of everything that was perfect, like lemons, and outside, and the scent of rain before a thunderstorm.

I kissed each hipbone again, and he raised his hips, pushing his fingers into his waistband and shoving at his pants. I didn't want things to go so fast, I didn't want to scare him off, but he was into this. He wriggled, I tugged, and between us we were down to our underwear, and slotted together perfectly. This time he was sprawled over me so he was the one in charge, the one in control.

"Are you sure?"

"Green," he murmured, "so green."

I assumed it was green for go, and if the kissing was anything to go by, I was right, but this was his show, and I was along for the ride. He reached for his cabinet, awkward, me holding him up, and leaned back with lube and condoms, a triumphant expression on his face.

"Will you?" he asked, and passed me the condom. I nearly lost it right there and then.

"We don't have to do—"

"I want to. It's been so long."

"I haven't coerced you into—"

"No. Please, Gabriel. Please."

I rolled on a condom, and he squirted lube in his hand and mine, and together we prepped him, stretching, loosening. The sounds he made were raw and filled with need. They were want and lust and love all wrapped up in one. He was on top, it was him taking the time he needed, and we kissed messily until at last I was inside him, the heat of him encompassing me and almost sending me over the edge.

We rocked against each other, and I alternated between tugging him down for kisses, and grasping his ass to slow the motion of *us* because I was getting close to losing my mind just from this contact.

"Gabriel…" he murmured, leaning over me, caging me, kissing deep.

The slide of me inside him was everything. Legs

tangled, exchanging groans, and warning each other we were close, I locked my hands with his, lacing our fingers, and we kissed with broken words as his orgasm captured him, and I'd never seen anything so beautiful as he came on my belly. I fucked up into him and yelled his name in my release. He collapsed on me, and I held him like the precious thing he was.

"Wow," he whispered when his breathing stilled.

We should move, but despite the wet mess between us after I'd softened enough to pull out, I decided I never wanted to move.

"Wow," he repeated.

"You're so beautiful," I murmured.

He smiled into another kiss. "You make me feel beautiful."

I quirked a grin at him. "Then my job here is done."

Chapter Sixteen

Gabriel

SOMETIME IN THE NIGHT, I'd cleaned us up, not wanting to leave Tiber's arms, but thinking ahead to us waking up together in the morning. When I moved he snuffled in his sleep and rolled over, but by the time I'd gotten back into bed he was back on his side, and I tugged him in to me, with me as the big spoon.

I hadn't gotten much sleep—never allowing myself to go to a place that allowed the nightmares in, so I slept in fits and starts, and each time he was still there and I still hadn't let him go. I could stay in bed forever holding him, but when the clock showed five a.m. I had to make some move toward getting out of bed. I had the report about the paw prints to check through again, administrative feedback from that course in Seattle, and most importantly, I wanted to make Tiber breakfast.

I managed to ease myself out from under him, with

small and gentle movements, and he only reacted once but the resulting movement helped me, as he rolled onto his front. Free of the sexy armful I'd enjoyed all night, I used the bathroom, hunted for a toothbrush, found a supply all wrapped, and borrowed some toothpaste. Then I headed for the kitchen and opened the back door, various dogs and cats doing their thing outside then joining me as I waited by the coffee pot, yawning as lack of sleep caught up with me.

I heard movement from the bathroom, the rush of water, and footsteps down the hall.

"Morning," Tiber said from the doorway.

I turned to face him with a ready grin. He was carding his hands through his hair, readying to tie it back, but before he could do that I headed over to kiss him into stopping, and slid my fingers into the silky length of it. I wished that he never put his hair back, despite the fact it was probably annoying, or even a health and safety hazard. Who knew?

"There should be a law against it," I announced the conclusion of my thinking.

He smiled up at me. "A law against what?" he asked, and gripped my waist, resting his cheek against my heart.

"You putting your hair up like that. Not that I'd ever stop you, because it's your hair and it's not for me to—"

He stopped me with a kiss. "That was an okay thing to say, Gabriel. Don't second-guess what you say to me when it sounds all sexy-cute like that."

"I don't mean to… okay… yeah." *Great. I made a mess of that one.*

"Jeff never wanted my hair loose, said it made me look

too… yeah." He shrugged as if that wasn't an evil thought for his ex to throw at him.

"Fuck him." I tugged him back to me again. "When I woke up, you rolled onto your front and all I could think was that your hair was so soft, and dark against the sheet, and I wanted to kiss you from the top of your head to your spine, and keep on going."

Fuck. Now I was hard, and this wasn't going to get either of us to work at all.

"That's one of the nicest things anyone has ever said to me," he said into a kiss, and then ducked away to check on the coffee.

We ate breakfast in fits and starts, between kisses and hugs, fussing over the animals, and exchanging a hundred good mornings, and then it was time for me to leave to get back to my place for a shower and a clean uniform.

"Can I come back here tonight?" I asked as we kissed goodbye. "No expectation, just to be here with you and the kids."

"I love that you call them 'the kids'," Tiber said, and detached Fudge from where she was on my shoulder. "I'll make dinner."

I walked down the path and turned at the gate. "I'll bring treats," I promised.

"You'd better."

He waved at me, I waved back, and I was still grinning like an idiot when I drove back into town. The smile followed me to the office, which was a dangerous thing because Hen pounced on me the moment I stepped inside.

"That is one hell of a smile, Sheriff. Good breakfast?" She winked at me, and I couldn't even attempt to hide my happiness. "Shame I have to ruin it, but someone's called in a vicious dog up on Lambert, details sent to your phone." My smile dropped and I turned on my heel with a call for Devin to come with me. A vicious dog? Lambert was a dead-end road that merged into the forest, and I tried to envisage the place on a map and wondered how close it was to where Billy had died and realized it was no more than three or so miles to Clear Creek Falls.

"You think this is it, sir?" Devin asked as he belted up.

"It could be another false alarm, but the call looks real," I said as I read the report. It had been filed this morning, a terrifying vicious dog, running loose. It all seemed like there was a chance Billy's death could be explained today, which would take the pressure off the wolves and make me a hero in Tiber's eyes.

We headed up the mountain toward Lambert, the road changing from blacktop to gravel, as we drew up to the last house before the road petered out.

"Owners are Rick and Lacey Grover, newly moved in, purchased the property from SA Alverstone," Devin read from his phone.

"Shaun Alverstone, I went to school with his son. It's remote up here." My head spun with memories of Shaun Alverstone Junior who'd long since left Prophet for the bright lights, and I wondered if he'd gotten on any better than I had. All the possibilities of living away from small town ties had been right there in front of us both, but it was me who'd come back all messed up. I hoped he'd done better. I hoped he had a career and a family, and was happy where he was.

We heard the dog a long time before we saw it, frantic

barking that was deep and loud, and with a hand to his arm, I stopped Devin leaving the car.

"Procedure?"

He blinked at me. "Assess hazards using caution for location."

The barking grew closer and we got our first look at the dog in question. It was big, and I didn't recognize the breed, but it was all teeth and attitude, and when it collided with our SUV the damn thing rocked. It disappeared, and then jumped up at Devin's window, barking ferociously as if doing that would get him inside.

"Holy fuck!" Devin scrambled away from the door and clutched the handle in shock as it jumped up again, teeth bared, and eyes wild. The barking didn't stop but then the damn thing was scratching at my door, the snarling a frenzy now as the animal was thwarted.

I laid on the horn to get whoever was supposed to be controlling the dog out of the house, flicked the siren when no one came out. At last after way too long, the front door opened and a woman sprinted out of the house, yanking up jogging pants with one hand, a leash in the other, and screaming at the top her voice. She skidded to a halt next to the car, and an epic battle ensued while she got the dog on the leash, and then she attached it to a thick chain attached to an anchor point in the ground. I sure hoped it was cemented in, but I wasn't getting out of the car. Not until the dog ceased barking, and the women stopped screaming at us about riling up her pet.

This was nothing like Tiber's pack of canines, no peace and respect, just temper wrapped in hysteria. The woman finally   stopped   shouting,   but   the   dog   remained hypervigilant, snarling in our direction, and straining at the leash.

Devin pulled out his taser, but I recalled the dog handler on our team in LA explaining that tasers weren't good for taking down fighting dogs.

"Tasers are dangerous to use on a dog like this, because as soon as you cut the power, it won't feel any more pain so it could get scared and run, or continue to fight and try to bite."

"What if…" He bit his lip. "I don't want to shoot a dog, sir."

I nodded. "It won't come to that, but just a note, we should probably have a tranquilizer gun to hand. Can you organize two, one each, when we get back?"

"On it, sir."

"Okay, I want you to hold back, keep the radio to Hen open in case. I've got this."

"Wait, no, sir, you're not going out there alone."

He was one determined rookie, as he opened his door. I caught his arm. "Body cams on, stay behind me, and if there's even one hint of the dog getting loose…" I rested my hand on my gun, which was a last resort.

Devin's eyes were wide. It wasn't as if we had animal control out here—it was up to me and Devin to deal with this canine menace. I'd never hurt an animal intentionally but if it came down to choosing between human and dog then I might be forced to make a choice I never wanted to.

I couldn't help the prickle of fear when the chain tightened as we stepped out of the SUV, or hearing the snarls and seeing flashes of big canine teeth. Was this how

Billy had felt in his last seconds as his attacker lunged for his throat? I felt queasy.

"What do you want?" the woman yelled, scraping her blonde hair back in a pony tail then taking out a phone and pointing it at me, recording. I didn't know where to start. "Why'd you go riling up my dog!" the woman snapped, defensive stance initiated. "Loki gets upset when we have people on our land."

I ignored that. "Officers Thompson and Randall, Prophet Sheriff's Department, and for the record we're currently parked and standing on your driveway, Mrs....?"

"Grover, although why you need my name—"

"Mrs. Grover, your dog should be restrained on open, unfenced property like yours. Hikers are on the trails not far past your house."

"My husband likes Loki to run free when he's away. Keeps me safe and the dog's doing no harm." She panned the phone to her now docile pet, all growling stopped, and then she huffed as if she'd made her point. I wasn't getting into a pissing contest over how not-docile her dog had been on our arrival, and whether this entire video would be up on social media as soon as we left. I had the chaos on the SUV cam, so instead I focused on details.

"How often does your husband work away?" Devin asked.

"Why do you need to know?" She eyed us with suspicion. "You have a warrant to come on my property and start asking questions?"

"If you answer it would be helpful."

She stared at us, and it was as if I could see her brain working overtime. "Some," she finally offered.

"How long has he been away this time?" I pressed.

"I'm not answering all these questions when I don't get why you need to ask them." She," she tilted her chin.

"We've had a complaint about your dog and—"

"Fuck's sake, I bet it was the neighbors. It was, right?" She threw a look down the road that I assumed was for Lenny and Betty Hamlin, the nearest neighbors. She turned the camera on herself. "I see you neighbors, always messing with us, causing trouble where there ain't none."

"How often is your husband away so your dog is loose?" I pushed as she focused her phone back on us.

"He's away maybe a few days a year. Like I said, it's not anyone's business but ours."

Next to me, Devin bristled, and I know he believed our uniforms and badges demanded respect, but that wasn't always what happened. Another learning experience for the rookie, and one I hated him to see.

"Mrs. Grover, it's our business when a dog is loose and not under control."

She smirked then. "Well, you can see, *Officer*, that he's completely under my control."

Her saying that the dog was under her control didn't discount the dog from hell being responsible for Billy, because how many days had it been running loose, away from the property and into the trees. Would the timing add up?

"How long has your husband been away?" I asked again, and her lips thinned.

"A week. He's over in Tacoma, and he'll be pissed when he sees this video."

I didn't give a shit what her husband thought, but my

chest tightened because Billy was killed on Friday—six days ago.

"What breed of dog is Loki?" Devin asked what I should have asked.

"Rhodesian Ridgeback." Lacey moved to stand between us and the dog. "I have all his papers, and he's chipped, and he wouldn't hurt a fly, so you've got no reason to be on my property." Next to me Devin made a sound, and I had to ignore his soft snort of disbelief. "Loki's a good dog—he's just boisterous is all. Don't know why the authorities have a problem with that."

Boisterous? That was one word for it. I didn't know enough about dogs to reconcile her Jekyll and Hyde pet lying docile now with the vicious guard dog that had scratched my car and threatened to harm me and Devin.

There wasn't much else I could do here. I'd follow up on the complaints, but was this a dangerous dog, or a guard dog doing its job that had crossed a line with us? We needed to research Rhodesian Ridgebacks and also talk to Tiber who might just be the font of all canine knowledge we needed.

"One last thing," I said, and her lips thinned.

"What?"

"Do you know Billy Odette?"

She kept her gaze steady, and I couldn't get a read on her. "The Makah killed by wolves?" she asked. "I'd never met him. No."

"And your husband? Did he know Billy?"

She glanced at Loki and back at me. "You'd have to ask him when he's back in two days."

Two days of Loki roaming around? That wasn't going

to fly. "I suggest you keep Loki indoors with you where he can guard you more effectively than roaming the neighborhood at large. Consider this an informal warning. My deputy will be up to check at random intervals."

"This is my property."

"I could get an order to have him removed from the property if you'd prefer that?"

"Jesus! I'll keep him inside."

What I wanted to do was take a sample of fur from Loki, but that was crossing a line without that magical warrant she asked us about. What I should *actually* do is visit again as soon as possible and bring Tiber with me.

She stared at us as we got back in the SUV, did a U-turn, and headed back to town, Loki rolling and scratching his back the same as I'd seen any other dog do. Devin was quiet and stared out of the window.

"Okay?" I asked and he turned, his face pale and his brow furrowed.

"I can't imagine something like Loki, or a wolf, ripping out a person's throat, the horror and fear of it... it's just..." He shuddered.

"I know." And that was about all I could say. "When we get back I want you to focus on the Grovers, find out what you can, dates of moving, trouble with the neighbors, that kind of thing."

"On it."

"And I'm going to talk to Tiber."

Chapter Seventeen

Tiber

"Hey," I said as I got into the SUV.

"Hey."

Gabriel smiled at me and glanced at my lips. I leaned over the console to give him the kiss he'd subconsciously asked for.

When I pulled back, he was grinning. "I'm liking this new boyfriend status."

"Yeah." I couldn't think of anything else to say that wasn't corny as hell, so I just wrapped my hand tight around his when he reached for it.

I was so bad at peopling. Thankfully, Gabriel didn't seem to care. I thought about last night, how I'd almost ruined the mood with my insecurities and the flash of memory I'd had of Jeff criticizing me. Ugh—when would I ever be free of him?

But Gabriel had been sweet. And the sex… surprising. It had been emotionally rich as well as physically off the charts. He was gentle and cared about my pleasure first, which was astonishing enough. But more than that, he'd been so loving, genuinely loving. I'd given up believing something like that was even possible. I couldn't give my body without losing some of my heart, and I'd begun to think I was the only man on the planet like that. But Gabriel had been present with me, body, and soul.

I'd seen it. I'd felt it. And I was becoming so invested it was scary.

I cleared my throat. "So. Tell me more about this dog. His name is Loki?"

"Yeah. Like I said in my text, the owner says he's a Rhodesian Ridgeback. And he jumped all over the car when Devin and I arrived, barking, and snarling like he wanted to—" Gabriel hesitated.

"Rip your throats out?" I prompted.

"That." Gabriel's tone was dark. "And it sounds like he was loose on the afternoon that Billy was killed. Do you know anything about the breed?"

"They make great pets. I've known a few. Very loyal to their owners. Not so excited about other people. But they're used as police dogs, and watchdogs, so I know they can be trained to be aggressive. And all dogs will protect their turf. If they're fearful of strangers, which can happen if they weren't socialized as puppies, they can be prone to biting. But killing?" I shook my head. "Well. Let's wait and see the dog. There is one thing though."

"What's that?"

I squeezed his hand. "I did some research after your text. Ridgebacks were bred in, obviously, Rhodesia, which is now Zimbabwe. And they were used to hunt lions."

Gabriel gave me a troubled glance. "What does that mean? Like maybe the dog thought Billy was a lion?"

I laughed. "Ah, no. But it does mean the dog might not be intimidated by a large animal like a horse. Unlike many other breeds. Of course, I doubt modern Ridgebacks are used to hunt lions, but the instinct might still be there."

"Hmmm. Just… stay in the car, okay? Unless or until the lady who owns him puts him on a chain like before."

I shrugged.

Gabriel scowled. "I mean it."

"Okay."

The dog, and his owners, lived far out at the end of a dirt road. Like Stone Whiteplume's cabin, the place was so remote it felt like a hideaway. It made me think about how many of these remote properties existed in the Olympics and what kinds of people might be hiding what kinds of misdeeds in these verdant woods. Of course, I was the last person on Earth to judge anyone for wanting privacy. I was a hermit myself. But maybe it was the deep shadows that the towering trees cast over the house as we pulled into the driveway that made the place feel more sinister than the home of a harmless introvert.

"Her car's gone," Gabriel said, as we pulled up to a two-story white house. "And the dog's not on the chain. Maybe she put him inside, like I told her. I hope so because—"

Something struck the driver's door with a loud crash and wild barking ensued. I jumped. A brown, short-haired dog, large and muscular, snapped and snarled at Gabriel's window. Fortunately, the glass held.

"Yeah. So, this is the dog," Gabriel said nervously over the baying of the hellhound.

"You don't say!"

Loki noticed me and ran around the front of the car to jump at the passenger window and give me the same slavering warning.

I ignored the dog's apparent fury and studied him. I reached for a kernel of calm and spread it throughout my body.

"Hi, Loki," I said in a normal voice, which he probably couldn't hear over his own barking. I clicked my tongue. "Hey, boy."

He had a large, triangular head and lots of teeth, which were bared. But his ears were back, eyes wide, pupils dilated, and—I moved my head to check—his tail was tucked between his legs.

I smiled at him. Clicked my tongue again. "It's okay. I've got treats." I took a dried salmon strip from my coat pocket. I held it so it was visible from the window and sniffed it excessively, pretended to lick it, sniffed it again, taking my time.

Wow, look at this treat! It's the best thing ever! Mmm.

The barking stopped. I held the treat up to the glass and sniffed again, exaggerating the motion of my nose. Loki appeared confused, eyes darting between me and the treat. Oh yes, he wanted, but he was still afraid.

I waited.

Loki sat on his haunches and licked his lips, staring at the treat expectantly. I opened the door.

"Tiber!" Gabriel sounded alarmed.

"Stay here." I got out and shut the door. I tossed the dog the treat and got another one from my pocket.

"Hey, Loki. Who's a good boy?" I cooed.

Loki was conflicted. He took two steps back, but he wasn't barking. I squatted down and smiled, holding the treat out. "It's okay, honey. You can take it. I won't hurt you."

He barked aggressively, just to show he wasn't gonna take any nonsense from the likes of me. I waited, holding the treat. He paced back and forth then slunk forward, snatched the treat, and dodged back. He turned to watch me.

"Hey, sweetie." My forearms were on my thighs, my hands open.

He wanted to come to me for pets. Or part of him did. I could see it in his eyes. But fear won out. He ran off and ducked through a hole in the boards of a shed.

I stood up and dusted off my hands.

"Don't ever do that again!" I turned to see Gabriel standing by the driver's side door, white as a sheet. He put away his gun.

"We're here so you can get my opinion on the dog, aren't we? Loki didn't kill Billy Odette."

"How do you know that for sure?" Gabriel came around and stood by me all big and puffed up, as if to guard me from any and all menaces.

"Because, first of all, he's protecting his turf here. He gave us hell because we came onto his property. He wouldn't be protecting his turf on a mountain trail miles from here. Even if he did wander that far, he'd be into sniffing out deer and running free, not attacking people.

Secondly, he's fearful. That's why he barks like that. Poor guy has probably been around very few people other than his owners. He has no idea what to make of us."

"But you said fearful dogs can bite," Gabriel pointed out, still looking around for the dog.

I smiled. "So you do listen to me."

"Shut up. Always."

"Yes, fearful dogs can bite. But what they really want is for you to show them you're okay so they can stop being afraid. When *you're* afraid, say you hear a noise in the night, and you get up to check, aren't you relieved to find there's no danger? No one likes to be afraid. Dogs are no different."

"But how did you know he wouldn't bite you when you got out of the car?" Gabriel insisted.

I shrugged. "His aggression was surface level. His body language showed me that he was really scared. So I knew when I moved towards him, his instinct would be to move away. This is an open space here, plenty of room to escape. Also: salmon. I gave him food. That's an alpha thing to do. An offer for him to be in my pack."

The dog in question poked his head out from the shed and bark-howled at us. Then he stared pointedly at my pocket and licked his lips.

"Tough guy," I told him fondly.

"Let's get back in the car." Gabriel's voice trembled..

"We should get samples while we're here, right?"

"You just said it wasn't him."

I raised an eyebrow. "I'm glad you'll take my word for it, but hard evidence would be helpful, wouldn't it, *Sheriff?*"

Gabriel grumbled, but he got his sample kit from the car. "I guess we should, since the owner doesn't seem to be around." Keeping one eye on Loki, he bent to take photos of a paw print near the driveway. I wanted to get samples of Loki's fur, even though it was clearly brown and the fur the coroner had taken off Billy was gray. Evidence was evidence.

I didn't see any furniture on the house's narrow porch nor any kind of doghouse or bedding near the chain. No place where a dog could find comfort. Instead, a heavy link chain was staked to the ground. Ugh. Some people didn't deserve dogs, though it appeared his owners let Loki run free at least some of the time. Maybe there was a bed of sorts in the shed.

I took a few steps in that direction and squatted down again. I took a salmon treat from my pocket and sniffed it, then held it out. I sighed, relaxed.

Loki came out of the shed. He had something in his mouth. A beat-up green stuffed bunny. He glanced at Gabriel warily—not a fan. He took a few steps towards me. His flanks trembled and his tail was tucked, but he was making an offering back—a toy. My heart melted.

"Is that for me? Thank you! Here. I'll trade." I held the treat in the palm of my hand. "I won't hurt you. Promise."

Loki slinked closer. In a flash he dropped the bunny, snatched the treat, and ran back to the shed. Whatever my dog-charming powers were, that boy wouldn't let me touch him.

I took the stuffed bunny and put it into a baggie. I hated to take it, but I hoped he had more toys in the shed.

And I'd bring it back once the lab got hair and saliva samples from it.

WE PULLED out onto the dirt road and I could see Gabriel was still tense and upset. I put a hand on his shoulder. "It's okay."

"How can I get you to not take chances?" he said. "This isn't the first time. You went to talk to Jimmy Bowie with Duke, even though I told you it could be dangerous. What if Jimmy had been complicit, and Duke had reacted badly? You had no backup."

"We were on a public beach."

"And then you agreed to meet with Jeff, who's a total abuser."

"In a public diner."

"And you went to see the wolf pack! In the woods!"

I rolled my eyes. "You knew we were going. Libby and I and Susan went. Susan had a tranquilizer gun if something had happened, which it didn't."

"But it could have. I'm just…" The SUV bounced over the pitted road and Gabriel grasped the steering wheel hard, his jaw tight.

I felt a flicker of anger and I was about to tell him that —surprise—I'd survived for twenty-six years without reporting every move to him. Then I noted the whiteness of his knuckles and the sheen of sweat on his brow.

I'd truly scared him. That surprised me a little. Gabriel loved dogs. I was surprised that he'd feared for my life with Loki. Then again, his bark had sounded vicious. And we had recently found Billy with his throat ripped out.

Damn. Sometimes I forgot that other people couldn't read animals the way I did.

"I'm sorry I frightened you," I said.

"I lo—I'm... Look. I'm crazy about you. Tiber. I never found someone I felt this way about. I want you around for a long time, okay? So please don't do anything stupid and die."

I gave a startled laugh. "Um. I promise?"

"Good." Gabriel's Adam's apple bobbed. Was he still that unnerved? He maneuvered around a pothole and shifted in his seat.

"What else is wrong?"

He gave me a wary glance. "Remind me, if I ever even think about keeping anything secret from you, that it's a fool's game."

I huffed. "Well you shouldn't anyway. So what is it?"

He licked his lips nervously. "Are you doing anything tomorrow? Like midday?"

"I have an eight and a ten o'clock client call, but I should be done by noon. Why?"

"It's the twins' sixth birthday. Sam's twins. Well, and Lori's. Obviously."

"Obviously."

"So there's a lunch thing at Sam's. And he invited me. I'd like you to come. If that's not too much. Or too soon. Or weird. Or anything." He seemed embarrassed.

Was I a bad person that I found his discomfort cute? But then I realized what he'd asked me, and—instant karma—I had my own discomfort.

Going to a family party? With four-year-olds? Me?

God, I hated social events. Especially ones in which I

was one of a small group and couldn't hide in a corner. And *kids*. Kids just blurted things out. Embarrassing things.

That was one reason why I preferred animals. No blurting.

I stared out of the window. Gabriel put his hand on my shoulder and rubbed his thumb across it. "Hey. You know Sam."

"Yeah."

"And Lori's great. Really. The twins will love you. But if you don't want to go, it's fine. It's just... you're important in my life. Fuck. Is that too much?"

I was important in his life. He wanted to include me in his family. My heart got heavy and full even as sweat prickled up my back and my stomach swooped at the thought of a goddamn birthday party.

I cleared my throat. "It's fine. Just let me know what time."

Chapter Eighteen

Gabriel

THE NEXT MORNING, I booked the samples in with Hen who organized a courier to have them taken for testing, then took a moment to copy Devin on everything. He reported back on what he'd found out about Mr. and Mrs. Grover and their dog Loki.

"Rick Grover, construction, past offenses for possession, no time inside, but his career is shaky. Lacey Grover on the other hand comes from a family with enough money to pay the mortgage outright on the property they live in. Extended family in Tacoma and down in Tucson, nothing much else to add, apart from the ongoing debate with their neighbors who insist that new fencing at the back of the Grover property is impinging on their land."

"The same ones who called in the dog incident."

"Yes, sir. Also, Orson's alibi for the time of Billy's

death checks out. He was at the hospital in Wenatchee on the day before and the day of the attack. We have witnesses and security camera footage if we need it. Finally, I've checked with all the park ranger stations in the national park, and also an organization that tracks wild wolf populations and so far, none of them are aware of a lone wolf in the area. I'm waiting to hear back on a couple but they're over near Winthrop, so I doubt any wolf they'd be tracking would have made it this far west."

"Good work."

"Also, I asked around town about Dell, like you said. He works sometimes for the lumber company. Seems to do okay for himself. As far as anyone knows, he and Billy Odette never said a word to each other. So, there's no motive there."

"Okay, keep digging. I'll be back in a couple of hours."

Devin nodded, but then he went straight back into research mode, and there was no reason for me to be standing and staring at him. I headed home, stripped off my uniform, showered and shaved, then with a towel around my waist, I stared into the battleground that was my closet. What did I wear to my first invited lunch with my semi-estranged brother, a sister-in-law I knew judged me for hurting Sam, and a niece and nephew who were curious about me but didn't know me too well? Jeans were good. I could do jeans—I had many pairs of similar jeans, and I wasn't immune to the fact my ass looked good in them. *Yep, I'm dressing to impress Tiber, for fuck's sake.* Eventually I was back at the closet dressed apart from the top. My entire closet was in the blue-gray part of the color wheel, and that seemed... I don't know... a cop-out? I had the niggling thought that I needed to be brighter for Tiber.

I rummaged for a shirt I recalled I had, finding it at the back wedged between two LAPD T-shirts. I should throw those out—no point in hanging on to reminders of a past I wanted to forget. I sniffed the red shirt and it smelled of washing detergent—had I ever worn it in Prophet? I didn't recall. It was a little wrinkled, so I ran an iron over it in my spare room, and when I buttoned it up and checked myself in the mirror, it fitted well and for a brief moment I felt as if I could be a new me.

But it wasn't the real Gabriel staring back.

A sudden flash of a red shirt I'd once worn, one more suited to my undercover persona, had my heart skipping. I stripped it off immediately and tossed it into the garbage in an instant. The me that had acted out being Zachary Owens had been loud and brash and in people's faces and wore a ton of bright shirts. That wasn't the real me—the real Gabriel—at all.

I sank to the bed, a more familiar soft grey top in my hand.

Yesterday in the SUV, I'd almost blurted out to Tiber that I loved him, and now I sat here unable to make a decision over a damn shirt? Before I said anything like the L word to him I needed to get my head straight. I needed to talk to Sam, or my therapist, hell, talk to freaking anyone I could and *then* talk to Tiber once I had all my ducks in a row. Anything to get all the jarring memories from ruining everything.

A knock on my front door interrupted my mini

breakdown, and I shrugged on the grey shirt, grabbed my wallet and my badge that never left my side, then headed downstairs. I opened the door with a flourish, and Tiber grinned at me, so gorgeous it stole my breath. He wore a gold T-shirt with the logo of a farm sanctuary on it, and his hair was still damp. I tugged him in, shut the door, and kissed him hello, pouring everything I had into the kiss and ignoring all the darkness lingering in the corners.

It left us breathless, and he'd wound his fingers into my hair.

"Hey," he said, and it was all he got out before I went in for another kiss. He laughed and then pushed me away. "We'll be late."

I wanted to say something offhand as if it didn't matter if we missed lunch, but this was important and I couldn't use sex as an excuse to avoid the one thing I'd been angling for.

I eased myself away, wanting to sink straight back into him, and checked my hair in the mirror. He rested his hands on my waist and peeked around the side of me.

"Gorgeous."

I sent him a smile. "Back at ya."

"I bought the kids a present each, or at least I repurposed something from the gift shop," he announced as I picked up the backpack with my small haul of gifts. I may have gone over the top with what I'd gotten but I had a few years to make up for, and Sarah and Aaron weren't going to be turning six every day.

He held up a couple of familiar cuddly toys, both dogs, both the spitting image of Duke, even more so because he'd replaced the neon collars I recalled with tiny ones the same color as Duke's—a bright red.

"They're mini-Dukes," he announced, and then poked them back into the bag. "I hope they're okay."

I kissed him to tell him that they were beyond okay, and he smiled into the kiss.

"Okay then."

We headed up to the Thompson Cabins, walking at a slow pace, and I enjoyed the fact that *miraculously* there was no heavy rain. Yes, it was damp and there was a gentle mist in the air, but at least we weren't experiencing horizontal downpours. We started out chatting about Duke, then the lack of rain, but the closer we got the more I was running out of the words, when all I could think of was talking to the family and dreading that Sam would say something about things I hadn't shared with Tiber.

"So you lived here all your life apart from the LA bit?" he asked as we drew closer.

"The house? Um, yeah, I was born in the back room, same as Sam."

"It must be nice to have a sibling," he said, almost wistful.

"I have two," I blurted. "Me, Sam, then Ezra who was the baby, and is at college." It occurred to me that I hadn't told Tiber much of anything at all about me if I hadn't talked about Ezra. He didn't seem shocked that I hadn't shared the extra brother thing before—maybe it was a non-event given we were still learning about each other.

"Aww, big brother Gabriel, kind of makes sense with you having older sibling vibes." I stopped dead, and he reached for my hand and laced our fingers. "You don't have to tell me what happened between you and Sam, but a heads-up on whose side I should be, and what I should be saying might be nice."

"It was all on me. I was the one who messed up with them," I said.

He patted my arm. "I was joking about sides. It's all good."

I glanced at my watch before tugging him off the path and into the cover of the trees lining the road to the cabins. Then I untangled my fingers from his and took a step back.

"So, cheat sheet on how I fucked up with them."

He was shocked. "Wait, no, Gabriel, that's not what—"

"No, let me. It's okay. When I realized I was gay, I couldn't tell my mom because she'd passed a few years before. I'd always been close to her, but she wasn't there anymore." Tiber's expression grew compassionate, but if he got all supportive I might just stop explaining, I held up a hand to stop him talking. "Dad was the religious type— brimstone, eternal damnation, all the classics—and it got worse after Mom died. So, when I told him I was gay, it was as if I'd told him I'd committed mass murder. He wouldn't let it go, near threw me out of the house on many occasions."

"Oh, Gabriel—"

"Thing is, I was messed up and all I could focus on was that Sam never stood up for me. In hindsight he didn't for a lot of reasons. Not only was he younger than me, but Dad was formidable. Still, that didn't stop me from feeling betrayed." Fuck. I sounded bitter. "So I left, went to be a cop, did my job, never came home. Sometimes because I couldn't, and if I could I always decided what was the point of facing any of my dad's small-town homophobia? Being gay in the microscopic world of Prophet had strangled me, but I've grown to realize it wasn't so much the town… just my dad."

"I'm sorry." He reached for my hand and laced our fingers.

"I found out throat cancer killed Dad, after it had happened. Sam had to deal with Dad, with being a substitute father to Ezra, plus getting married, having kids, running the family business. I sent back money every month, thought that made things better, but it was too late to be a brother, so I thought maybe I could come back and be a friend. Or fix things."

"So that is what you're doing? Back to fix things?" Tiber wasn't judging me; he was summarizing what I'd just said.

"Fix being a brother and an uncle at least," I said with honesty.

He stepped closer to me and pressed a kiss to my chest, right over my heart. "Let's go do that, then." He sounded strong, but I could feel the tension in his hands. I knew he wasn't the best with meeting new people, and I wanted to reassure him everything was okay. Instinct told me that he was putting a brave face on things, and I loved him for what he was willing to do for me, and needed to give him something back.

"If I mess up, if the family argues, if anything makes you feel uncomfortable, then we'll leave," I murmured.

He sent me a smile that spoke volumes. "Nah, it's okay. We'll be brave together."

We finished the rest of the short journey in silence, holding hands, and every step we took I felt a little calmer, and by the time we reached the decorated front door with two sixth birthday banners, I was smiling. Maybe telling Tiber everything that happened to me might make me feel lighter, but I wasn't ready to burden him with that yet.

Soon.

Before the love-yous.

"Uncle Goober is here!" Aaron called from a side window before vanishing. I knocked on the door.

"Goober?" Tiber asked.

"They can't pronounce Gabriel, but Goober is a new one on me."

The door swung open, and Sam was standing there with his face painted as a clown. "Don't say a word," he warned. I made a sign to zip my lips. "Come in, welcome to the madhouse."

He and Tiber shook hands, and then it was me and Sam, and somehow we did an awkward kind of bro hug thing.

"Uncle Goober!" Aaron called as he skidded into the hallway, and memories of Ezra doing the same thing on the polished wooden floor hit me like a plank of wood. I stumbled, Tiber settling me with a hand to my back.

"Goober! Uncle Goober!" Sarah added and the two of them rushed over, faces painted, to grab my legs. I went to a crouch, my heart spilling over for my niblings as they took hugs from me and pressed sticky kisses to my cheek. I'd missed so much thinking I was doing the right thing, when all I'd done is not been here for the best and worst of times. No wonder my brother was pissed at me. He had every right to be.

"Goober?" I mouthed at my brother, who bit his lip to stop from laughing.

"They can actually say that," he said with a straight face, and then smirked. I liked seeing a smile on his face— it reminded me of better times. "I'm not saying it was my idea but…"

My heart felt lighter for a moment, as if maybe I was closer to him forgiving me for the things I'd done.

Or not done.

"Presents!" Aaron climbed me like a tree, wrapping his hands around my neck. I hoped to hell I'd gotten the presents right, because what if typing *gifts for six-year-olds* into a search bar was not the right way of finding gifts? Then Sarah wanted the same experience, because she tugged at my jeans and with Tiber's help I finally had my arms full of my niblings and I was so damn happy I could burst. Forget the memories, or the terrors, or the fears, or the case, I was in my happy space, with my niece and nephew in my arms, my brother smiling at me, and Tiber leaning on me as if to hold me up.

"Food first!" Lori announced, and somehow me and the kids made it through the narrow doorway into the front room—the good room as my dad used to call it—all set up for a sixth birthday, which appeared to include using every primary color known to man. Tiber fetched my bag of gifts, and placed them on a chair inside the room, and still the kids didn't want to get down.

Or was that me not wanting to let them go?

We collapsed in a heap on the sofa, or rather I collapsed and made sure Sarah and Aaron weren't squashed, and then it seemed as if food was first, and I hadn't realized how much I needed a plate of nibbles, or how much I loved Sarah picking the cucumber out of her salad and giving it to me.

"Aaron saw your prison," Sarah began, and I could tell from her voice where this was going. "I wish I could see it." She used a wistful tone and her gaze was not on me but on a far point as if she wasn't talking to me specifically. I recalled Ezra used to do that, wander into rooms, and announce to no one in particular that he wished someone would take him to the park. I want to say it didn't work, but Ezra had been my shadow and I would have done anything for him.

I left him. He was a teenager when I left him with an ill father, and a brother who had so much on his plate with the stables.

My good mood slipped, but I pushed the shift away.

"I don't actually have a prison," I began, but Sarah frowned, and I backtracked. "Sure, get your dad to bring you down and we'll lock him inside."

The kids loved that, rolling around in laughter as their dad pretended to be shocked.

We had cake and we sung "Happy Birthday" all off key and smiling. The kids loved their jigsaws, books, games, but they loved the stuffed dogs Tiber gave them. more, particularly when they realized they were miniature Duke-dogs. They loved visiting when I had Duke, but for some reason I'd always avoided having them down when Tiber was there. The same Tiber who was now lying on his front on the floor, reading a book to Sarah and Aaron about animals in a wood, and using all kinds of voices.

"Can we talk?" Sam asked, and indicated outside the room with a nod.

"Sure," I said, as if the exact thing I wanted to do now was talk. I followed him into the kitchen, where he added a new filter to the coffee pot and then leaned back against the counter. "The kids love having you here."

"I love being here with them, thank you for inviting me."

"I didn't invite you," he said, crossing his arms over his chest. "It was Lori's idea."

"Oh, okay, yeah, I get that." I knew how much I'd fucked up, and I didn't expect for a moment that Sam and I were sunshine and roses.

"I wanted to but then..." He sighed, uncrossed his arms, and shoved his hands into his pockets. "I have this block. I have a wall I come up against and I know it's tied in with Dad, and Ezra, and then you. I mean, Ezra wasn't old enough to be the recipient of Dad's pulpit speeches, so he's better adjusted than you and me, but still, he resents you because I made him that way."

I nodded, feeling as if my little world of hugs with my niblings was coming to an end. What was I going to do? Stand here and wallow in the awful parts, or open up and share something honest. I shut the kitchen door, closed it tight then stayed there gripping the handle just in case.

"I understand."

"Do you?"

"Yeah, of course I do, Sam. I left you, and I could have come back on occasion but then when I was undercover, I was so deep there were days I forgot my own name," I began, and he kept his gaze steady on me. "I have so much I could tell you, but I love you, Sam. You and Ezra were my entire world, and the stupidity of me running didn't make sense to me until I couldn't come home. I can't tell you any more for now, and maybe never at all, but it hurt me to do what I did, it nearly killed me. I was close to losing everything, Sam. You have to know I would have come home if I could have done it without putting your life in danger. Or Lori and the kids, and that I would have been here in a heartbeat."

He closed his eyes for a moment, then we were locked in an intense face-off, so many emotions passing over Sam's face, it was as if he couldn't decide which one to land on.

"I do love you, Sam. You and Ez. You're my brothers and at the low points when I thought I might…" My voice cracked, and I couldn't even use the word die. "I wanted to come home."

"I know you love me," he said. "So does Ez in his own way, I just… I trust you, so let's move on from this, and I don't just mean me, I mean you need to stop looking at me as if you're about to cry."

I raised an eyebrow. "I'm so not doing that," I countered.

He huffed a laugh. "You so are." He made a face, all frowning and miserable. "Hey, my name is Gabriel and I'm a hero in a funk."

"Ass," I muttered, but I let go of the door handle and took a step toward him. In seconds we met in the middle and hugged. This was me clinging to my brother because he'd been one of the things that had kept me sane back in LA, and I needed him to know that without being able to elaborate. The door crashed open, niblings, Lori, and Tiber all joining in the hug. When we separated, the biggest debate of the party began, kicked off by one single sentence from Sarah.

"Dad, Tiber says he can get us a dog."

I couldn't help but laugh at my brother's expression of horror.

We left a little after five p.m., loaded up with containers of cake and party food that would give us sugar rushes for at least a week. There were no messages from Devin, no emergencies, but also no information that might solve the case of what killed Billy Odette. Still I felt relaxed, lighter, knowing what I'd told Sam, and how the next person I needed to talk to was Tiber.

Then maybe I could properly sleep at his place without thinking I was going to have a nightmare.

"Your family is cool," Tiber said as we walked down the hill juggling the leftovers. "Sorry about the dog thing."

"Please don't apologize. It's been a long time coming, and I know Sam is only pretending horror. "

"Is he though?" Tiber laughed.

We walked on in companionable silence, and eventually we reached my SUV, and I packed the leftovers in there. "I need to get back to work but we could meet up this evening, and then maybe…" It was now or never, and I took his hand, and laced our fingers.

"Maybe?"

"I have parts of things I want to tell you, about my time in LA."

He stepped up to me, hugging me close, his face against my neck. "Come to my place?"

"Yes." That was the best offer I'd ever heard, but Tiber's cell vibrated as we hugged, which stopped us kissing in the street.

Which was probably a good thing.

Right?

Chapter Nineteen

Tiber

I WAS STILL SMILING at Gabriel when my phone rang. I took it out of my pocket and glanced at the screen, expecting it to be a telemarketer, but the display said *LIBBY SMITH*, I answered.

"Hey, Libby. What's up?"

Sobbing came from the other end of the phone. I pulled out of Gabriel's arms. "Libby? What's wrong?"

Her voice was ragged. "Dell and four other m-men. They…"

"What? What did they do?"

Horrifying images of dead wolves swam into my mind. *Please, God, no.*

"They were here. They—they wanted me to tell them where to f-find the wolves. They had guns. I wouldn't tell them, but—"

"What is it?" Gabriel asked.

I gave him a troubled glance and pressed the phone to my ear. "Where are they now, Libby?"

A hiccupped sob. "I wouldn't tell them, Tiber. But one of them saw the painting on my easel. It shows the wolves at the little falls off the South Fork trail. They recognized it and t-took off. It's not far from their den. Oh, Tiber, we have to stop them!"

I gave Gabriel a dire look. "I'm with the sheriff. We'll head them off. Thanks, Libby." I hung up. "Dell and his buddies are going after the wolves."

Gabriel's face was red with anger. "Where are they?"

"Get in the car. I'll show you."

THE SOUTH FORK trailhead was very basic, without even a porta-john. Not many hikers knew about, or cared for, the short, steep hike. But two pick-up trucks were in the small gravel lot. The weather had turned, and the surrounding trees swayed and moaned in the wind. Dried leaves skipped across the gravel. I got out of the SUV and zipped up my light raincoat against the cold.

"That's Dell's truck." Gabriel nodded his chin at a white pick-up with a flag bumper sticker as he got out of the driver's side. "And I think the other belongs to Ned Crumper. He's the local UPS man."

"Great."

I was alarmed when Gabriel, who already wore a handgun in a side holster, took a heavy-duty shotgun from a back compartment in the trunk. His face was grim.

Christ, I hoped this didn't go badly. I turned for the trail.

"Tiber."

I stopped and glowered at Gabriel, already knowing what he was going to say. "No."

He rolled his eyes. "Please. Stay here."

I crossed my arms. "You asked me to consult on this case. I'm consulting. Besides, it's Dell and Ned and a few other townies up there. They won't shoot a human being." Nor a wolf—at least, not unless it was over my dead body.

"But if they're shooting wildly, you could get hit."

"Okay. So you go first." Not very brave of me. But it was better than being forced to stay in the car.

Gabriel sighed. "Fine. But *stay behind me.*"

He led the way up the trail, the shotgun in hand.

We were nearly at the little falls when we heard two loud bangs. Gabriel started to run and I sprinted after him. We rounded a bend in the trail and saw a group of four guys up ahead. An older, gray-haired man had his gun at his shoulder, eye at the sight, as if he'd just fired. A tall, skinny guy was gazing into the woods with binoculars. The other two had hunting rifles at the ready. One of them was Dell Prosser in a neon orange puffer vest, and the other guy was in his thirties, obese, and wearing camo. I didn't recognize him.

"What's going on here?" Gabriel bellowed.

The four men started at the sound of his voice. The man who'd been firing grimaced, shamefaced. "Er—hey, Sheriff." The obese man put his hands up as if Gabriel was about to rob him.

We reached the group and stopped a few feet away. Gabriel held out an arm to block me from getting ahead of him. As if I wanted to get any closer to these assholes.

Dell stuck out his chest. "We're doing our civic duty since you don't seem to have the guts to do it, Sheriff."

The other men looked at each other nervously but didn't say a word.

Gabriel's eyes flashed with anger. He took a step closer to Dell and pulled himself up even taller. "Your civic duty is to stay out of police business. You all know we're in the middle of an investigation. My office has sent out several updates in email—and posted them on the town's website —so I'm sure you're all aware."

"That's not good enough!" Dell said, not backing down an inch.

Gabriel ignored him and continued. "The entire Clear Creek Falls area has been blocked off. There's no danger to anyone."

"As if those wolves are gonna hang out at that one spot with their thumbs up their butts," Dell scoffed. "They can go anywhere they like, Sheriff! We've all got family to protect. Not to mention the tourist trade. Right, John?"

The name triggered my memory, and I recognized the gray-haired man as John Slater, who ran the only gas station in Prophet.

"You have to admit, Sheriff," John said solemnly, "We ain't seen any results from your end."

"It's been one week!" Gabriel said, exasperated. "These things take time. And there *has* been progress. Fish and Wildlife, and Tiber here, our local expert, have already studied the wolf pack. And gotten samples from them."

I spoke up. "We now have paw prints of every wolf in that pack, and they don't match what we found near Billy's body. It wasn't them!"

Gabriel shot me a warning glance, and it occurred to me that I might be disclosing information he didn't want disclosed. Oops. But I was pissed.

"Tiber's right," Gabriel said in a calmer tone. "So far, the investigation does *not* point to the wolves. But we'll know conclusively soon enough."

"Paw prints!" Dell sneered. "That don't mean anything. Those trails at Clear Creek Falls have all kinds of hikers and dogs. Any prints you found there don't mean a damn thing."

"It was right next to the—" I began.

Gabriel cut me off with a judiciously nudged elbow. "You'll know more when I know more. Now that's all there is to it."

I pressed my mouth shut. I kept thinking I could employ logic with Dell, as if he were a reasonable person. But the last thing I wanted to do was interfere with Gabriel's job.

"I heard a gun discharged. What did you shoot?" Gabriel demanded.

John winced. "Er— probably nothing. I thought I saw something white, but I think it was just a big rock."

"Do you realize these are public trails? And we're only about a mile as the crow flies from a campground. Discharging a weapon down a road or a public trail is *illegal*, John. You leave me no choice but to run you in."

"We were defending ourselves!" Dell said.

"From a rock?" Gabriel asked.

"We didn't know it was a rock, obviously! It could just as easily have been those wolves coming in for an attack."

"Yeah, Sheriff, it could have been. We just got a little

het up," said the tall man who'd been holding the binoculars. I thought he was Ned, the UPS man, and he appeared nervous at Gabriel's not-so-veiled mention of arrest.

"We didn't hit anything," said the young guy in camo.

"We've got rights!" Dell said. "Just because you've got a… whatever it is… goin' on with this professional animal lover, that doesn't mean you can brush this off, Sheriff. This is serious business." He shot me a disgusted look.

I gave him a smile that I hoped was as cold and spiteful as I felt in that moment. He twitched his nose in disdain.

"Billy Odette was killed by something!" John agreed.

"And we want it strung up in town where we can all see it, so we know it's a done deal," said Ned.

They all nodded.

They wanted to see a dead wolf strung up in town? Fuck them. Fuck them all.

Gabriel stared them down. "This is my investigation, and I'm running it by the book. This is not the wild west. And I will not tolerate vigilantes in my town. *Period.* Now, is that perfectly clear?"

"There's no way you can prove it wasn't them wolves," Dell said.

"In fact, Dell, the DNA test results will be conclusive, one way or the other," Gabriel shot back.

"DNA report?" Dell made a face as if he'd never heard of anything so ridiculous. "What does that even mean?" But I noticed he'd gone pale.

John spoke up. "You mean, the coroner can do tests on Billy to see what killed him? Like on those TV shows?"

"It's all part of the process. The *legal* process," Gabriel emphasized.

Dell gaped, stumped for words. Sweat had popped out on his brow and his gaze darted between me and Gabriel. "T-that won't prove anything. Like I said, there's all kinds of traffic where Billy was killed. Animals in the woods. Anything could have been through there. This is a cover-up!"

Gabriel wiped his hand over his face—a sign of extreme frustration. He started ticking off points. "Okay. Here's the deal. Number one: this is not hunting season for anything, and certainly not wolves. Number two: even if it were, you'd need a license. And number three: as I said, it's *illegal* to discharge a weapon on a trail in Washington state. I could run you all in right now."

John and Ned glanced at each other. They deflated, and John held up his hands, raising his gun to point skyward. "I can't afford any trouble, Sheriff. I didn't mean to do anything wrong, I'm sorry for firing from the trail. Dell just thought… well…"

"Yeah, we'll go, Sheriff. No need to ticket us or anything," Ned pleaded.

"We have rights!" said Dell.

Gabriel glared at each one in turn. They all appeared worried or contrite—except for Dell. "What you have is two minutes to vacate the area, head back to your vehicles, and go home. Or I *will* arrest you," Gabriel said in his hardass voice.

"Come on, Dell," said John. "I told you this was a bad idea." He and the other three started to walk away.

"Sorry, Sheriff," said camo-guy as he left.

"I still say it's the wolves!" Dell offered as a parting shot. The four of them headed down the trail. Dell glared over his shoulder at me, as if it were my fault.

Gabriel called after them. "If I catch you out in the woods again shooting off guns, you're facing jail time. No questions asked!"

They disappeared around the bend.

Gabriel sighed and relaxed. "Christ. I think you have the right idea, not working with people. I'm sorry about this. About what Dell said."

"Not your fault he's a stone-cold idiot."

Gabriel grimaced. "I don't understand why people can't wait a few fucking days to hear the facts."

"Dell. That's why." I looked down the trail where he'd disappeared. "There's something about him…" I wasn't sure how to put it into words.

"What, Dell?"

"Yes, Dell."

"You think he's lying?" Gabriel sounded curious now.

I gritted my teeth, frustrated. "I'm not good at reading obfuscation. Secret agendas. Animals don't have that bullshit."

"True."

And that was why I'd been so vulnerable to Jeff.

"You think Dell has a secret agenda?" Gabriel prodded. He relaxed the arm that carried the shotgun so it pointed at the ground like a lowered flag.

I shrugged. "There's just something about him. About this whole crusade. Like the day we found Billy, he insisted on going with us instead of with the two other guys when we split at the bridge. And then as soon as you found the body, he was shouting *wolf! wolf!* before you or I even thought about it. Why would he even go there? What does he have against wolves?"

"I don't know. *Peter and the Wolf* scared him when he was a kid? His mom used to read him *Little Red Riding Hood* every night?"

"It's not funny, Gabriel."

"Sorry." Gabriel smiled. He grasped my arm with his free hand and rubbed. "I guess he did jump to it pretty quick. And he's sure been a loudmouth about it ever since. The man's fixated."

"Right?" I let Gabriel tug me a step closer but I kept staring after the men. They might not be visible anymore, but they were foremost in my mind.

"So what? I admit, there's something hinky about him. But Devin checked him out, and, as far as we can tell, Dell didn't even know Billy. So what would his motive be? And even if he had a motive, I don't think he has a dog."

"I'm sure all dogs are forever grateful," I snarked, still looking in the direction of the departed posse.

Gabriel took my chin in his fingers and made me face him. We stared into each other's eyes for a long moment, sharing silent questions.

"He sure didn't like it when you mentioned the DNA tests," I pointed out.

"Probably just stuck on his own idea," Gabriel said.

But I wasn't so sure that was it at all.

I'D DRIVEN downtown for the birthday lunch, so Gabriel dropped me off at my car, and I drove myself home. It was after five, and I only had a few hours of daylight left to get the dogs out for a walk. They'd been alone since that morning and I needed to feed them too and let them out to pee.

I was almost home when I spotted two crows in the middle of the road. I slowed down, expecting them to fly away as I approached. But they didn't. They stayed on the asphalt, ignoring my vehicle.

I stopped and rolled down my window, waved a hand at them. "Shoo! Go on."

Instead of leaving, a third crow flew in and joined them on the road. They weren't pecking at anything that I could see. Not cleaning up roadkill. They stood there. One of them cawed at me.

I was tired, and I was still pissed off about Dell. I wanted to get home, back to my safe space. My hermit abode. I glanced up ahead towards my house. It was at the top of a rise and from where I was stopped, I could see the second story of the house, set back from the road.

There was a car in the driveway. I blinked, not trusting my eyes. But yes, I could see the roof of a blue vehicle. In my driveway.

Who the hell was that?

Dread sparked in my gut. It wasn't Gabriel, and it wasn't Libby's car, and it wasn't a delivery van. I thought about Dell's challenge on the trail. *Just because you've got a... whatever it is... goin' on with this professional animal lover.* That look of disgust.

Prophet was a liberal community overall, but I knew

there were right-wing elements in town. That blue car wasn't Dell's truck either, though. Still. What if he'd come with someone else? What if they intended harm?

I backed up a few feet and pulled off onto the shoulder. I sat there for a moment, staring at that car. But I couldn't wait there all day. And I didn't want to bother Gabriel over what might be nothing.

I got out of the car and snuck along the side of the road to my driveway, pausing behind the big oak tree in the yard.

The blue car in the driveway was a sedan. The license plate had a rental company's logo on the frame. That was even more confusing.

I didn't see anyone, neither inside the car nor in the yard. But from the house I heard frantic barking. The pack knew a stranger was around. I darted to the back of the car, hunched over. I peeked around the side.

There was no one at the front door or in the yard. Nada.

Then someone appeared, backing around the far side of the house, bent over doing something. The person stepped around the corner and I got a good view of them.

It was Jeff.

He was splashing gasoline from a big red container around the foundations of my house.

I couldn't believe it. I literally could. Not.

For several seconds, I couldn't breathe. Then I took out my phone. I filmed him. I filmed him pouring gasoline under my bedroom window, crushing the little flowers in front of it with his big, stupid feet as he went. I filmed him as he poured gas all around the front stoop. The tip of his tongue stuck out in concentration. I watched the image on the screen as I filmed him, still unable to believe it was happening.

That son-of-a-bitch. Seriously?

He reached the nearest side of the house and shook out the last of the gas. He tossed the empty can behind him and took a step back, studying his handiwork. Then he reached into a coat pocket and pulled out... a book of matches.

Oh hell no.

My state of disbelief finally shattered. I shoved my phone into a pocket and, with a primal yell, jumped up and ran for him.

He startled and dropped the book of matches. His face went ashen when he saw me. He held up his hands in placation. But fuck that. I had never thrown a punch in my life, but I threw one now. I got him in the jaw. And maybe it wasn't the strongest punch in the world, but it was still satisfying to see him stagger back and put his hand to his face. "Tiber! Wait! This isn't what it looks like!" He rubbed his jaw.

"You have five seconds to get off my property!" I yelled. "You fucking fuck!"

His face crumpled. "Oh, honey. You need to move back to Portland! You don't see it now, but this is for the best. Hiding yourself away like this isn't healthy. And with the insurance money—"

"You were going to burn down my fucking *house*? With all my animals inside?" I was incandescent with rage.

His gaze shifted guiltily to the house. "Oh. Um. Are

they in there? But there's a doggie door or something, right?"

What a clown. *Are they in there?* As if he couldn't hear them barking like mad. And of course he intended to kill my animals too. Because that was yet another thing that was mine he couldn't control and that kept me tied to Prophet.

I stood there, fists clenched at my side, breathing hard. I was so furious, I felt as if I might explode. "I got video of you doing it, you sick fuck." I held up my phone, thumbed to forward the video, and selected Gabriel's name. "And now my boyfriend, *the sheriff*, has it too. Get in your car, Jeff. Drive away. And don't ever, ever, *ever* come back. Or, I swear to God, I will email a copy of you playing happy arsonist to every email account at St. Vincent's. We'll see how much they admire you then!"

He gaped in shock. "What? You wouldn't—Now come on, sweetie. I just love you so much. Is that a crime? Okay, maybe I went too far. I can see that. But I had the best reasons."

I was shaking. "I hate. Your guts. Do you hear me? *I hate you.* I could be cold, naked, starving, and broke, and I'd still kill myself before I'd ever go back to you. How can I make it any more fucking clear?"

His face did something dark and ugly. Spittle flew from his mouth as he screamed at me. "You don't get to leave me! I'm the one who leaves! You're nothing, Tiber. Nothing! You're a weak little pansy pissant!"

"Good! Then you won't mind getting the hell out of my life! Now go before I let my dogs out and sic them on you!"

It was a bluff. My dogs were not biters, never would be. But he glanced uneasily at the front door, where the barking recommenced, loud, and furious. Jeff marched to his car and opened the door.

"Fine. I'm done trying to help you. You can have your boring, pathetic little life, Tiber Russo." He got in.

I walked to my front stoop and stood there, scowling, arms crossed, until his car had disappeared from sight. Then I slumped. The odor of gasoline made me gag. And I couldn't help but get a terrifying vision of what *could* have happened, with the animals trapped inside.

If I'd been five minutes later…

Tears prickled my eyes and I unlocked the door. Four dogs and two cats rushed out. I fell to my knees and embraced them as best I could while Leo stood at the end of the driveway and barked his little head off in warning.

"You're okay," I repeated, over and over. "It's going to be okay."

Chapter Twenty

Gabriel

I FILED the paperwork on the idiots with guns shooting on the trails, and then there was nothing else to do but end the day. It had been a high attending the party for the twins, a low with Dell and his *friends* causing chaos, but now I had an evening where I could chill and hug Tiber and not think about the possibility of someone being killed by a stray bullet.

I sent a text to Tiber asking if he wanted anything specific from the mercantile then headed there anyway determined to pick up as many snacks as I could for me and Tiber, plus for the whole bunch of kids. When my cell vibrated in my pocket I had a handful of lettuce and dog treats, and I juggled it all, expecting to see a list of things we needed for a night in, or just Tiber's usual, *we're all good*.

It was a video in my messaging app, and it was loaded enough so I could see trees, but it stuttered and stopped, perils of being stuck in the veg aisle of a store with limited wi-fi. I expected it was a joke or something, it could keep, and I found a basket and dumped in the snacks I'd found, plus popcorn, and I almost made it to the counter when I turned and headed back for cat treats—Patch would never forgive me if I forgot her, given she'd adopted me and spent most of her time around me on my shoulder.

There was a line at the checkout, two people in front of me, and I was happy to chill and wait, pulling out my cell and checking whether what had loaded of the video was any clearer in the brighter lights at the front of the store.

That was Tiber's place, and I bet it was another look-where-the-hell-Frank-ended-up story, and I turned down the volume and pressed play, just to enjoy another one of Frank's mishaps. But it wasn't Frank.

It was…

Someone was at Tiber's place? Creeping around?

The line moved and I stepped forward, exchanging a quick hello with someone I recognized from the rez.

Then eyes back on the video and all I could think was, what was the person doing? I cursed the small screen and the light and my eyesight, and peered at it. This wasn't anything to do with Frank, this was Jeff at Tiber's place, and he was messing about under the kitchen window. What the hell was he doing?

Wait. The fuck? Was he trying to get in? Tiber wasn't inside given he was recording, and I didn't have to turn the volume up to imagine his reaction.

I dropped the basket where I stood, and sprinted out of the shop, straight to my SUV, turned up the volume and replayed the video even as I peeled out of the parking.

With the sound up I could hear the way Tiber's breath hitched, I could sense his fear. I saw him move closer, I heard the slosh of something, and then Tiber zoomed in on Jeff. What was Jeff doing?

It made awful sense when I saw the red gasoline can.

I hit 911, ID'd myself, asked for Fire, Paramedics, back up, and fishtailed off the main road.

Please let me be in time. Please.

I floored it, tearing up the hill, the SUV bouncing wildly over potholes and swaying as I jerked to a stop. I expected to be greeted by flames, with everything I loved being burned to the ground, but it was quiet. Weapon drawn, I jumped out of the car, stalking to the gate—no sign of Jeff or his car.

"Jeff's gone," Tiber said from the shadows, and I crossed to him, holstering my gun, and pulling him close.

"Fuck," was all I managed as Tiber buried into my neck and clung to me. "Tiber. Fuck." I could have lost him, I'd misjudged Jeff, this was all my fault, I thought I'd scared him off, but he was dangerous and he'd made me believe he'd left town.

I fell for it.

The sound of sirens grew closer, and still I didn't move, and still Tiber gripped me and didn't let me go.

"Sir?" Devin was here, the volunteer firefighters were here.

"Jeff Strickland tried to torch Tiber's house," I said, and that was enough for Devin to take control. I should have been directing, ordering, searching for Jeff, but Tiber wouldn't look at me, wouldn't look at his house, and the dogs were all around us, Duke lying between us and the firefighters, and the flashing blue lights.

"They've got him, sir," Devin said. "He got as far as Sappho. He's been detained pending whatever you tell me, what do you want me to do?"

"There's a video," I said, and dug into my pocket. "Of what he did. He was going to…"

Tiber tensed, and lifted his head. "Burn my house to the ground, with all my animals inside. He didn't care who he hurt, he just wanted me homeless and vulnerable so I'd go back to him." He shuddered and I gripped one arm, as I handed over the phone to Devin.

"Have him arrested for attempted arson." I ordered.

Devin nodded, then held my phone up to my face to unlock it. I didn't care what else he found on there, it was mostly photos of my niblings, Tiber and our little family, and our home.

Tiber stepped over to his front porch stoop, his legs going out from under him, the pack surrounding him, leaving me enough space to sit with Tiber and hold him again.

"It's okay," I murmured in reassurance. "I'm sorry. I should have arrested him before."

Tiber snorted a laugh, a bitter, regretful sound. "On what grounds? He never did anything that could get people to take me seriously, he convinced everyone he was harmless, but now look." He waved at his house. "Now he's done this, and I'll testify, and he'll get help or prison time, and no one else will have to go through what I went through."

"I should have arrested him—"

He kissed the words from my mouth. Then gripped me tight. "It's over now. For real."

Patch wound around my leg, but pressed against Tiber as if the cat knew it was Tiber who needed it. Tiber had needed me, and I'd let him down.

"Sir?" Devin went to a crouch, "I've forwarded the video—they confirm he's under arrest."

He was joined by Lucas Quinnel, our chief volunteer firefighter, who nodded at me. "It's safe to go inside, we've washed down the entire perimeter and checked the roof. It's all clear."

"Thank you."

"Uhm, also, there's this big-ass turtle in the bushes by the tree. Is that usual?"

"Tortoise," I corrected when Tiber was quiet. "Frank."

Lucas half smiled, his face lit from the side by the blue lights of the truck. "For what I know about tortoises, Frank seems okay. I think he tried to high five me, either that or he was dancing."

"Thank you. I owe you one."

Tiber and I sat for ages on the stoop, Duke standing guard, the entire family around us. I hugged Tiber close and tried not to imagine what it would be like if I'd been too late, if Jeff had succeeded in burning the house, and the animals…

Tiber buried his face again, his shoulders tight, and guilt began to consume me, one stupid thought at a time.

I should have been sure he left town!" The weight of my failure was heavy and suffocating. When everyone had left, when it was just me, Tiber, and the kids, I couldn't move—I wanted to be the strong one, but I couldn't let go of Tiber, I was frozen.

It was Duke who got us to move, nudging my arm, whining, pushing at Tiber, and it was Tiber who got to his feet first, me close behind.

"I need to check on Frank," Tiber murmured, using the flashlight on his phone to locate Frank who was none the worse for wear as I stood there in a daze.

We headed inside, closed the door, fixed whatever the animals needed, I petted Patch, hugged each dog, even tracked down Renfield who was fast asleep in the linen closet and seemingly oblivious to everything that was happening around him.

We were getting ready for bed, and Tiber was quiet, and my guilt was all-consuming.

"I'm sorry. I didn't see how bad…"

"No one did," Tiber said, and grasped my hands, lacing our fingers. "I thought he'd leave, I didn't realize—"

"This is not on you—I should have been watching out for him."

"We're okay, we're safe. I need sleep."

We undressed, but it wasn't right, everything was off, I felt guilty, Tiber was exhausted, I'd nearly lost him, he'd nearly died, and all I wanted to do was hold him and never let him go. We got into bed, he turned into my arms and we hugged for the longest time.

"I can't imagine a life without you," I whispered, "I love you Tiber."

Only, he couldn't hear me because he'd fallen asleep in my arms.

Chapter Twenty-One

Gabriel

THE FIRE WAS ALL-CONSUMING, *tearing through the building as I stood there with a gun to a stranger's head. Was this Tiber's home? Was this from before? Why was the heat so close?*

"Zach! Do it! Take the gun and shoot him." *I whirled on the voice, but couldn't see through the scarlet mist, or hear through the crying and begging from the man at my feet.*

"*I'm not Zachary Owens anymore, I'm Gabriel Thompson. I'm a cop. You're under arrest!*"

"Gabriel! Wake up!"

"Zach, baby, *all you have to do is kill him. Just put the barrel right up against his temple and pull the trigger. You know you want to.*"

I don't want to hurt anyone, I don't want to kill. The sound of a gun echoed in my nightmares and I spun to find where the noise was coming from, tracking the echoes as they reverberated in my thoughts, seeing the blood splatter on the wall, unconsciously searching for the point of impact, brain and bone shattered in front of me.

"Gabriel!"

Someone knows my name, someone is calling me. My cover is blown. I'm unarmed now—where did the gun go— where is Cyrus? Another shot, and this time someone screamed, shouted.

No! No!

"Gabriel!"

Tiber? *You have to get out of here Tiber! You shouldn't be in my nightmare! Run! They know my name, I have to get out of here! I can't hold him anymore, I have to let him go! Cyrus is trying to kill me. I'm sorry. I'm sorry. Forgive me, I didn't mean to—*

"Gabriel! Wake up!"

The nightmare released me, and I scrambled to sit, clawed at the covers around me, sweat dripping, blood in my thoughts. I flung myself out of bed and away from a wide-eyed Tiber, falling to my ass on the hard floor. Duke was there, butt planted between me and Tiber, staring at me, and somewhere in all of this another dog was whining.

"Jesus." I yanked at the covers I'd taken with me, crawled onto my front and tried to stand, but my legs were like jelly and I was limp with exertion.

"It's okay, Duke," Tiber said, and then slid off the bed and down to my side in an instant. Adrenalin spiking again, I crab-walked back from him until my back hit the dresser, but he didn't come close to me, simply stayed with Duke, and waited for me to calm down. The remnants of the nightmare clung to me, all of the images and sensations still vivid in my mind. My breathing was ragged, harsh, as I tried to get oxygen, and a cold sweat coated my skin as I shivered in the otherwise warm room.

I tried to shake off the persistent fear, but it was as if the blackness of the dream had seeped into the corners of the room and there was no space for anything else. I squeezed my eyes shut, hoping to block out the twisted scenes I'd played on repeat in my sleep, but the same unsettling images flashed before me over and over. I hadn't been in time to save anyone, and then they'd wanted me to kill, and the gun in my hand... shit... the gun. I flexed the fingers of my right hand, almost able to imagine the weight of the weapon there, and my muscles tensed as my hand trembled. The nightmare had felt so real, and even though it was something my mind had created, and I wasn't in danger, the unease it left behind was hard to ignore, because the aftermath of these nightmares left me feeling vulnerable, and exposed to the terrors that, thank fuck, only existed in my imagination.

Minute by minute Tiber watched me, and Duke whined. My heartbeat began to steady. The vivid details of the nightmare blurred at the edges enough so I could think rationally.

"Shit." I scrubbed my face with the heels of my hands. "Shit."

Tiber wriggled a little closer, Duke moving with him, and I had nowhere to go to even if I wanted to, but somehow I didn't feel trapped. For the first time after a visiting nightmare, I craved contact—even if I didn't deserve it.

The intensity of the nightmare is only as strong as I allow it to be.

I repeated the mantra a couple of times in my head, attempting to channel my therapist's advice. He didn't have a solution for the nightmares because what caused them was buried way down in my psyche. Until I sifted through my memories and came to terms with them, then they'd never go away.

"Hey." Tiber used a gentle tone, and stopped a few inches from me, taking up position on the diagonal from me with his legs out in front of him and his feet inches from mine, Duke slinking between us and then resting his head in my lap. The light of the bedside lamp was a halo around them both.

"Hey," I answered as Duke let out a soft whine and butted at my stomach. I rested a hand on his head and then stroked his ears which were soft as silk. "I didn't mean to… do that." I waved my free hand toward the bed.

Tiber shrugged. "We all have nightmares," he said, and tapped my foot with his, leaving it next to mine, a touch that meant everything. I was humiliated and weakened by the fear in my head, and all of it had happened in front of Tiber.

He couldn't know the nightmares were so bad that some nights I couldn't let myself sleep, let alone how stupid I'd been for letting myself fall into such a deep sleep with Tiber right next to me. Abruptly it hit me—in my nightmare I'd lashed out, and I panicked.

"Fuck." I searched Tiber's face for injury. "Did I hurt you?"

Tiber shook his head. "Duke woke me up," he said, as

if that made everything okay. "Did you know that animals can sense when something's not right even when you're asleep?" I shook my head, I mean, I guess I was aware of that on some level, but I liked hearing Tiber talk. "When you were deep in a nightmare, and you were experiencing fear and distress, Duke was scratching at the door, and he woke me up."

Had he really felt me having a nightmare, through a door?

"You were calling out," Tiber said matter-of-factly.

"What did I say?"

"I couldn't make sense of any of it, but Duke heard, and I was half awake, then I let him in, because I didn't know what else to do."

Fuck. Had I scared Tiber? So much for explaining about the city, and what I'd done—he'd seen the effect it had had on me when I was asleep. The nightmare must have been triggered by that business with Dell and his buddies firing shots into the trees and then, Jesus, Jeff and the threat of fire. The stress and fear had sent me to the darkest places.

"He just wants to give you comfort and support," Tiber said, and stroked his hand through Duke's tail which twitched as if he might wag it.

"Did I scare you?" I asked.

"Me or Duke?" Tiber joked, or at least I think he was joking.

"You."

"No. You didn't scare me." He stood, using the bed to steady himself, and then held out a hand. "I want to try something."

I took his help and he tugged me into a hug and then eased us back on the bed, pulling the covers back over us.

"I don't want another nightmare." I panicked.

"You won't," Tiber murmured, then whistled for Duke to come up on the bed. Duke stared up at us, whined, unsure why he was being asked to go up on the big comfy thing when he wasn't usually allowed when I was visiting. But I could see what Tiber was trying to do—maybe Duke could be my emotional touchstone, wake me if I fell too deep into sleep. We settled back down, my skin still warm, my head like cotton wool, and then, instead of me spooning Tiber, he reversed the hold, so it was him cradling me, with Duke in front of me.

And only after Tiber's breathing had evened out, and only when I could be sure that there wasn't a single nightmare left in my head for tonight, I slept.

I WOKE up to an empty bed—well empty of Tiber at least, Duke was staring down at me with an expression of doggy happiness, his breath just this side of yuck, but his fur soft to touch.

"Go find Tiber," I instructed, which was the only way to untangle myself from the covers given Duke was standing on them before he jumped down and padded away. I used the bathroom, brushed my teeth, all the while Patch stared at me, and then clung to my shoulder as I headed out to the kitchen. Tiber glanced up from a notebook when I walked into the kitchen, and gave me the most beautiful smile, as if last night hadn't happened at all and I hadn't probably scared the shit out of him.

"How are you feeling?" he asked, as I pressed a kiss to his forehead, and encouraged Patch from my shoulder, who left in a huff, tail high, which gave me the chance to make coffee, then sit next to Tiber.

"I feel okay. Tired, but, okay. I'm sorry—"

"Don't apologize." He took my hand and squeezed it. "It happens to us all."

"I'd like to talk about it with you, the bits I can't forget, the parts of what I did that make me who I am."

"Now?" he asked and peered at his watch, "I want to, only I have a call scheduled at nine with a terrier in Vermont. Well not the terrier, but the owner who insists their dog is a reincarnation of Elvis and wants reassurance that when he howls all night he's channeling the man himself."

I blinked at him. "You're kidding."

He shook his head, and smirked, "Nope. I need to share some of the crazier calls I've had with you. How about I tell you some tonight, and maybe we can talk about your dreams as well."

I nodded, a sudden fear gripping me. "I'll bring pizza. Are you really feeling okay? With the whole Jeff thing?"

He squeezed my hand again. "Yeah. I don't want to talk about that. Or think about it."

"Okay."

"No pizza… I'll cook tonight, and I thought…" He wrinkled his nose, and paused to stare at his coffee. "I had an idea, and you don't have to if you don't want to but…" He held out his hand, a key in the palm. "My spare. I thought you could bring some stuff over, if you like?

Clothes I mean. I can clear out a drawer and some closet space and—"

I took the key before he could change his mind, then kissed him, and he melted into my arms.

"Even after my nightmare last night?" I asked after we separated, both kind of dazed.

He knocked elbows. "Particularly after last night."

I didn't know what he meant by that, but I had a feeling the invitation was less about me being the sex god of his dreams and more about him thinking I needed help. But I wasn't proud; I'd take it. And maybe we both needed me to stick close after what had happened with Jeff.

I headed back to my house, and after I'd showered and pulled on a clean uniform for the day, I packed a case of things, one of my spare uniforms, some T-shirts, jackets, and realized as I packed that I already had a whole new set of toiletries in his bathroom.

This wasn't me moving in, but it was the promise of more.

———

"DNA RESULTS ARE BACK," Hen announced as I stepped into the station, "Devin's waiting."

Hope buoyed my steps as I went into the incident room and pulled the door shut behind me. It was such a small space, and I'd never worried about its coziness before, but now with our second big incident in six months maybe we ought to expand the office sideways to give us a better space.

Or maybe that was inviting trouble.

"Morning, sir."

He nudged a coffee and one of Hen's muffins toward me, but my stomach was full of butterflies in anticipation of something that might close this case.

"Morning. What did they find?"

Devin's eyes sparkled. "Get this: the hairs they found on Billy's body were part gray wolf, part *Czechoslovakian Vlcak*. I looked it up, and it sounds like we're dealing with a wolf-dog hybrid, or as the internet calls them Wolf-dogs." He scrolled a screen on his laptop and I saw it was a notes page. "Bred for security, also inconsistent and difficult to predict behavior... inheriting wild instincts and behaviors from the wolf side of their lineage... training and socialization can be challenging because they have a stronger prey drive, a higher need for space and mental stimulation. Also, they could look to challenge the pack leader, or owner, which means an unstable situation."

"What in hell's name is an animal like that doing here?"

Devin cleared his throat. "In addition the blood/tissue tests, including the saliva from the animal, show no signs of rabies. All the results and analyses have been copied to us and Fish and Wildlife."

"Okay, let's get Susan on the phone."

He dialed the direct number, put it on speaker, and I heard a familiar voice. "Fish and Wildlife."

"Morning, Susan. Sheriff Thompson over at Prophet, we have the results here."

"I was just checking through them myself."

"Thoughts?"

"I'm reluctant to summarize too much without closer

reading, but off the record, I don't think this is a wild animal, and certainly not one in its natural habitat. This animal was very specifically bred by someone. I mean, a *Czechoslovakian Vlcak* is already a wolf-dog hybrid, and the DNA results indicate it's been crossed again with gray wolf genes. It's possible that it's a pet that escaped and is now living in the wild. Or maybe someone dumped it in the woods, someone who got it as a puppy and then couldn't manage it when it got older."

I thought of Loki and his snarling and snapping. "Or, it could also be someone's dog that they let run loose?"

"Sure, that's a valid option. Whatever it is, we need to find it because it's a danger to everyone."

"We haven't had any more attacks."

"That you know of, Sheriff. The forest is a big place, hikers, campers, who knows what is happening out there."

Jeez, that was a thought I couldn't allow myself to linger on. "True. But you'd think we would have heard something. Why would the animal attack Billy and no one else? Sort of argues against it being an animal just roaming in the woods. Was Billy in the wrong place at the wrong time? Was he targeted? Was it just a tragic accident?"

"Valid questions, Sheriff. All valid."

"No sign of rabies though." I took the one good thing.

"That's a good sign for sure. But rabies vaccinations in hybrids are complicated, because there has been no vaccine developed and approved for use in wolves or wolf-dogs."

Fuck. Another thing to add to my list.

"Anyway, Sheriff, I'll work my contacts in other states.

Meanwhile I suggest you look closely at the community around you for dog ownership, and so on."

We ended the call, and I sat back in my chair, hitting my head on the wall.

Yep, we *really* needed a bigger room.

"Track down any and all breeders of these *Czechoslovakian Vlcak* dogs. Find out if any puppies have been sold to anyone in the Prophet area in the past ten years or so. I want to know everything about this breed, and anything we have on the nature of a wolf-dog."

"On it, sir."

"And…" How did I ask this without losing my cool.

"Jeff?" Devin accurately read my expression. "Forks PD are holding him based on the video—they wanted to know who is managing the case and if he should be transferred back to Prophet."

Oh hell no.

"I need to tell them we don't have the capacity to deal with that." Fuck. The last thing I wanted was to have anything to do with Jeff at all. I knew at some point Tiber would need to face Jeff, but for now I could keep him away from Prophet. Away from him. Away from me.

"Sir? Do you want me to tell them?"

Relief flooded me at the thought of someone else taking the load, but that wasn't fair on my rookie. "I got it."

I made the call quick, clean, gave them my statement as well as Tiber's number so they could get his, told them to link me in if they needed additional information, and then Jeff Strickland was no longer Prophet's problem, or at least he wasn't until the wheels of justice turned. I took my muffin and coffee back to my office and shut the door, the rush of information about the dogs, added to the nightmares, plus Tiber saying we should talk and that I should leave clothes at his space, and abruptly it was all too much to process.

So, I sat in my safe space, sipped my coffee, and stared at the wall.

And tried not to think of anything at all.

Chapter Twenty-Two

Tiber

HAD I really asked Gabriel to move in with me?

Crap. So much for taking it slow. We'd only recently dipped a toe into boyfriend territory. What the hell was I thinking?

I put a bag of carrots into my basket. Added a head of lettuce. Now for the pet aisle at the Prophet Mercantile.

It was just that, when I'd witnessed his nightmares, I'd understood the dark circles under his eyes, the exhaustion that sometimes leaked into his expression. It wasn't due to the case or because he worked long hours. It went much deeper than that. And I'd known that Duke could help him. I'd known that *I* could.

And, if I could help him… if I could ease his mind, how could I not?

An image of Jeff pouring gasoline around my house flashed into my head like a sucker punch.

Okay. And maybe I didn't want to be alone at home

right now. That wasn't fair to Gabriel, asking him to move in because I felt vulnerable. Except I sensed he wholeheartedly concurred. Hell, he'd probably stand guard in my driveway with his shotgun all night long if I let him. Anyway, that wasn't the main reason.

It's not moving in. It's just leaving some things at my place. Spending more time together. It's not a freaking wedding. Chill.

Right. And the thing was, I wanted it more than I feared it. It was going to be okay. *Just breathe, Tiber.*

I went up to the register to ring out and One-Eyed Jack yawned sleepily. "Hey, bruh."

"Bruh. Late night?"

He smiled. "Yeah. Watching horror movies. The wife hates them and she won't let the kids watch 'em, so I can only indulge when everyone else is in bed."

I smiled back. "What'd you watch?"

"*Slash/Back*. It's, like, alien monsters invading Alaska and these badass Inuit girls take 'em out. Pretty decent."

"Sounds—" I froze. Out the front window of the market I saw Dell Prosser, in his white pick-up truck, drive past. He was headed out of town. I got a clear view of him in the driver's seat, and he was scowling.

"Bruh?" One-Eyed Jack rang up my last item.

I had seconds to decide. I could either go with the flares my gut was sending up *immediately*, or it would be too late.

"Sorry. Can I come back for this? I gotta run!"

"Sure?"

I left One-Eyed Jack looking confused and raced for my car.

I managed to catch up with Dell's truck. I hung back, not wanting him to notice me. I wasn't sure he knew what kind of car I drove, but I wasn't taking chances. When he turned off onto a side road that headed into the woods, I followed.

I had to hang back even further on this road, since there was no traffic. I nearly lost him at one point, when I went over a rise and his truck was no longer visible ahead of me. But there was a turn off to the right, and I saw his truck down that way, bouncing along the rutted track. From then on, it was all dirt road, and it was easy to hang back and follow the plume of dust his tires churned up instead of the truck itself. For miles.

It went on and on. I began to wonder if Dell knew I was following him and was leading me on a merry chase. But then I got a flash of his truck turning right up ahead. I slowed down, and when I reached that spot, I saw a long driveway with a plywood-and-chicken-wire gate. The dust still floating in air beyond the gate confirmed Dell had gone that way. I braked to a stop and considered the situation.

I couldn't see anything down the driveway. It went uphill and to the right, giving no indication of what was at the end of it. But all along the property boundary that paralleled the road was chicken wire fencing. And then there was that gate. Of course, the owner might raise cattle. Or have horses. Fences weren't uncommon. Still, dread prickled the back of my neck, and my stomach was tight. I knew Dell didn't live out here. So why was he here? Who was he visiting?

I took out my phone to call Gabriel, but I had no

signal. Nothing. Damn it. My internal mapping system wasn't the best, and I'd been focused on Dell's truck and not getting caught following him, so I had no idea where I was.

I could just drive away. Tell Gabriel about it. But could I lead him back here?

Fuck it. I should at least take a peek. I backed up my car and pulled it off the side of the road into the shade of some big cedars. When I got out, the wind gusted, raising the hem of my yellow rain jacket, and sending my hair whipping into my face. I had a tie in my pocket and I put my hair back. The branches of the cedar waved frantically at me and there was a *whooooo* sound as the wind railed. A crow cawed angrily from a branch.

"I'm just gonna take a look," I said out loud. I wanted some idea of what was down that driveway before I dragged Gabriel or anyone else out here. And no point in being a chickenshit about it.

The gate wasn't locked. A simple rope looped over a hook held it closed. I slipped inside and reattached the rope behind me.

I stuck to the woods to the right of the driveway, eyes, and ears alert, and moved deeper into the property. The driveway ended at an open dirt area with numerous buildings. There was a one-story, ranch style house, painted a faded green and junked up with bits of cars and old appliances in the front yard. Dell's truck was parked in front near a Jeep with camouflage paint. A separate two-story building, perhaps a large garage or workshop, stood to the right of the house. I saw a small arena beyond that, like a horse paddock. And there was heavy, chain-link fencing abutting the garage structure. I could only see one side of it.

I studied the chain-link fencing. Unlike the cheap chicken wire surrounding the property, this was made from serious material with large posts cemented to the ground and thick steel links at least ten feet high. It almost looked like a pen of some—

An animal trotted into view inside the fencing and my heart lurched as icy fingers spread down my limbs.

It was a wolf. Oh God. They'd captured the wolves. How? How had they managed it?

And then, with a jolt. I realized it wasn't the wolves. At least, it didn't resemble any of the wolves I'd seen when Susan and I had gone out with Libby. This animal was darker in color, more of a charcoal gray body with creamy paws. But he was too far away. I had to be sure.

I glanced around. If I cut across to the fenced area from here, I could be seen from the house—if anyone was watching. But if I could get to where the garage blocked me from the house, that would take care of that problem.

I skirted the property, staying in the trees. It was hard-going, and I ran into some barbed wire fencing that had been smashed down at one point, and it caught the leg of my jeans. I got free and continued on.

Why did they have wolves?

Who lived here?

What in God's name was Dell up to?

When I'd worked my way to the right, and was out of sight of the house, I had a better view of the kennels. Because that was what they were—kennels. There were six separate fenced-in dog runs, each with several dogs. A shelter made from pine boards where the dogs could go inside had been built at the end of the kennels that attached to the garage, but a number of the animals were outside. On closer inspection they were most definitely *not* Libby's wolves. They had white legs and underbellies, like the wolves, but their top coats were charcoal to black. Their heads seemed bigger to me, their ears larger and more upright. They paced in their kennels with restless energy, not happy to be confined.

If they were not Libby's wolves, what were they? A different species of wolf? Wolf-dogs? Some dog breed that looked like a wolf?

Whatever they were, the person who lived here was breeding them. The kennels were permanent enclosures with cement floors, large posts, high chain-link. This was not amateur hour.

I checked my cell phone again for a signal. Nothing. I slipped it into a pocket. My brain was going to some dark places. Something here was wrong. I loved dogs. And I loved wolves. But there was something *really* wrong with this setup.

If someone was breeding animals out here, why did no one know? And what did Dell have to do with it? Why did he blame the wolf pack when he knew *this* was out here?

I didn't like the conclusion that led me to.

But I needed proof. I snapped some photos of the kennels with my phone, but it wasn't enough. All they showed was animals that might be wolves securely confined. There was a side door to the garage at the end of the building. It had a little step in front of it and a porch light to the side. A small, grimy window revealed a stack of books. An office, maybe. Answers? Probably.

Did I dare check it out? Would the animals in the kennels send up the alarm if I tried?

The compound was quiet. It was mid-morning and this side of the garage was in the shade. If someone had been inside the office, the light would be on, I was pretty sure. It wasn't. And Dell was at the house. So presumably whoever lived here was in there with him.

And the wolves or wolf-dogs? At the end of the kennels was a small shed that would block their view of me if I approached the door the right way. I wet a finger and held it up. The wind was blowing to the north, towards the door. They wouldn't smell me either.

The memory of Dell's smug face at that town hall meeting decided me. I moved further north through the trees. When I was at what I judged to be the perfect spot, I slunk from the trees and ran for the door.

It was unlocked. I cracked it open slowly, peeking inside. There was no one in the small room, and it was an office. A large, steel filing cabinet was to the left and a messy desk to the right with a huge coffee mug on it and an open bag of cookies. I slipped in and let the door close behind me.

My palms were sweating. I didn't want to be in here long. I had neither the time nor nerves for a massive search. I just wanted something…

I scanned the desk, running my hands over the contents as if I could glean information via osmosis. There was a finance ledger, a flip calendar featuring dirty jokes, a screwdriver, and various tools. I moved a folder and found a small stack of tri-fold brochures wrapped in a rubber band. *Blazen Guard Dogs.* On the front was a wolf or wolf-dog that looked like the ones in the kennels. It was attacking a stuffed dummy on a stand. I closed my eyes.

Fuck.

I pulled one out of the stack and opened it. Wolf-dogs. *Elite security dogs… policing… protection…* home defense. A paragraph in bold said they came fully trained with *keywords* that would cause them to attack. Priced at five grand a dog.

I felt sick. I raised my head to get some air and saw, out of the dirt-speckled window over the desk, yet another part of the compound. That arena I'd glimpsed beyond the garage was a fenced-in area with an obstacle course and a row of those stuffed, human-shaped dummies.

They were training these dogs to kill.

A wave of fury and nausea came over me. God, I couldn't even think about it. I couldn't. I stuffed the brochure into my pocket and got the hell out of that building.

I stood on the little stoop outside, taking gulps of fresh air. The breeze helped, cooling the sweat on my face, washing away the stale horror of the little office.

Only the wind was coming from the south now. *The south.*

Then the wolf-dogs went crazy.

One of them slammed the chain-link fence to my left, on the other side of the shed, barking and snarling like a creature demented. The entire pack sent up a battle cry of rage. Terror washed over me.

I ran for the trees. I dared a glance back and saw that

all the wolf-dogs in the kennels were going nuts. They'd smelled me, and now they saw me running, and they flung themselves against the fence, desperate to get at me. A few were attempting to climb it, paws in the chain-link openings, and doing a damn good job of it.

Shit. Shit!

I ran as hard as I could. One part of my brain said that running would stimulate the wolf-dogs' prey drive. And that was all well and good. But if they caught me, I was pretty sure I'd be dead. Visions of Billy with his throat ripped out swam through my mind, giving me a burst of panic-fueled adrenaline.

I was nearly at the trees when I heard shouting and then a gunshot. I glanced behind me. Dell and a man I'd never seen before—younger, brown hair, flannel shirt, deadly expression—were running towards me from the house. And in front of them were…

Two of the wolf-dogs. Loose. They came for me like charging lions, expressions lethal.

I was a dead man.

Chapter Twenty-Three

Gabriel

IT WAS late by the time I got off work. I hoisted the duffle over my shoulder as I headed for Tiber's front door. I stopped to pet Frank, who had escaped to the front yard again, and could almost make out which dog was barking in which tone. One word from me and the cacophony stopped and instead became scratches at the door—seemed the kids were eager to get out and I waited for a moment.

Tiber's car wasn't in the drive, and I had the key, but was it right to use it now? What if Tiber regretted his decision to let in the cop with the issues? I turned the key over in my palm, the scratches were becoming whining. I was being stupid—he'd given me a key, and I could at least go inside and maybe he'd just give me that Tiber smile—the one that lifted my heart and made all my anxieties vanish.

I knocked on the door anyway.

Just in case.

I unlocked it, and stepped into the chaos of every single member of Tiber's pack whimpering and whining. I made my way through them to the back door, opening it and letting them spill out to relieve what appeared to be hours of pee. It wasn't like Tiber to leave the animals so long that they were so grateful to be let out. A nose nudged my knee and I realized Duke was back, sitting at my side and staring up at me with his big brown eyes.

"Where's Tiber?" I asked, his ear pricking and then flattening. He whined at me, and I went to a crouch. "Did he leave you to deal with Patch all day hmm?" Talking of Patch, claws in my neck and the heavy weight registered, and there was Patch meowing in my ear. I got the feeling I was being told off.

Duke clung to me in his own way, becoming my shadow as I took off my uniform and hung it on the back of the door. The closet space wasn't ready for me yet, but there was a drawer, so I tipped my underwear in there, added my own charger to what had become my side of the bed, then stepped back and almost on Duke's tail. I flailed, catching myself at the last minute and went to a crouch again when Duke started to whine.

"What's wrong, buddy?" I asked, and Duke began to pant. "Duke?" I stroked his head, Patch leaping down from me and pressing herself against Duke. "Are you worried about Tiber? He's coming back you know." It broke my heart to even contemplate that Duke was suffering from separation anxiety, and recalled what I'd read about dogs understanding the passage of time. Duke might remember

Tiber leaving the house, but would he understand how long he'd been away?

"What would Tiber do?"

I sat on the floor, back to the wall, Duke leaning on me, then flopping down with his head in my lap, and I wrestled to get my cell out of my jeans, scrolling to Tiber's name and connecting. It rang for a while and then went to voicemail, a simple message asking people to leave their number if they needed help with pets.

Okay, so he was busy somewhere. "Daddy's busy," I told Duke, and stroked his silky ears. He huffed at me, pawed at my leg, and that didn't help my own anxieties any. I fed everyone according to the feeding list, broke up a couple of squabbles over shared food, lifted Patch out of the way because he was hassling Duke. "You don't even like dog food," I explained as I carried him into the yard and placed him with gentle care on the garden table. He eyed me with the kind of disdain that only a cat could give, and then wandered down the garden and into the forest behind. Not that I could see him as he went toward the trees and I realized night was closing in.

Something was niggling me.

Something I'd missed.

I went back into the kitchen, my canine shadow almost tripping me up, and stood in the center of it.

What had I missed?

Why was I getting as anxious as Duke?

I turned a full three-sixty, my gaze finding nothing amiss, no sign of a note—not that I expected to be apprised of everything Tiber did, but he did say we'd have dinner tonight? Maybe he messed up his nights? Maybe he was at the grocery store shopping? I stopped the circle right back at the feeding schedule, and something jumped out at me. Ferdinand needed antibiotics for an ear infection, and it was marked as three times a day. Breakfast was ticked, but there was nothing for the midday mark but an empty space. I traced the days, nope, every previous day had three checkmarks, and my chest grew tight and my heart sank.

"Where are you Tiber?"

Panic and fear took hold.

God. Was it Jeff? Come back into town and causing trouble? I called Devin but no, Jeff was still in custody in Forks. That was one panic dealt with, but I couldn't shake the fear that gripped me. I called Libby as I locked up, put Duke on a leash, and went out to the car. I hope to hell that her and Tiber were talking wolves and had lost track of time.

"Is Tiber with you?" I asked without as much as a hello.

"Hello, Sheriff. No, I haven't seen him today. Is everything okay?"

"Sure, I just meant to ask where I was meeting him," I lied.

Who else could I call? Hen was a master gossip, maybe she could put feelers out for Tiber? *Yeah, good idea, lets set Hen on Tiber—he'll love that. Not.*

I made it back into town, and Duke was growing more agitated, whining, and then as we passed the mercantile he began to bark, hopping from paw to paw. I stopped the car, glancing at the store, movement catching my eye, a line of crows on the roof.

"You think Tiber is here?" I asked Duke, not for one moment questioning that I was asking a dog a question. Duke barked once more, staring at the store. "Fine, I'll stop and ask," I explained as Duke sat back on his butt and whined. One-Eyed Jack was out removing his open sign from the sidewalk, so I hurried up to where he was working before I could feel stupid that I was translating barks into Duke having any idea where Tiber was.

"Hey, long shot, but is Tiber in there?" I glanced past him into the store, but I couldn't see Tiber nor his car.

"Nah, he was here earlier, but he went running off after Dell," One-Eyed Jack said. "Left all his groceries if you want to pick them up?"

I ignored the fact the man implied I'd want groceries, as if he knew Tiber and I were a thing and instead focused on the running off part. "What do you mean 'after Dell'?"

"Dell went flying away from town, faster than a streak of piss, and Tiber followed him."

Fuck. Now my brain was in hyper-anxiety mode and heading for meltdown. Did Tiber intend to confront Dell, on his own? What would Dell do? He was a big man with a short fuse.

And what if he *was* up to something nefarious, like Tiber suspected?

Hell, had I ever known Tiber to be wrong?

"When was this?" I managed to ask.

"Oh, this morning. Maybe ten."

Shit. Shit.

"Which way did they go?"

One-Eyed Jack pointed to the main road that ran through Prophet, which didn't help at all. In fairness, *out there* was a vast wilderness that I had no hope of searching to find one man.

Okay, everything is fine. Totally fine.

"Did you try his cell?" One-Eyed Jack asked.

I nodded, and stayed polite even though what I wanted to do was tell him that of course I'd tried his freaking cell, but that would be exposing my panic and that wouldn't help anyone.

I hurried out of there with a polite thank-you, and then grabbed Duke from the car and headed to the office. Now what?

There was no sign of Hen, but Devin had just gotten back from wherever he'd been, shrugging off his slicker. Only then did I notice how wet I was, running from pillar to post without a coat.

"Tiber's missing," I managed to force out, and the smile Devin gave me slipped.

"Where?"

"If I knew that—shit, sorry… He followed Dell Prosser out of town, and all I know is that he's been gone since ten this morning, he missed giving Ferdinand his meds, and the dogs don't like it, and Duke…" I pointed at my feet as if Devin wouldn't have noticed Duke right there.

"Okay." Devin glanced at the topographical map of the area surrounding Prophet and then back at me. "Where do we go… where do we even start?"

Okay. I needed to think this through. If this was a normal person, not someone I loved, what would I be doing? Did Tiber's car have a tracker? Not that I recalled. Was his phone in use? I called him again, this time it went straight to voicemail and I left an even and calm message that didn't hint at the fear I had.

"Hey, Tiber, call me when you get this."

Now what? We didn't follow the rules of someone not being declared missing until so many hours or days had passed—this was a small town and missing was pretty obvious from hour one. I'd have to wait for him to call me back, but maybe I'd head out and drive around.

"Sir?" Devin tapped my shoulder and pulled me from my thoughts, "I might have a lead on something."

"On Tiber?"

He blinked at me. "No, the case, but…"

"Spit it out, Rookie."

"I have a weird feeling about all of this," he admitted.

"That is instinct, Devin. Talk to me."

"You know how you asked me to contact breeders of *Czechoslovakian Vlcak*? Well one of the breeders I called was a guy in California. He said he wouldn't sell puppies to someone in this area, because, I quote, there's a breeder in Washington state so they'd likely go to that guy instead. That breeder is over in Duvall and his name is Sampson. I left a message. Want me to try again?"

"Go."

Devin held up the phone and copy pasted the number waiting for it to connect and then putting it on speaker phone.

"Sabrina Sampson." The voice on the other end was that of a young woman.

"Sheriff Thompson, Prophet."

"Hello Sheriff, I was just about to return a call from your office about the Vlcaks?"

"You know someone?"

"Yeah, I do know of a guy over there on the Olympic Peninsula dealing in Vlcaks, but my dad refused to sell him any of our puppies. Said he didn't like the smell of it."

"What do you mean?"

"I only know what Dad told me, that he met this home security-slash-survivalist guy at a Vegas convention. He had a booth, marketing that he was raising guard dogs that were a crossbreed of wolf and Czechoslovakian Vlcak. Guess Dad thought he was training them to be vicious. You have to be careful with Vlcaks, but they're good dogs."

Training them to be vicious? Vicious enough to drag a grown man from a horse? Fuck.

"This guy—do you have a number at all? Or a name at least?"

"I'm not sure I can—"

"I can certainly get a warrant if you need me to," I said.

She sighed. "Blazen Guard Dogs, Washington state, that's all I have; guy's name was Merrik, not sure if that is a first or last name."

"Thank you for your time," I finished. Devin was typing away, face intent.

"According to the Washington Business Bureau, Merrik Walters owns Blazen Guard Dogs, 15001 Old Creek Passing. Don't know that road, but I have it on GPS. You want me to go talk to them?

I was torn—I needed to find Tiber, and then Devin cursed under his breath.

"What?"

"You'll never guess who is listed as co-owner of Blazen Guard Dogs?"

"Who?"

"Dell Prosser."

Fuck. Dell was tied to the dogs, Tiber had followed Dell out of town. Was it possible that Tiber was up at this place?

I gave Hen Tiber's key, which I'd had for less than a day. "Can you ask Libby to stay at Tiber's place with the animals?"

"Sure.".

Then to Devin, "Let's go."

Duke sensed our urgency, jumped straight into the SUV and over the back so I could attach his harness, and then with Devin navigating we headed out to Blazen Guard Dogs. I didn't have any space to panic because I was driving in the rain, and the roads were slick. They were local enough to us that I should know the name, but then, the road we took was well off the beaten track

We drove for thirty minutes, following the GPS. Each rut in the road forcing me to slow down was like a physical blow. Then Duke barked at something on the shoulder, we saw Tiber's car parked in the shade of some trees, and Devin jumped out. I hoped to hell Tiber was in there, reading a book, taking a nap, but Devin shook his head.

"Engine's cold, it's locked up tight."

"Fuck." I stared into the dense forest, and the tangled undergrowth and tasted blood in my mouth as I bit my lip. "Where are you?" We carried on down the dirt road, finally coming to a security gate in fencing surrounding the place. No entry signs warned us to stay away, but I could hear distant barking, and Tiber could be in there.

"Sir?" Devin asked, and we exchanged grim looks. We were both armed, but I unlocked the new tranquilizer guns, and we took one each.

Then, we headed inside.

Chapter Twenty-Four

Tiber

"HE'S STILL UP in the tree, Mer."

"No shit, Dell."

I opened my eyes. The sky was gray and overcast, the wind gusted, and rain was imminent. It was almost dark. It felt like I'd been up in the tree for days. Had it really only been since that morning?

When the two wolf-dogs had been set after me, I knew I couldn't outrun them. I'd seen a tree with good climbing branches not far into the woods from the kennels, and I'd gone up it. Yes, it was a trap. I knew I'd be cornered. But there was no way I'd make it to my car or the road, so it was either get my throat ripped out right then and there or climb the tree.

I'd chosen the tree. For a moment, I'd thought the two wolf-dogs could climb. They half ran up the tree, snapping and snarling, in their frenzy to get at me. But gravity had taken hold, and they'd dropped back to the ground. They'd been there ever since, pacing at the base of the tree, watching me intently. Drooling.

Dell and his buddy had gone away and come back a half dozen times by now to see if I was still there. I was losing count—along with hope.

A body-wracking shiver went through me as despair wrapped me up in arms even colder than the oncoming night. I had a thin raincoat on, and I was freezing. Fuck.

"This waiting is bullshit," Dell complained. "I still say we just shoot him."

"How many times do I have to say it, Dell?" said the brown-haired man impatiently. Dell called him Mare or Meyer or something like that. "A bullet hole means murder. We're sticking to the plan! He's gotta come down eventually. He ain't got no food or water up there. When he does, Helo and Raz'll kill him. Then we'll dump him close to Clear Creek Falls, and it'll look like another wolf attack."

"But look at him! He's, like, Indian or something. Bet he can sit up there for days."

"So what? It's not like anyone can hear him calling for help out here. What difference does it make how long it takes him to die?"

"But what if he dies up in the tree?"

"Then we'll get a ladder and pull him down! Jesus, get a grip, Dell. We're supposed to be partners in this thing. Don't lose your nerve now."

"I'm not! But those DNA tests could be a problem. What if they figure Billy wasn't killed by that wolf pack? Like, for sure?"

"I told you: our dogs are part wolf, so the DNA tests

never will figure out anything *for sure*. That's the whole beauty of the thing! This'll blow over, we'll collect our money from that Makah dude, then we have that job in Idaho. That one pays fifty grand. So put on your big boy panties and play it cool."

They continued to argue as if I couldn't hear. They'd been *paid* to kill Billy with the wolf-dogs? And someone in Idaho had hired them to kill too? What kind of sick person would think up a business like that? I listened for more clues, but they just bitched at each other. Too bad I'd never get a chance to tell Gabriel what I'd heard.

I adjusted my hold on the tree trunk, shifting my weight to get a little relief from where the branch I was straddling pressed into my balls. I rested my head on the bark. My parched throat ached. If it rained, maybe I could collect some water in my palm.

I could use my belt to secure my hands around the trunk so I could sleep without falling tonight. With enough rain, and assuming I didn't die of exposure, I could live for *days*.

Yeah. Great. This was not the way I'd pictured the end.

Fuck, I didn't want to die.

I thought about my mom. She would be devastated. I was her only child. And who would take care of her when she got too old to take care of herself? That was my job.

I thought about my pack. I'd taken them all in, promised them I would be there forever, that they'd found a safe home. What would happen to them now? To Leo? Ferdinand? Gracie? Patch? Fudge? Renfield? Would they end up in some shelter, separated, and maybe languishing unwanted or even be put down? And what about Frank? Would any shelter take a huge tortoise? And Duke, sweetest boy ever, who'd just started to heal from the loss of his previous owner, Mike. What would another shattering of his world do to his ability to trust? I wanted to be there for them. *I'd promised.*

Could I hope that Gabriel would help them all?

Gabriel.

Just this morning, while shopping at the mercantile, I'd had a little freakout about asking him to move in a few things. Now, I could think of nothing I wanted more in this world than to sit with him on the couch every night, with all the animals around us, holding hands or leaning against one another, watching a martial arts film—his favorite—or a thriller—mine.

I wanted to know what it would be like to wake up with him every morning. I wanted to see the nightmares fade from his eyes. I wanted to see the gray emerge at his temples. I wanted *him.*

How long had I loved him? I'd known that night in the diner, sitting with Jeff, and stealing glances at Gabriel, that *he* was where I belonged.

Why hadn't I told him?

And what kind of fucked up fate had brought us together only to have it end just when it was starting?

I should have at least texted him about following Dell. There'd been time before I'd gotten too far out for a signal, but I hadn't thought of it.

Gabriel was right. I did take stupid chances. I'd do anything to take the last one back.

Rain struck the top of my head and my raincoat clung to me. I shivered again, hard. I wanted to wrap my arms around myself, but I was afraid to let go of the tree. My mind was far from clear. I didn't trust myself not to wobble and fall.

I raised my head and looked down. Dell and the other guy were gone again. It was dusk and raining steadily— cold, fat drops. But my wolf-dog sentinels were there, one on each side of the tree. They were both male, I'd noted earlier. One had laid down, resting. The other was sitting on its haunches, staring up at me. When our eyes met, he shifted his front paws expectantly and licked his lips. A low growl sounded in his throat and his upper lip quivered, threatening to bare his teeth.

Ironic that I, the so-called dog whisperer, would be killed by a canine. Was that like a dentist dying from an infected tooth? I'd tried to communicate with the wolf-dogs earlier, but without success. When I tried to connect with them, all I got was a red rage, pain, flashes of snapping jaws taking down prey.

These poor creatures had been trained to be aggressive, to destroy above all other instincts. They were like that movie, *The Manchurian Candidate*. They didn't know what they were doing. They acted by rote, doing what had been drilled into them. They served the man who controlled them with an iron fist.

I thought of how that training might have gone, given the flashes of agony I'd felt from them, and shuddered. Some trainers used aversion tactics like fear and pain. Things like cattle prods and shock collars, berating and beating, or withholding food until the dog displayed the desired behavior. I had no doubt that the owner of Blazen

Guard Dogs would stop at nothing to create his killers. Poor things. It wasn't their fault.

I studied the wolf-dogs again. They were beautiful animals, really. They looked enough like wolves that most people would mistake them for one. I thought about what I'd learned of wolves in my studies. How they weren't natural allies with man and didn't turn to them for help or comfort. They were wild creatures and they neither wanted or needed anything from our species.

Were these hybrids more wolf or more dog? Was there anything inside them to reach out to? How loyal were they to their owner?

"Hey, guys," I said in a low and friendly voice. "Are your names Helo and Raz? I'm Tiber."

This made the wolf-dog that had been lying down sit up. They both growled at me menacingly, teeth bared.

"You wanna hear about my dogs? No? Cool. The one I've had the longest is named Leo. He's a little guy with a mondo attitude. I found him when…"

I told them all about Leo. Then Gracie, and Duke, and the others, one by one. Hell, talking warmed me up a little anyway. And at some point the wolf-dogs got bored and stopped growling and snarling as I yapped away. One of them laid back down again. The other paced towards the compound and back, as if searching for his master. He licked his lips.

"Hungry? Me too. I wish I had something to feed you, but I don—" I was about to say I didn't have anything, but I realized that wasn't true. I didn't have food for *me*, no. But I had dog treats in my pocket, because I always had dog treats in my pocket.

Were they not going to come out and feed these guys? Maybe they reasoned that the hungrier they were, the more they'd enjoy eating me when I fell. Nice.

I dug out the handful of treats I had on me and tossed them to first one wolf-dog then the other. It wasn't as if they'd do any good buried with my corpse. The wolf-dogs snatched them out of the air and swallowed them whole, then eyed me as if thinking I was a lot larger and juicier than those silly Milk-Bones.

"Sorry. That's all the food I have."

The wolf-dog who was watching me danced his front paws once at that. As for the one lying down, his ears perked and his head shot up. What had I said?

"Food? Do you know that word? Food."

They both stood and stared in the direction of the compound, panting.

They knew the word all right. Food, of course, was not coming. But that made me think. What had I seen in the brochure? Keyword trained. Of course. If they knew the word for *food*, they likely had one for *attack* as well. And for the opposite of that—standing down.

"Stop!" I said loudly.

This brought their attention back to me and set off angry barking.

"Down!" I tried. They growled.

"Back off!" Nothing.

"Chill!" Nope.

I tried every other word I could think of. But the wolf-dogs grew more and more agitated. Probably they didn't care for me yelling nonsensical orders at them. And, when I thought about it, a smart trainer would choose words that weren't commonly used to prevent accidental triggering of the dogs. Something like *Zenith*! I sighed. I'd never guess it.

"You know what? Let's forget that for now and talk about something nice. Where was I? Oh, Frank. Let me tell you about Frank. See, he's an African Sulcata, and he was just a little hatchling when he was imported by an exotic pet shop in San Diego...."

I laid my head against the bark and talked on. I told them about all the animals I had now, and, when I ran out of things to say about that, I told them about other animals I'd known, going back to my parents' vet clinic days.

I talked to hear the sound of a human voice. I talked because I was still alive and still capable of speech. I talked and even shed a tear or two as the rain poured down.

Below, the wolf-dogs waited.

Chapter Twenty-Five

Gabriel

I DIDN'T LIKE this one little bit.

Finding Tiber's car abandoned didn't sit right with me, and the remoteness of the location had my Spidey senses on overtime.

Devin and I had both slipped on bullet-proof vests, I could see the apprehension in his gaze as he stared down the road. "Body cams on."

"You think we're walking into something?" he asked as he fiddled with Velcro then reattached his body cam, thumbs up from me when I saw the recording light showing.

"I don't know," was all I could give him.

"You think Tiber's okay?"

Fuck, I hope so. "I don't know," I repeated with patience. The last thing my rookie needed was for his boss to go full tilt at whatever we found just because the man he loved might be in danger. For all I knew he could be around here with Dell Prosser drinking coffee and shooting the damn breeze.

I didn't think so.

My gut instinct told me this was wrong.

We drove to the gate, reversing up to it, nose to the road for quick exit, but blocking anyone from leaving, then headed for the gate itself. I pressed a button on a security box, but the wires to it lay loose in the weeds so it was just for show. Okay, so that was a clue this wasn't a high-tech operation, still there were signs warning us to stay out, even one that suggested there was an electric fence, but that was bullshit. The gate had a simple rope loop for closure—so much for a secure compound that no one could get into. I exchanged glances with Devin who was wide-eyed and on his toes fighting the rush of adrenalin I was sure he was experiencing.

"Follow me, do what I do. Take things slow, okay?"

He gave one more bounce and then took a deep breath, exhaling it harshly. "Sir."

I tapped my radio, hoping to hell we connected. "Sheriff to dispatch."

"Dispatch, go ahead," Hen replied.

I breathed a sigh of relief. "We're at the address, it's quiet, but I need backup."

"On it." She paused, and didn't ask why I wanted backup, because I had no good reason other than my gut telling me something was wrong. "Did you find Tiber?" she asked.

"Organize the backup," I repeated, and had to end the call, because I didn't have time to explain, in case the fear got to me that Tiber was in the compound hurt, or worse.

"Something's not right," Devin murmured, his gun already drawn, same as me. It wasn't only the sound of distant barking, snarls, and yelps, that made this wrong. It was the lack of people and the loose lock. "A fenced compound, warning signs to stay out, yet we can just walk in?"

"Maybe they're sloppy, maybe they don't care," I summarized. If Dell Prosser was anything to do with this then it made sense it wasn't slick—Dell wasn't a criminal mastermind.

Or maybe whatever they have in there is dangerous enough to handle any intruders.

Why had Tiber followed him out here? What the fuck was going on? The deepening gloom of dusk made eerie shadows as we headed down the driveway. Devin tightened his grip on his gun and stuck close to my wing as we crossed a parking area strewn with bits of engine and car parts. There were two trucks, one I recognized as Dell Prosser's, the other I didn't. We climbed the steps up to the door of the one-story home, then took positions on either side of it. I took a breath to center myself before I leaned over and rapped my knuckles.

"Sheriff's Department, open up."

We couldn't go barreling in—we didn't have a warrant, we had no probable cause, but the same instincts that had kept me alive undercover were making my skin prickle. Was Tiber in there? In trouble? I strained to locate noise but all I could hear was a show with canned laughter. When I focused, I couldn't get a sense of Tiber being in there, and what the fuck was that all about? What part of me was so tuned to Tiber that I knew he wasn't in there?

We headed around the back of the house with caution, peering in windows. In the kitchen there were signs of inhabitants, mugs, plates in the sink under the window, music on a radio, and the TV was on showing a re-run of a stand-up comedy show. We couldn't see much else.

"Empty," Devin summarized.

Next we checked out the rest of the compound, and I made a point of moving so our body cams picked up everything. Anyone who watched the footage would see two cautious officers doing what they should—despite me wanting to run through the entire compound searching for Tiber and kick down every single door or barrier we came to. The barking grew louder and when we reached the source of it, we found a run of kennels, each complete with a single dog—a single, frustrated, angry, dog.

More like wolves.

Wolf-dogs.

They were huge and snarled and snapped at the wire around their runs, vicious, and thank god there was wire and metal between us and them, because if they came after either of us, we were dead. One of them alone was big enough to yank a man from a horse, and rip his throat out, but imagining all of them on top of us. I couldn't help the shudder, and I felt sick at the thought of their teeth…

"Did one of these kill Billy?" Devin asked as we checked out the kennels.

"Seems right," was all I had to say, because the coincidence was too big. "Cover me," I ordered, then pulled an evidence bag from my jacket, moving closer to the nearest empty cage, of which there were two, and grabbing a few hairs from the chain link as fast and efficient as I could, ignoring the frenzy of the dog in the next cage trying to get to me. I sealed and pocketed it, then joined Devin. "We need to widen the search."

"You really want to split up?" His tone was verging on nervous, and I liked that he wasn't all about going off and being a hero. He'd go far by keeping his head straight.

"No. Stick together until backup arrives, we just need to head out to the trees." I said this with confidence, but any kind of backup could be an hour, or more, so it was me and Devin up against however many of these wolf-dogs were here, plus an unidentified number of humans. Memories of another time where I was facing hell, flooded my thoughts. Panic gripped me and I took a deep breath and pushed it down, forced it so deep inside that it couldn't hurt me today. I needed to find Tiber, and this wasn't the time to lose my shit.

What if he's hurt? What if I'm too late?

I can't lose someone else.

The ghosts of the past haunted me and made my chest hurt and my head spin, but I refused to let them paralyze me. Not today.

"Sir?" Devin gestured with the gun, and I glanced over to where he was pointing. We'd walked away from the dogs and there were two paths, heading out into the trees, one with a tangled mess of undergrowth blocking most of the way, the other wide open. This far from the kennels, the noise from the dogs was deadened by the closing canopy and twisted undergrowth, but I tried to steady my breathing, ignoring the overwhelming surge of fear that Tiber was in trouble. As an officer, I was trained to stay focused, to maintain composure even in the most dire of situations, but one thought about Tiber being hurt somewhere, and I was losing focus.

"Okay, kid, we're going to—"

I stopped, the sound of crashing through the undergrowth, cursing, a loud argument, and I tugged Devin into the second path and hid behind the trees.

"… fucker can stay there all night."

"Fuck's sake, Merrik, he'll die of hypo-whatever, when you get cold and shit." That was Dell's voice, strident with a hint of stupid.

"Yeah, so?" I didn't recognize the second voice, but now knew his name—Merrik.

"So wouldn't that show up in a thing?"

"What thing?"

"Where they cut the body open—it will show he wasn't ripped to death by dogs first."

Merrick scoffed. "You don't know what the hell you're talking about. Stop trying to second-guess every goddamn thing."

They appeared in the clearing, both in hunting jackets, both armed with pistols and rifles, and I waited until they were past us before elbowing Devin in the side, indicating what I was going to do, and then stepping out with my gun pointed right at them.

"Drop your weapons."

The two men whirled to face us, Prosser's mouth open in a yelp of shock, the other man already going for his weapon and diving to the side behind a pile of firewood. Prosser was frozen in place, as the first bullet from the other man's gun embedded in the tree behind us.

We split, Devin diving to the ground and taking

Prosser with him, already holding him ready to cuff, out of the line of fire, which left the other guy for me.

"Give it up!" I ordered. "Sheriff's office, we have backup."

"I don't see no backup!" the guy shouted, and his voice seemed more distant. Where was he going?

Gun loose in front of me, aimed high, I edged around the wood, but he'd moved away, backing to the kennels, firing at me but missing by a wide margin.

"Stop!" I ordered again. "Drop your weapon or I'll shoot."

I had a dead aim on him, one in the center mass would take him down, but he was wild-eyed and scrabbling at the cage. I took a shot to the side of him, the bullet kicking up dirt.

"Stop! Drop your weapon!"

He scrabbled with a lock on the cage, his actions frantic. "Throat! Throat!" he yelled at the dog inside, who was right up against the wire, and who snapped at the man's fingers, getting hold of skin, the man screaming, and attempting to yank his fingers back. He was trying to get the dog out, and shouting, and then he screamed again. When he freed his fingers there was a spray of blood in an arc above his head. He dropped the gun in the other hand and went to his knees. I kicked the gun away, as he rocked, his hand missing two fingers, flat against his chest.

I cuffed his uninjured hand to the empty cage, checked what was left of his fingers on the other as he cursed and rocked, and cursed some more. Instinct had me checking for arterial blood, but it was stumpy and oozing and I didn't think he'd die from that alone. I wrapped his jacket around the wound for now.

"Where's Tiber?" I shouted.

"My hand! My hand!"

I circled back to Prosser who was sitting on the ground, cuffed to his truck, Devin's weapon pointed at him.

"Where's Tiber?"

"I ain't saying nothing!" he yelled at me.

I went to an immediate crouch next to him, pressing my gun against his temple. "Where. Is. Tiber?"

Prosser snarled up at me, madness in his eyes. "Down the trail," he said, and then the madness dropped, and he grinned. "You can't stop them."

"Them who? More of you?"

Prosser huffed a laugh. "Dogs. They got him."

My heart cracked. Two empty cages, two dogs? They'd hurt Tiber? No. That wasn't possible.

"Stay here," I ordered Devin.

"But—"

"Stay here, eyes on these two, report to Hen. I'm going after Tiber." I checked my gun, pulled out the tranquilizer gun as well, and double handed with weapons I jogged down the trail. I heard Tiber before I saw him, talking like he did to Duke, and I sped up, skidding around a corner and there he was.

Tiber.

Walking toward me, two wolf-dogs at his heels, trotting along with him nice as you please. Somehow my beautiful, wonderful boyfriend had connected with two of the dogs and they were just there, panting a little, but docile and controlled.

I didn't care what my body cam showed, I didn't care where we were in this relationship of ours, I ran to him and gripped him hard.

"Fuck!" I snapped, and yanked him close to me, one of the dogs whining.

"It's okay, I'm okay," Tiber said, but his voice wavered, and I could feel his fear and pain. He was freezing, soaked to the skin, and I hugged him tighter as he shivered.

"Let's go," I said, and half tugged, half encouraged him to head back towards the compound. I needed to find a blanket or something.

Merrick's face went slack with shock when we walked out of the woods. "The fuck!" he yelled, then quietened when the two dogs trotted over and sat down in front of him.

"What's the kill word then?" Tiber asked, going to his knees, and putting an arm around each dog's neck. "Tell me."

"No! They'll kill me, they'll kill you."

"What is it? Kill? Nah. I bet that's a word you use a lot. Destroy? How about a body part? Arm? Thro…?" The dogs tensed; Tiber tensed. *I* tensed.

Merrik yelped. "Stop it!"

"Leave off," Tiber murmured, and the dogs relaxed, as did the caged dogs close by, even the one with Merrik's blood soaking his muzzle. "You've hurt them all," Tiber murmured, shivering, his tone dripping with sadness. "You twisted these beautiful animals, abused them, and trained them to kill, and I hate you for that."

"Fuck you," Merrik snarled.

Tiber put the wolf-dogs into a kennel, and we left Devin to guard the prisoners while we walked back down the driveway to the SUV. I grabbed a blanket from the back, wrapped it around Tiber's shoulders, pulling his hair out of the way and holding him close.

He was alive, and I held him and felt every shivery breath he took.

I held him when backup arrived, and we watched them carted off Merrik and Prosser.

I held him when a van from Fish and Wildlife arrived.

And I held him when he cried.

Epilogue

Tiber

"TAKE THIS, UNCLE GOOBER!" Sarah shoved her trick-or-treat bag at Gabriel so she could hold out the skirt of her costume and twirl for me.

"Oh, wow. Cutest witch ever!" I declared; eyes wide.

She gave me a feisty little scowl. "Not cute. Scary!"

"Scariest witch ever!" I amended.

"Not as scary as me!" Aaron put up his ""paws" and growled menacingly. His tiger costume was homemade with orange and white-striped fuzzy fabric and matching paint on his face. Adorable.

"Yikes. Please don't eat me!" Gabriel said, and we exchanged a smile.

Aaron roared louder and feinted towards Gabriel, but Lori put a hand on his shoulder. "Okay! Enough of that. *Nice* tigers get more candy. Let's go, guys!"

"Yay, candy!" Aaron yelled, switching from tiger back to boy in a heartbeat.

We headed out with Aaron warning us not to step on his tail, and Sarah announcing loudly that she hoped no one was lame enough to hand out hard candy.

God, it had been years since I'd been trick or treating. I think the last time was in elementary school. I was the kid too shy to go up and knock on someone's door. But I loved Halloween. I normally spent it cooped up watching horror movies. It was exhilarating to be downtown tonight, hanging out with beings of my own species, enjoying the kids in their costumes and the decorations on Main Street. Hay bales lined the sidewalk along with scarecrows and pumpkins of every shape, size, color, and carving—from scary to silly.

Prophet held trick or treat in the businesses downtown so kids could get their candy on, and every place had stayed open late. Grounds for Joy gave baggies filled with M&Ms and candy corn to the kids and chocolate-covered coffee beans to adults. The mercantile featured One-Eyed-Jack and his wife dressed as Bigfoots passing out caramel apple kits to make at home—apples included. And at the sheriff's office, Hen, in an Oompa Loompa costume, was in the lobby, passing out packets of sour fish. "Our Sheriff's favorites!" she cooed, giving Gabriel a wink.

He rolled his eyes, but a smile danced on his lips. Technically, he was on duty, and wore his sheriff's uniform, in case anyone got too rowdy downtown. But it was a happy, peaceful crowd and everyone was having a good time.

When we reached the art gallery, an older man handed us decorated cookies while Libby Smith, dressed in an elaborate witch costume, had a station set up on the sidewalk offering free face painting. She was dabbing orange on the nose of a little boy when we walked up, but she put down her brush to give both Gabriel and I a hug.

"There are my heroes! Why aren't you dressed up?"

"I'm on duty," Gabriel said, shoving me under the bus.

I gave him a glare. "And I'm not twelve."

Libby blew a raspberry. "Do I look twelve to you? We all deserve a night to not be ourselves. Come back in a few minutes and I'll do your face, Tiber."

"Could be hot," Gabriel said with a twinkle in his eye.

I laughed. "Uh, no. I'm pretty happy being myself these days. But thanks anyway, Libby."

She sighed. "Fine. Then I still owe you. Let's do lunch this week, okay?"

"I'd like that," I said, and was surprised that I meant it.

It would be understating it to say Libby had been relieved when we'd proved her wolf pack had nothing to do with Billy Odette's death. Susan too and—so she told Gabriel—the entire Fish and Wildlife Department. They'd even cracked a bottle of champagne.

But I hadn't gone with Libby to see the wolves again. As wonderful as it had been, I figured they deserved their privacy. If I were a wolf, that was the way I'd want it.

When we'd hit up every business on the street, we wandered back towards the diner. They'd commandeered the parking lot next door and had strung up lights and put out picnic tables. The night was fair—not too cold and no rain—so families gathered there after trick or treating. For five bucks, you were allowed in where you could take a seat and grab hot cider, coffee, or hot chocolate plus various baked goodies from a buffet table decked out in black and orange.

The evening was, in a word, perfect.

Gabriel, Sam, and the kids went up to the buffet while Lori and I grabbed a picnic table. She scooted close to me on the bench seat. "I haven't had a chance to ask you about your charming of the wolf-dogs. You should have heard Gabriel go on about it. After ten minutes of ranting and fuming over you *risking your life*, he was all admiration for your mad skills."

I gave a little scoff of a laugh. "They were trained using keywords, so I just had to guess the right ones. Hell, I was up in that tree long enough to write *War and Peace*." The memory made me sad. "Those dogs weren't evil. They were just trained that way."

"Still." Lori shuddered. "When I think of what they were capable of... I'm surprised they weren't put down."

I, too, had been surprised that cooler heads had prevailed, especially given how riled up the town had been over Billy's death. But Gabriel—because that was the kind of man he was—went the extra mile and found a guy in California who rehabilitated fighting dogs and other so-called *irredeemably aggressive* canines. He agreed to take all the wolf-dogs from Brazen Guard Dogs and work with them. The kennels had been shut down by the county, all the animals removed, and Merrik and Dell were now in jail pending trial for murder.

Apparently breeding and training wolf-dogs for security wasn't enough. They'd planned a whole side business as hired hitmen, killing people, and blaming it on wild wolves. Which was as sick and horrifying an idea as anyone ever dreamed up. Thank God it hadn't worked out the way they'd planned.

Orson Travis was in jail, too. His bank records showed he'd paid Merrik ten thousand for Billy's murder. And maybe the fact he'd gotten caught was part of Stone Whiteplume's magic. After all, he'd said if the victim didn't deserve the curse, it would bounce back and bite the curse maker in the ass. I liked to think so, anyway.

"So, you have to testify at their trial, huh?" Lori asked. "That should be exciting."

"Yeah, because I was born for the spotlight," I quipped. "But that's in January, so I'm not gonna even think about it until after all the holidays."

"Wise man." Lori gave me a fond smile.

I'd expected to be testifying at Jeff's trial, too. But I should have known he'd wriggle out of it. Because he hadn't lit the match, technically no crime had been committed. Jeff claimed he'd never intended to light it, that he'd known I was watching all along, and had only meant to scare me. I could have pushed the case anyway, but it would have been difficult to prove in court, especially given Jeff's ability to charm a jury, and his mom's ability to pay for a high-priced lawyer.

But I still had the video, and Jeff was terrified I'd send it to his employers. Whatever excuses he made up, it was still a bad look. He'd begged and pleaded and promised he'd never come near me again. I believed him. He didn't love me; he'd just thought I was an easy target. He knew better now. He'd be on to some new, unfortunate guy in Portland. I wished I could have put Jeff in jail, but he'd get his karma someday. Of that, I felt certain.

The crows told me so.

"Speaking of holidays," Lori said, "I hope you'll spend Thanksgiving and Christmas with us."

Something warm and unbearably squishy stirred in my chest. "That's sweet of you. Thanks. But my mom's coming for Thanksgiving."

"Bring her along."

"Not sure the pack would forgive me if I didn't cook Thanksgiving dinner at my house. The smell of the turkey is the best thing in the world, you know. Aside from getting scraps."

Lori shrugged. "So come over to ours, with your mom, for Thanksgiving dinner, and make a turkey at yours the day after. That way the pack'll get more 'cause you guys will have gotten your fill."

I laughed. "You're quite the problem-solver."

"You learn that skill when you have twins." She laughed, but then grew serious. "Sam and Gabriel are just starting to reconnect, and Ezra is coming home for Thanksgiving. It's important to Sam to be with both his brothers, so it's important to me. And you're important to Gabriel. You make him happy, Tiber. And that translates to a man who is better able to be a brother and an uncle. Not that I don't like you for your own sake..." She patted my arm.

"No, I get it."

I watched Gabriel juggle three hot to-go cups and laugh at something Sam said, and I did get it. Totally. I'd do whatever it took to help that man.

It had only been three weeks since we'd discovered the wolf-dogs, but Gabriel had slept in my bed every night since, Duke by his side. Already the shadows under his eyes had faded and the darkness that sometimes swam in their depths rarely made an appearance.

"What happened to him in LA?" Lori asked thoughtfully.

I sighed and glanced at her. "I'm not sure. He's told me a little. But not much."

"Same with Sam. Well," she said with an upbeat lilt. "It's over now. And he's home. So, it's all good, right?"

"Right."

Then I thought of Jeff and how he'd found me and felt a trickle of unease. The past didn't always stay in the rearview mirror. Sometimes it came back. Maybe I should buy Gabriel one of Stone Whiteplume's *fuck off* pouches. And one for myself too. Just to be sure.

Because if the past ever came looking for Gabriel Thompson, God help us all.

The gang came back from the buffet table loaded with plates and cups.

"Uncle Tiber, we got you cookies! But you can't have any of my cupcake," Sarah announced seriously as she flopped a paper plate onto the table.

"Sarah!" Lori gasped.

I grinned. "It's okay, Mom. She's setting boundaries." And when she called me *Uncle* Tiber, Sarah could have anything she wanted. Ever.

Gabriel slipped in, putting a cup in front of me. "I figured you for a cider man."

"You know it."

He sat with one leg on either side of the bench seat and too close for anyone to mistake us for friends. And there he was, the sheriff—*my* sheriff—in his uniform with my favorite five o'clock stubble and a gorgeous twinkle in his eyes. He stared at me for a beat, then leaned in for a simple kiss.

I felt my face heat. "You're on duty."

He chuckled. "You are my duty, Tiber Russo."

I felt a glow of love so strong I had to take a sip of cider not to choke up. I glanced around the table and wondered how the hell a cranky hermit like me had ever reached this moment.

Truly one of life's mysteries. But for now, I'd take it.

THE END

Next in the Lake Prophet Mysteries

Zenith

Coming soon.

Gabriel's past stalks him in Prophet; threatening to destroy everything he's building with Tiber, and jeopardizing the safety of the town.

How to Howl at the Moon

Sheriff Lance Beaufort is not going to let trouble into his town, no sir. Tucked away in the California mountains, Mad Creek has secrets to keep, like the fact that half the town consists of 'quickened'—dogs who have gained the ability to become human. Descended on both sides from Border Collies, Lance is as alert a guardian as they come.

Tim Weston is looking for a safe haven. After learning that his boss patented all of Tim's work on vegetable hybrids in his own name, Tim quit his old job. A client offers him use of her cabin in Mad Creek, and Tim sees a chance for a new start. But the shy gardener has a way of fumbling and sounding like a liar around strangers, particularly gorgeous alpha men like Sheriff Beaufort.

Lance's hackles are definitely raised by the lanky young stranger. He's concerned about marijuana growers moving into Mad Creek, and he's not satisfied with the boy's story. Lance decides a bit of undercover work is called for. When Tim hits a beautiful black collie with his car and adopts the dog, its love at first sight for both Tim and Lance's inner dog. Pretending to be a pet is about to get Sheriff Beaufort in very hot water.

Howl at the Moon Series

1. How to Howl at the Moon
2. How to Walk Like a Man
3. How to Wish Upon a Star
4. How to Save a Life
5. How To Run With The Wolves
6. How to Love Thine Enemy

What Lies Beneath (Lancaster Falls 1)

In the hottest summer on record, Iron Lake reservoir is emptying, revealing secrets that were intended to stay hidden beneath the water. The tragic story of a missing man is a media sensation, and abruptly the writer and the cop falling in love is just a postscript to horrors neither could have imagined.

Best Selling Horror writer Chris Lassiter struggles for inspiration and he's close to never writing again. His life has become an endless loop of nothing but empty pages, personal appearances, and a marketing machine that is systematically destroying his muse. In a desperate attempt to force Chris to complete

unfinished manuscripts his agent buys a remote cabin. All Chris
has to do is hide away and write, but he's lost his muse, and not
even he can make stories appear from thin air.

Sawyer Wiseman left town for Chicago, chasing the excitement
and potential of being a big city cop, rising the ranks, and making
his mark. A case gone horribly wrong draws him back to
Lancaster Falls. Working for the tiny police department in the
town he'd been running from, digging into cold cases and police
corruption, he spends his day's healing, and his nights hoping the
nightmares of his last case leave him alone.

<hr/>

The **Lancaster Falls** Series

Also By Eli Easton

For a full list of ebooks and links please scan the code above or
visit eliseaston.com

Also By RJ Scott

For a full list of ebooks and links please scan the code above or
visit rjscott.co.uk/rjbooks

Meet Eli Easton

Having been, at various times and under different names, a minister's daughter, a computer programmer, a game designer, the author of paranormal mysteries, a fan fiction writer, and organic farmer, Eli has been a m/m romance author since 2013. She has published over 30 gay romances.

Eli has loved romance since her teens and she particular admires writers who can combine literary merit, genuine humor, melting hotness, and eye-dabbing sweetness into one story.

Website & newsletter - elieaston.com

facebook.com/100008994061782

x.com/EliEaston

amazon.com/stores/Eli-Easton/author/B00CJUKM9I

bookbub.com/authors/eli-easton

goodreads.com/7020231.Eli_Easton

Meet RJ Scott

RJ is the author of the over one hundred and sixty published novels and discovered romance in books at a very young age. She realized that if there wasn't romance on the page, she could create it in her head, and is a lifelong writer.

She lives and works out of her home in the beautiful English countryside, spends her spare time reading, watching films, and enjoying time with her family.

The last time she had a week's break from writing she didn't like it one little bit and has yet to meet a box of chocolates she couldn't defeat.

www.rjscott.co.uk | rj@rjscott.co.uk

Newsletter - rjscott.co.uk/rjnews

facebook.com/author.rjscott

x.com/Rjscott_author

instagram.com/rjscott_author

amazon.com/author/rj-scott

bookbub.com/authors/rj-scott

goodreads.com/rjscott

pinterest.com/rjscottauthor